The Candela of Cancri

ALSO BY J.C. SIMMONS

FICTION

Blood on the Vine
Blind Overlook
Some People Die Quick
Icy Blue Descent
The Electra File
Popping the Shine
Four Nines Fine
The Underground Lady
Akel Dama

NONFICTION

Ernest Miller Hemingway: A Workbook

The
Candela
of Cancri

JC SIMMONS

iUniverse, Inc.
New York   Bloomington

The Candela of Cancri

iUniverse books may be ordered through booksellers or by contacting:

iUniverse
1663 Liberty Drive
Bloomington, IN 47403
www.iuniverse.com
1-800-Authors (1-800-288-4677)

ISBN: 978-1-4502-5757-2 (sc)
ISBN: 978-1-4502-5756-5 (dj)
ISBN: 978-1-4502-5758-9 (ebk)

Printed in the United States of America

iUniverse rev. date: 09/15/2010

This book is for Jim Bennett

Acknowledgments

Carolyn Matthews Simmons: The finest thing ever raised on a Mississippi farm and for making it all possible.

Lisa Jones: My "Editor in Chief." She has always been a part of the process.

Jeanne Kroker: My "West Coast Editor."

Debbie Bennett: For seeing through the haze.

Tom Honea: Friend, classmate, gridiron teammate, and fellow writer. An amazing insight into all things literati. Remember his name.

John Mutziger, D.O.: For keeping me alive to pen this work, and bringing the reality of medicine to the fore.

Rick Shackelford: For always being a friend, and the "Shack" of these novels.

Edgar Grissom, M.D.: A friend of forty years who started me on this path. His insight into the Royal R. Rife frequency generator and its medical effectiveness kept this novel grounded in reality.

A special thanks to the following people: David Germany, Pauline Matthews, Carol Shackelford, Pat Webb, Bill and Emily Jordan, Bill Graham, Jack Tannehill, John Evans, owner of Lemuria Books, Mike Doran of Southern Literary Agency, Marcel Mitran, Raul Villarreal, Lisa Hancock, Tom Gerald, Julie Grissom, Sarah Mutziger. To all those aviators with who I shared a cockpit. To all the friends who read the books and made helpful suggestions, you know who you are. For all those who I have forgotten, my apologizes.

PROLOGUE

The old woman lay corpse-like in the neatly made bed, her breathing slow and weak. Her hair was scraggly, brittle, and thin from the chemotherapy. Weighing no more than ninety pounds, she had fought a brave and hard battle, but she was losing the war. The stomach cancer had spread to the liver, lungs and lymph nodes, and probably to the brain. The last CAT scan showed it was time to stop treatment. The oncologist gave her no more than six months.

I sat on the side of the bed and held her hand. From time to time she would open her eyes and smile at me, but say nothing. The Siamese cat lay beside her head and would leave only to eat or use the litter box. It was as if the animal knew that she was desperately ill.

"I'm going to call J.D. and have him bring the Rife machine. It's worth a try."

She opened her eyes, nodded.

"It can't hurt and it's noninvasive. Traditional medicine has contributed all it can. Even Doctor Mutt (her family physician) is satisfied you have done all that is possible."

She turned her head and looked toward the cat.

I went to the living room and made the call.

. . .

J.D. Ballard arrived with the Rife Frequency Generator later that afternoon and we gave her the first treatment.

It was a simple machine, generating sound waves aimed at killing cancer cells without causing harm to healthy tissue. One held onto two metal probes while the machine generated the correct frequency that literally imploded the cancer cells which would then be absorbed into the body and expelled along with other dead cells. Repeated treatments were necessary. The machine always worked. There were no failures. Sometimes patients died of other causes, but not from the cancer targeted by the machine.

The Royal Rife Frequency Generator is the best kept secret in modern medicine. It is also illegal for any medical professional to use it to administer treatment, even though it would save hundreds of thousands of lives.

The American Medical Association, in their infinite wisdom had determined the machine was "nonsensical hagiography, medical quackery, and pseudoscience."

It is a battle that has waged since the nineteen thirties at great expense to the health of the general public.

• • •

Exactly seventy-five days after her first treatment, the old woman was found, to the utter amazement of her oncologist, to be free of disease. Cancer would not kill her.

Chapter One

Slamming the book closed with great anger, I threw it on the table beside the chair and stared at the fire in the stone hearth. Unable to sit still, I went to the kitchen and watched cold rain lash into the windowpanes, the woods outside rendered as grey watercolor smears by the streams cascading down the glass. I wanted a drink, but I had not eaten all day. I was no longer hungry. It was as if all visible life in these woods had slowed to a stop. The only movement remaining between these four walls was my pulse, beating rapidly and desperately in my veins.

Deciding to forego alcohol, I, instead, made a pot of coffee, went back and stood looking down at *Ernest Hemingway: A Descriptive Bibliography*, recently published and authored by Dr. Edgar Grissom. He had, with this work, destroyed my entire collection of first edition books by the Nobel Prize-winning author. With the exception of *The Old Man and the Sea,* not one of the books sold to me as "first edition, first issue" were as proffered. Even the dust jacket of *The Old Man and the Sea* was a lie. The artist, Adriana Ivancich, credited by the publisher, Scribner's, was not the one who illustrated the cover, but her sister, Francesca.

I wanted to curse Grissom. This would cost me thousands of dollars. But one can't shoot the messenger. I wanted to blame the booksellers. However, they were only working with the information available to them from an old and incomplete and poorly researched bibliography.

The only one to truly blame was myself. The information was out there. I could have dug it up. Grissom did. My anger subsided somewhat. The only thing I could think of to say was, "Thank you Dr. Grissom and you can kiss my ass." I can say this with a smile because Edgar is a personal friend of mine.

The only consolation to this whole Hemingway bibliography thing is knowing that book collectors and dealers around the world will have the exact same reaction as I have had today.

· · ·

After looking at the drawing of the dust jacket of *The Old Man and the Sea*, I sat down and began to read the novella. 26,500 words of pure literary genius. At one time this work was to be part of a long trilogy Hemingway wanted to do about the sea, the air, and the land. It never happened. Life intervened, as it does to all of us sometimes.

At a break, I studied the dust jacket again, admiring the stark simplicity of the drawing that depicted a small fishing village as seen from a hill or Watch Tower—maybe the Finca Vigia. The browns and greys, dull against a vast blue sea, nets stretched and skiffs at anchor. The whole scene I have admired since 1952 drawn by someone other than the nineteen year old raven-haired Italian beauty Hemingway had such an infatuation with that he brought her and her family to Cuba for extended visits. There she, Adriana, promptly had an affair with the Finca's Majordomo, Rene Villarreal. An affair so beautifully written about in *"HEMINGWAY'S CUBAN SON"* authored by Rene and his son, the artist, Raul Villarreal.

I finished the read-through of the novella and was happy. I'm always happy when I catch the giant marlin with the old man and fight the battles with him and dream of the lions on the beach.

The fire settled suddenly and an explosion of sparks rose upward into the chimney. I put the dust jacket back on the book admiring Lee Samuels photograph of Hemingway on the back cover. I do not know when this photo was taken, but he appears to be about the same age then as I am now. For some reason this also makes me feel good.

Carefully placing the book back in the glass case, I look over the Hemingway collection and think that even though the value of them has decreased tremendously, not a word written in them has decreased a penny.

. . .

Desperately needing some company, I went to the phone and dialed my closest neighbor, Rose English. "Let's cook some red meat and drink some claret."

"It's raining."

"Standing rib marinated in my fridge. We can oven-grill it. Bring my cat when you come."

"I have company," she said with exasperation in her voice.

That threw me. Rose never has company.

"It's a big roast."

"Come here. We'll cook it in my oven. Bring a bottle of champagne."

"I can do that. Half an hour."

Champagne? Rose was beer and whiskey. Maybe her "company" was the champagne and caviar type.

After a quick shower, I loaded the meat and wine into my truck and drove the two miles in pouring icy rain. The weather was changing. The air is heavy and polluted with gunk that makes your lungs act like dehumidifiers and your head like the collection tank. Now the sky was uneasy, thick clouds boiling down from the northwest in the fading light telling of the cold front clashing with warmer air of the Gulf of Mexico. The day was dreary and seemed with portent.

When I parked in Rose's driveway, she turned on the porch light. There were no other vehicles and I wondered how her "company" had arrived. Rose was my friend. She welcomed me to this rural environ fifteen years ago when I moved my aviation consulting business from the capital. Now nearing seventy, Rose is a cattle farmer, never married, tough as an old leather boot and with a heart as big as Texas, especially where it concerns her animals and friends. When she wants to, she is one of those women who can charm a ten point white tail buck into becoming a hat rack. She is not kind to fools and if you ever make her your enemy, you soon regret it.

To this day I have no idea why she befriended me. I have thought about it often and can find no other answer than, like a wandering bull, she feared for my safety in a country where one could be easily hurt or killed by making the wrong moves or saying the wrong thing, for this part of the world was not too far removed from slavery.

Kicking the bottom of Rose's door, my hands were full, I yelled for her to open it for me. She did, with a smile. Water dripped from my forehead.

"Here, old woman, take the tray with the roast before I drop everything."

"You always need help, don't you?" She took the tray, laughing.

Setting the champagne, dinner wine, and a bottle of Martel cognac on the kitchen counter, I asked, "So where is this company? They leave already?"

"No, she's in the living room. Come, I'll introduce you."

"Let's get the meat cooking first. I'll put the champagne in the fridge and open the dinner wine so it can breathe."

Rose nodded, shoved the standing rib into the oven and made no snide comment about me wanting to "breathe" the wine.

Following her into the living room, which was dim-lit with only a small lamp, I watched a women stand from the couch and extend a hand.

"Jay, meet Susannah Ward."

She looked around thirty. She was slender, and her fine straight nose, hollowed cheeks, and thin lips gave her an aristocratic look. Her light blond hair had recently been styled in the windswept look, but with the humidity and rain it appeared damp and mussed.

She smiled, a dazzling porcelain event showing a glint of a silver bridge tied to a canine—a postmodern smile, a kind of deconstructed dental reconstruction.

After we shook hands, she stared at me really hard. Things got quiet and still and awkward. The stillness was so intense it seemed loud—was palpable, like something floating there between us, a new element created by both of us searching for relief.

She reached up and tucked a stray lock of blond hair behind an ear adorned with a diamond earring that turned the dim light into rainbows darting here and there.

"I'm sorry, Miss Ward. I'm not usually this ambivalent. It's just that I have a feeling we know each other."

"So do I, Mr. Leicester. It's the strangest thing."

"Well, you two sit and I'll bring some hors d'oeuvres. As soon as the champagne cools, we'll get Jay to open it. Dinner will be about an hour."

Susannah sat on the couch wearing a blue, pleated skirt and black pantyhose. She not only crossed her legs, but crossed them again, toe under ankle. She sat blinking her eyes, moving her hands slowly, like a cat does its paws while purring.

Rose brought the snacks, sat them on the coffee table. "The champagne should be cold enough. Jay, would you serve it, please."

Rose saying "please." I was confused. It was as if I'd shown up for some painful dental work only to find a sign on the door reading "Dentist dead." It felt like an episode of the Twilight Zone.

Pouring the sparkling wine and bringing the glasses on a tray, I handed Susannah one.

"Thank you," she said with a smile that made my heart accelerate.

Rose took her glass and sat on the couch next to her guest. I sat across from them. My cat, B.W., emerged from the darkness and jumped into my lap. He had been staying with Rose while I was out of town for a couple of days. A big Siamese, weighing over twenty pounds, there was not an ounce of fat on him. Rose gave him to me when he was six weeks old after my German Shepard of many years died. He has taught me much.

"Oh, he's so beautiful," Susannah said, with an inflection sounding much like a purring feline.

"Yes, he's quiet a character. He's still pissed at me for having his balls cut off, but he tolerates me, most of the time."

Susannah laughed.

"Don't be so crass in front of company," Rose admonished.

"It's okay, Rose," she said. "Speaking openly without reservation makes me feel at home, comfortable, like I'm among friends."

At that, B.W. jumped down, went and smelled around her feet, as if trying to figure out how she'd managed to cross her legs twice. She reached down and picked him up, put him in her lap. "My, he is a big boy."

B.W. settled in as if he'd known her all his life.

Susannah rubbed the big cat and tasted the champagne. I watched for her reaction, wanted to see if she knew anything about wine. Rose suggested that I bring it. There had to be a reason, for she did little, if nothing, merely to impress people.

Susannah seemed to immerse herself into the wine. She stopped petting B.W., gazed deeply into the flute, watching the tiny bubbles rising through the gold liquid. In the dim light of the room, her eyes glimmered like stars reflected in a narrow well.

Her eyes found mine. "You a wine person, Jay?"

I liked the way she said my name. Hell, I liked the way she did anything.

"I know little about it; however I do enjoy a fine wine with good food."

"Liar." Rose looked at Susannah. "The man has a cellar under his house with cases of wine gathering dust."

Susannah laughed. "I worked in the retail end of a large wine company. We handled only the very best for an exclusive clientele. I was able to taste some of the worlds finest."

"Lucky you."

"Yes, lucky me."

"So talk to me about the champagne."

She looked intently into the glass at the golden liquid as if it would offer some intrinsic knowledge. "My guess is this is a non-vintage, a true champagne. All chardonnay, from one of the better producers. Made by the 'methode champenoise' process. Maybe a Roederer or Tattinger."

"Tattinger."

I was impressed with her evaluation.

Smelling the wine deeply, she continued. "I've tasted a lot of their vintage years and frankly don't see a big difference, except in price, but vintage is superior to non-vintage only if the producer has chosen superior batches of wine."

The lady was knowledgeable. I wish now I'd brought a better wine for dinner.

Rose served the meal in the dining room, something she did only on special occasions, making me wonder about her relationship with Susannah Ward. The standing prime rib roast was wonderful and the Stag's Leap Napa Valley cabernet sauvignon from a mediocre year went well with the meal, the candlelight reflecting the brilliant red color on the white tablecloth.

"You going to be here long or you passing through?"

"I'm leaving in the morning, on my way to Colorado."

"I didn't see a car, are you flying out?"

"I'm traveling with a friend. She's visiting her family in Philadelphia and dropped me off here."

That explained the absence of a vehicle.

"Why do you have to be so curious?"

"I'm just making conversation, Rose."

"It's okay. I don't mind." Her tone was soothing but the candlelight illuminated a wet gleam in her eyes. A hundred tiny flames shimmered in her gaze. "My father and Rose were friends. He was an auctioneer at the cattle barn in Forest. My mother died when I was eight years old.

He did the best he could as a single parent to raise me, but by the age of fourteen I was doing drugs and boys. He asked Rose for help. She took me in for a year, straightened me out and I have loved her ever since."

Another one of Rose's strays, I thought, remembering Alella, a young girl from Mexico she took in and salvaged, until I got her killed. There was a lot I did not know about Rose English, but at the moment, I could not have been more proud of her.

Coffee was served in the living room.

"How about you, Jay? You and Rose know each other...?"

"Same as you. She found me wandering around in these woods on the verge of great peril. Took me in, pointed out what I should and shouldn't do, who I should and shouldn't associate with, and gave me a cat. We've been friends for the last ten years."

Susannah laughed. Even Rose smiled.

Something about this auctioneer's daughter intrigued me. I had no idea what. I'd just met her, knew nothing about her, but it was like we'd known each other in another life.

Finishing the coffee, I sat the cup and saucer on the table beside the chair. Rose got up, took all the cups to the kitchen.

"You know, Susannah, it's early, if you're interested, I'd like to show you my cellar, and anything else you'd like to see."

She made an effort to look in my eyes, searching for any traces of madness.

Rose came back and sat down, looking at both of us. "What is it?"

"Jay wants to show me his wine cellar."

Rose looked at me incredulously. "Why do you always have to be the stick that stirs up the hornet's nest?"

"What?"

"I'm sorry. I assumed Rose told you."

"Told me what?"

"I'm on the way to Golden, Colorado for my next assignment, to the Catholic Order of Pueblo Del Este. I'm a nun."

I wondered if there was a Newtonian law to one's mistakes, a set of reactions that ran like the bending of space and time. Maybe Einstein was right with his general theory of relativity.

Rose's eyes sparkled with mischievousness. I guessed she'd done this on purpose. But how could she have known I'd make a play for Sister Ward? She was not a mean-spirited person, but she loved to put me in a position of embarrassment. She delighted in it. Sometimes I thought it was to set me back in my place as a normal person in society, take away some of the arrogance that I was sorely guilty of exuding.

For the next half hour the two women kept talking about everything until the other stuff in between got lost, as when, on Memorial Day in a cemetery, one got distracted from the graves by the flags and flowers. I contemplated my hand, noticing the jagged scar across one knuckle from where Johnny Sassone bit me during a high school football game. Then I looked at both hands, after fourteen years as a defensive player all ten fingers had been broken, some twice, a couple three times. Football is a violent sport.

"Well ladies, I think I'll gather up my cat and head for the little cottage in the wildwoods."

Rose's eyes found me and smiled. It was a face that was friendly, patient. She gave the impression of a woman who was waiting for something to come.

Susannah stood, shook my hand. "It was a pleasure to meet you, Jay. If you're ever near Golden, be sure to give me a call. We're in the book." She held onto my hand. "Remember, do not let the shadow of the lost object fall across the ego."

"Yes, enjoy the Rockies. They are magnificent."

Rose walked me to the door.

"I'll never understand you, old woman."

"Good, that's the way I want it. Sleep well." She had a gleeful smile on her face.

Putting B.W. in the front seat of the truck, I shut the door and sat for a moment. It was raining softly, the kind of rain that reminds one of the optimism of red roses or the fearlessness of a host of daffodils.

At the cottage, I poured a knockout glass of cognac and lit one of the big Charlemagne cigars, my mind reeling back and forth, back and forth, shuffling fears and hopes until it could no longer take credit or blame for anything living or dead. The red tip of the cigar glowed and faded like a drunken firefly.

Finishing the cognac and cigar, I headed for bed. As I drifted into dreamland, an old woman came to my bedside and placed a hand on my forehead—she spoke of the future as already past—then she put her fingers to her lips and left the room.

From the files of Dr. R.T. Hamer, southern California: 1934

Eighty-two year old man from Chicago with a malignancy all around his face and neck. It was a gory mass. Just terrible. Just a red gory mass. It had taken over all around his face. It had taken off one eyelid at the bottom of the eye. It had taken off the bottom of the lower lobe of the ear and had also gone into the cheek area, nose and chin.

In six months of treatment with the Rife Frequency Instrument all that was left was a little black spot on the side of his face and the condition of that was such that it was about to slough off. His skin was clean again, just like a baby's skin.

Chapter Two

It was a bright, soft morning. The air was cool; while on the porch my breath blew into vapor mimicking the steam rising from the coffee cup. A chill defined the boundaries of each shadow from the deep woods.

A dark sedan passed by on the road in front of the cottage headed in the direction of Rose's house. It returned shortly. Susannah Ward headed for the convent in Colorado, I thought. Godspeed, Sister, I wish we'd met long ago—maybe we did. B.W. meowed at my feet. Reaching down, picking him up, I said, "Well old boy, there goes the past and the future." The cat squirmed to get down and headed for the door. He could care less about my existential thinking. He was hungry.

Inside, I poured some dry cat food in a bowl. The big Siamese turned up his nose, set looking at me as if asking, "The recession so bad that we can't afford tuna?"

I opened a can and poured it over the dry food. "Enjoy, my feline friend. That's all you'll get today."

The phone rang. Probably Rose—wanting to tell me that the nun was gone and to gloat a little at her well-executed plan to frustrate the local bachelor. But no, it wasn't Rose.

It was Hebrone Opshinsky. "Take a ride with me."

"Where are you?"

"Key West."

"Where might we be going?"

"Texas."

"Big state. Mode of transportation?"

"I sold my boat. Need to deliver it to Port Lavaca."

This stunned me. Hebrone Opshinsky would never part with his beloved Wheeler sportfisherman. He loved that boat, had spent decades restoring and keeping it shipshape.

"Pick me up at the airport, one o'clock this afternoon. I'll get J.D. to fly me to the Island."

We hung up, and I called my friend, J.D. Ballard.

"Can you fly me to Key West this morning?"

"Why not. Anything else you'd like? Maybe a trip around the world, stop in Afghanistan, see how the war is going against the Taliban and al-Qaeda?"

"Hebrone sold his boat."

There was a pause, then, "Did he lose a bet? Is he dying?"

"Will you take me to Key West?"

"We can leave in an hour."

"I'll meet you at the hangar."

Packing a ditty bag, my mind was assailed by unconnected memories, a storm at sea, ice on an airplane wing, a wet towel in a motel room, a Habit hiding the face of a nun in a darkened church.

Throwing a pair of crew socks in the bag, I noted they were so worn I could put them on from either end.

Parking in Rose's driveway, I grabbed B.W. and headed for the door.

"What's wrong?" Rose asked, emerging from the rear of the house.

Handing her the cat, I said, "It's Hebrone. I don't know how bad. J.D. is flying me to Key West."

"Is he hurt?"

"No, worse. He sold his boat."

"God---men!"

"There's no way to know how long I'll be gone. Look after the place and him." I pointed at the cat.

"Call me tonight."

"If I can."

She turned on her heel and walked away holding B.W. like a new-born baby, leaving a silence both uneasy and amused in her wake. I headed for the small grass runway we jokingly refer to as the "Union, Mississippi International Airport."

J.D. Ballard stood beside his favorite toy, a 1980 Cessna Citation 1SP. He'd bought it from an advertising agency in Jackson, the state capital, when they upgraded to a larger jet. My aviation consulting company sold the ad agency the Citation a few years ago. It was in immaculate mechanical shape and, with new engines, was a safe, easy to fly, economical, short field airplane for a retired radiologist.

Ironically, Cessna Aircraft was celebrating the 40th anniversary of the maiden flight of the Citation 500. On September 15, 1969, an old friend, pilot Milt Sills and copilot J.L. LeSueur flew the first Citation prototype from Wichita Municipal Airport—now Mid-Continent Airport—on a one-hour, 45-minute sortie. Originally named the Fanjet 500, a vice president of marketing convinced Cessna to rebrand the jet as the Citation, after the thoroughbred racehorse that won the Triple Crown in 1948. The six-passenger, 400 mph Citation, priced at $695,000, was the best-selling business jet of all time in its first year of production.

J.D. was a square-framed man of sixty, with a slender face and dark brown eyes highlighted by long lashes. His auburn hair was cut close and showed no grey. He was the kind of person who always seemed glad to see you. Recently retired from medicine, he spent his time on a small farm enjoying life and pursuing his passion for flying, fine food and wine, and hand-rolled cigars. He developed a theory that one should live each day as if it were their last. However, in the preceding few years he had developed an obsession with the life and times of a man named Royal R. Rife, a medical scientist who lived in the early part of the 20th century. It was an obsession that affected him profoundly, enough so that he would spend time with his pastor to help with the dilemma.

It involved a controversial cure for cancer that remained outside the mainstream of modern medicine.

We shook hands.

"She's full of fuel and the preflight is complete. Batteries are charged, so we don't need a power cart. Weather is good in Key West and I filed direct at flight level 350. You want to fly?"

"No. I'll act as your copilot and will sign you off for a proficiency check, if you wish, assuming you do not get lost and land in Cuba."

Still holding an FAA (Federal Aviation Administration) check pilot designation on the Citation, I could give type ratings, annual proficiency checks, and initial and recurrent training in the aircraft. However, when J.D. bought the airplane, I insisted he go through the FlightSafety training syllabus. It is an extended course using classroom, flight simulator, and time in the actual aircraft. I felt he could benefit from the extra training, especially since he planned to fly the Citation single-pilot on occasions.

"You don't mind if I walk around this bird, do you? Check to see if the wings and tail are still attached to the fuselage. Be sure you removed the pitot covers and the gust locks."

"I would expect nothing less from you. Oh, by the way, we have a passenger who will ride along with us, keep me company on the trip home. Here she comes, now."

A black H2 turned onto the road to the hangar. It was one of those civilian built, useless pieces of urban scrap iron the rich and stupid buy thinking they are driving something resembling an actual military Humvee. They are not.

It parked next to my truck and the occupant opened the door and stepped out. H2 not withstanding, the driver was a thing of beauty. She was a tall, delicately featured woman with black hair spinning down to her shoulders, intense eyes set in a thin Sephardic face. Striding easily over to where we stood with the agility of an athlete, I guessed her to be a runner. Her small dark eyes flashed at me for a moment like a hawk lasered on a rabbit from five hundred feet above.

"We ready to fly?" She directed the question to J.D., ignoring me.

I sensed she was an aggressive person, and on close inspection, not so young as she appeared from afar. From her I anticipated mean-spiritedness, vituperation, hypocrisy, and the other uncivilized behavior that is characteristic of those gripped by high emotion but without a clear understanding of facts. However, I've been wrong before with first impressions.

"Jay, meet Dr. Nancy Wiseman."

She reached out and shook my hand. It was a firm grip and her palm was warm.

"So this is the infamous Jay Leicester. I've heard a lot about you, some good, some not so good."

She was older, I guessed mid-fifties. Her face was drawn, and her eyes looked as hard as little black diamonds.

"You have me at a disadvantage, Dr. Wiseman. I've never heard of you."

"Please call me Nancy. I'm on the board of the Cattleman's Association in Philadelphia with Rose English and Shack Runnels. Between those two and J.D., your name comes up—a lot." She laughed and her eyes softened.

"You cannot believe a word any of them say about me. Lies, all lies."

She laughed an infectious laugh. I could see the attraction J.D. saw in her.

"Nancy runs a family clinic in Philadelphia."

"You're an MD?"

"D.O."

"Ah, an Osteopath."

"Don't tell me you have something against Osteopathic Medicine?"

"On the contrary. I came within signing my name on the dotted line of going to Osteopathic school at Downers Grove, Ill. My college roommate begged me to enroll. Both of our MCAT (medical college admission test) scores were the highest of the year. I visited the campus, just west of Chicago. It was tempting, but I elected to play in the NFL and then aviation."

"I may just like you, Jay Leicester. I had not planned too."

"Let's load up," J.D. said.

"Do you two—pilots—think you can find Key West?" The doctor said. "If not, I'll be glad to show you the way."

J.D. buckled himself into the left seat while I secured the cabin door.

"I must warn you, Jay, Nancy has a commercial license and is type rated in the Citation."

I was beginning to like this D.O. more and more.

Picking up the checklist, I said, "I'll read'em, you do'em."

J.D. nodded.

"Parking Brake."

"Set."

"Control Lock."

"Off."

"Oxygen System."

"Checked."

"Switches and Circuit Breakers."

"Checked."

"Throttles."

"Off."

"Battery Switch."

"On, voltage checked."

"Generator Switches."

"On."

We continued through the thirty-three items on the Before Takeoff Checklist. One cannot and should not expect to execute them from memory. That is why they print Checklists. Complacency in a cockpit has an unpleasant habit of becoming perilous. I have survived some twenty thousand hours aloft by asking a simple question before every flight; What if? What can go wrong, and if it does, what do we do about it? In a cockpit the most dangerous moment during an emergency is when fear and disorientation make it impossible to think. But a pilot must do something, even if it's wrong. This is the moment when training pays off.

There have been situations, other than flying, where if someone had asked the question what if, what can go wrong, the outcome may have been different: Making an investment in a portfolio of sub prime loans. Booking passage on a hydrogen-filled dirigible. Signing a nonaggression pact with Hitler. Deciding to bomb Pearl Harbor. Claiming to the world that you have weapons of mass destruction when you do not. What can go wrong?

Taxiing to the very end of the three thousand foot grass runway, we turned around to depart to the west and had to wait while four golfers cleared the far end. The airport borders the local country club and, with few takeoff and landings, is a favorite driving range for the duffers.

I read the takeoff data to J.D. "V-speeds are: V1-105, Vr-105, V2-115, Vfs-125, and Vse-146. Vref for emergency return-108. Fan speeds: Takeoff-91.4, Climb-88.8." Accelerating quickly, we were airborne within fifteen hundred feet, climbing out into a clear sky.

I watched the ground recede. It was the kind of morning that makes you feel that life is worth living. We cleaned up the airplane, went through the Climb checklist, and I tended to the radio communications. Finally cleared up to flight level 350 (thirty-five thousand feet), we were able to relax and enjoy the view. It was a gorgeous and unexpectedly sunny day. The cold front from yesterday had cleared the area. We could see the back side of it far off to the south and west. On the ground the winter colors shifted from brown to green and back again offering a cubist view of the world. Rectangular farmland shifted as if in a mirror, flattened, and then fell into the horizon.

Here was where I belonged. In the electric silence of the air, I felt I could hear the chorus of Handel's "Messiah," in full orchestra, trumpeting all its glory inside my head. At once, I felt puny and insignificant before the vast and scarcely comprehensible scale; a man alone in the vastness of the sky. I often feel there is an underlying simplicity to God's plan that continues to elude us all.

Up here, in the rarefied air, the boundary between life and death shrank so much that it was little more than a membrane, thin and clear. With hardly a step, one could make the transition. Who was I? Why was I here? Jay Leicester, aviation consultant. My career as a line pilot for a regional carrier lasted for twenty-five years. When offered early retirement after a merger, I jumped at the chance, and opened a consulting business. After ten years, I had enough of city life, bought a farm in the central part of the state, built a small cottage, and ran the business from there. It's been a good ride. I've met some interesting people, enjoyed the quiet times of the rural life. Now I was on my way to help an old friend deliver his beloved boat to a buyer. Something was very wrong. After the death of his girlfriend, Hebrone Opshinsky only had two loves in life, his full-blooded wolf, named Savage, and his Wheeler sportfisherman. He would never part with either unless something drastic had occurred.

Hebrone had been my friend for over twenty years. We met on a dark and evil night after a woman was murdered on a boat I was staying aboard in a marina in Biloxi, Mississippi. Hebrone was the night manager of the marina. He helped me and, later, saved my life. We became close after that.

As a young man, he joined the Army and served as a "grunt" in Vietnam. There are many jobs in the military. The war machine is vast and complex and ever changing. Some see no combat, some see too much. Some are introduced to the dark side. Such was Hebrone. Trained as an assassin, he killed one hundred and fifty-two enemy combatants---by hand, up close and personal. His existence was denied by our government. He wore no uniform, carried no I.D., and worked alone. He killed because his country wanted him too, because he was ordered to. The target was not of his choice, but that of our government and military leaders. After two tours of duty, his service was no longer needed, our cause was lost. His last kill was a Viet Cong Colonel responsible for the slaughter of sixty-one American soldiers in an ambush during the last month of the war. Forty-eight hours later, Hebrone was mustered out of the Army and walking the streets of New Orleans, Louisiana. There was no reindoctrination to civilized society, no visits to psychiatrist, no offer of help of any kind. He turned to alcohol and other drugs, drifted from one menial job to another, finally ending up on the Mississippi coast and in trouble with the law. A lawyer, Guy Robbins, helped him clean up, found a judge who was an ex-marine to listen to his military history and cut him some slack. Placed on probation, he detoxed and started to straighten out his life.

When we met, I was surprised at how youthful he seemed, as he was my age, and possessed the athleticism and energy of a much younger man. His manner was curt most of the time. His face was open and handsome, with a proud jaw line and a strong nose, the whole framed by neatly trimmed sideburns. Only the defiant gleam of his dark, hooded eyes belied the killer inside.

I could not comprehend the mental fortitude required to endure what he had seen and done. Something had to be fundamentally broken after the war in his psychic, some kind of primal dislocation between cause and effect, resulting in a numbness wholly understandable, necessary even, given the events, but which had the effect of allowing him to live with the memory of the killing. I once asked him if he ever had flash backs. "Yes, I do," he said. "But they are of a girl I knew in high school."

. . .

"Citation One Juliet Delta, descend and maintain flight level 240."

"Roger, One Juliet Delta out of 350 for 240."

Opshinsky once told me that early on, while "in country" he noticed the best performance from our young troops occurred when the enemy was trying to kill them, which led him to propose that such intense motivation would serve to improve the performance of our government leaders, or at least weed out those who couldn't run very fast. I tended to agree with him.

"One Juliet Delta, descend to FL100, contact Miami Approach on 133.5."

"Roger, down to ten thousand, Miami on 133.5, One Juliet Delta."

"Okay, Captain Ballard, descent checklist. Defog Fan."

"On."

"Pressure and Rate."

"Set."

"Altimeter."

"Out of 18,000, set and checked."

Tuning in the Key West ATIS (Automatic Terminal Information Service), I listened to the data. "They are landing to the east today. Winds are 33 at 10 knots, skies are clear, altimeter 30.06."

J.D. smiled. "Nice day in Key West."

"Hello Miami, One Juliet Delta with you, level ten thousand."

"November One Juliet Delta, descend to six thousand and Ident."

"There you go."

"We have you radar contact out of nine thousand. Contact Navy Key West on 124.025. Information Charlie is current."

"Navy Key West on 124.025. We have Charlie. Good day, y'all."

We landed on runway Nine and taxied to the FBO on the west end of the airport. Hebrone was waiting out front of the hangar.

Inside, over coffee, J.D. introduced Nancy and Hebrone. They eyed each other like two boxers, but were cordial.

J.D. placed a fuel order and filed a flight plan.

Walking them out to the Citation, I thanked him for the ride and told Nancy it had been nice to meet her and to please not let J.D. get lost trying to find Union International.

We watched the jet depart.

· · ·

Turning to Hebrone, I said, "Now, my friend, talk to me."

From the files of Dr. Milbank Johnson, San Diego, California: 1935

Patient: Tom Knight presented with carcinoma over the malar bone of his left cheek. Location of tumor enabled us to observe and measure from the start to finish of treatment with the Rife Frequency Instrument. Cure complete in three months. Details of treatment and of pathological examination are documented for your purview.

Chapter Three

Following Hebrone out to an almost new double-cab Ford Pickup truck, I asked who it belonged to, for I knew he had never spent a dime on a vehicle in his life.

"Smash was driving it when he disappeared. It's registered in his name. Nobody claimed it, so I've been driving it. The candy lady probably gave it to him."

Smash was the nickname of Andrew Bullard, a friend of ours who was lost at sea, along with a very rich lady who inherited a fortune from her family whose wealth came from a large candy manufacturing conglomerate. He was delivering her and the yacht to the Caribbean. They were caught in a vicious storm near Puerto Rico. No bodies were ever recovered.

"So what are you going to tell the police if they stop you?"

"That the truck belongs to Smash. What can they say?"

"Where are we going? The marina is the other way."

"I've rented a house not far from the submarine pens. Little, two bedroom cottage on the water."

"I was looking forward to staying aboard the Wheeler. What about Savage? He's never been a landlubber."

"Savage is dead. Somebody poisoned him. It's why I rented the house. I couldn't stay aboard without him, and why I sold the boat."

"I'm sorry, Hebrone. You want to tell me about it?"

"Maybe later."

"Stop by Tony's. I'll buy you a drink."

Hebrone looked over at me. "Good idea."

We had to park two blocks away on Whitehead Street, just down from the Hemingway house and museum. Duval Street was crowded with tourist and the side streets were full of cars with license plates from all over the U.S. Ocean liners docked at Mallory Square, offloading two thousand souls at a time. Good for the economy, bad for the island. I was lucky to have lived in Key West when it was a quiet island with a terrible economy, but a wonderful life style, populated with native Conchs, fishermen, and a few seasonal tourists. The biggest thing happening on the island was Mel Fisher and his quest for treasure from shipwrecks. He finally did find his treasure, but at great personal cost.

Captain Tony's is the original site of Joe Russell's "Sloppy Joe's Bar," made famous by Ernest Hemingway, who would finish writing each day and plod barefoot from his home to the bar and spend time observing the local clientele. Contrary to popular myth, Hemingway was not a drunk who drank himself into a stupor each day, but a man who enjoyed a drink and the company of Key West friends. He tolerated neither phony nor rheumy, and many of his characters were drawn from the people he observed in the establishment.

We entered the dim-lit, cave-like bar and a booming voice from the back bellowed, "Jay Leicester, as I live and breathe. Come sit yo'self down. I gone buy you a drink."

This was "Skinner," a giant of a man who was so black he shined. He had worked at Captain Tony's since it opened. Tony took him in after a knee injury ended a baseball career with the Pittsburg Pirates. He and I had known each other for twenty years. On more than one occasion Skinner poured me into a cab and sent me home when I was young, living on the Island, and flying for a startup airline. He was six foot three inches, three hundred pounds, and feared nothing. One day I was swimming off the Mallory docks with one of our Airline Captains when he was bitten by a large barracuda, severing the femoral artery.

When I yelled for help, Skinner, without hesitation, dove into the water and assisted me in dragging the man ashore. In spite of our efforts, the Captain bled out and died, but Skinner was the only one of many on the dock who responded to our need.

"Where you find dis one at, Cop'en Shinsky?"

"Wandering around on Duval Street eyeing all the lovely girls."

"You both be wanting some fine gin and tonic with fresh lime, I bet?"

"You'd be correct, Mr. Skinner."

We sat at the bar next to Captain Tony's wife's skeleton that hung next to the cash register. She has been there since the doors opened. So many rumors throughout the years have clouded the truth of the bones. What that truth is, no one knows. Tony took it to his death. What does amaze me is that the skeleton is real and no authority has ever questioned its origin. Ah, Key West.

Two men entered the dim-lit bar, and one could tell from their dress that they were fishermen fresh off the boat. Also as obvious, this was not the first bar they'd visited since docking. From their boisterous actions with other patrons, they were regulars at Captain Tony's. I watched Skinner reach under the bar and pull out a small Billy-club that reminded one of a miniature baseball bat. The end had been drilled out and lead poured into the hole. Skinner looked at me and, with his eyes, pointed to Hebrone and shook his head. All experience inoculates us with the ability to sense the environment in indefinable ways, and nothing is better at honing the senses than the threat of danger.

The two men started around the bar to where we were sitting. The one leading the way was short and stocky and his hair appeared to have been cut by a blind person. His cheeks were permanently flushed and reddened by scores of tiny broken veins. He was a burly, florid, red-faced man who glared at the world from beneath eyebrows that resembled a pair of ferocious caterpillars.

The one following was younger, his features fine-boned, his nose sharp, his ears too large, the overall effect comical. He was cadaverous, and his teeth seemed to be fighting to escape his mouth. He exuded the enthusiasm of a Doberman Pinscher dog. His speaking voice came complete with exclamation marks and the accompaniment of waving arms.

I had a strange feeling as if a story was unfolding that was controlled not by me but by destiny.

The burly man approached Hebrone. I could smell him from ten feet away. It was the aroma of dead fish, stale tobacco, cheap whisky and dried sweat.

"Well, well, if it ain't the Wolf man. Where yo wolf, Wolf man? He guarding yo little antique boat?"

There was sarcasm and something else I couldn't quite pinpoint in his voice. It could have been anger or a threat or simply teasing.

The younger man laughed. "Antique boat, ha, ha."

Hebrone turned halfway around. The light streaming in from the front door imparted a white-hot luminescence to his face. He glowered at the fisherman like a sullen kid at a hated step-father.

"Raton, best you leave," Skinner said, holding up the Billy-club. "Ain't gone be no trouble in dis bar today."

"What you gone do, big man? Hit Raton wid dat club? I'll gut you like a fish you ever come near me wid dat thing." He pulled out a knife from a sheath on his belt and waved it at Skinner.

Starting from behind the bar, Skinner bumped the cash register, shaking Tony's wife's bones. They rattled like an Eastern Diamondback. It would have been comical in any other setting.

In a moment of time I can only describe as a blur, Hebrone was off his stool, Raton was on the floor, his buddy holding his hands in front of his chest and backing away. Hebrone held the knife, his eyes looking at a place far from Key West and Captain Tony's bar. I feared for what might happen next.

Standing, I pointed at Raton's pusillanimous pal. He had backed all the way to the door. "Get your friend and leave. Now!"

Skinner eased up beside Hebrone. "It's fine, now, Cop'en. Gimme dat ole knife and I'll fix us another drink."

Turning, I shouted, "Hebrone!"

He returned from wherever he'd been and looked at me.

"It's over. Give Skinner the knife."

He looked at the big bartender, at the knife, and then at the man on the floor.

"It's okay, Cop'en. We fine, now. De man, Raton, he don't know about Savage being poisoned. He didn't mean nothing. He drunk is all."

Raton pulled himself from the floor, rubbed the back of his head, glared at Hebrone. "Can I have my knife back?"

"Come by tomorrow. You can get it when you sober. Now go on, get out of dis bar."

We sat back down on our stools and Skinner made fresh drinks.

"Ole Raton been at sea for the last two months. He didn't know about the bad thing with Savage. He still pissed about the wolf biting him when he tried to get aboard yo Wheeler one night while you out of town. He knew you had some gin onboard and all the bars were closed for the parade. Dat's why he acting like he is today."

We finished our drinks, thanked Skinner and started out the door, headed for the rental house on the water.

"Cop'en Jay, before you go let me show you something."

I followed him into the storeroom at the back of the bar.

"You got to watch Cop'en Shinsky. I'm worried about him. He gone do a terrible thing."

"What are you talking about, Skinner?"

"Dem people poisoned Savage, he knows who dey is. He gone kill'em, and it gone be slow and as painful as he can make it. It's a black mood he in. You got to try and stop him."

Skinner sat down on a stack of Jack Daniels whiskey. His face furrowed, sweat rolled down his forehead, making his skin shiny and ebony-looking.

"We're leaving in the morning to deliver the Wheeler to Texas. Hebrone sold it to someone in Port Lavaca."

He pulled a neatly ironed and folded white handkerchief from his pocket, wiped his face.

"I know, Cop'en. Lot of people wants to buy the Wheeler when word got around it for sale. He rejected a bunch of'em, even though they offered more money. He waited until he found a buyer along the Texas coast."

"Why?"

"Dem people poisoned Savage, dey spoiled, rich folks from Houston. He gone deliver de Wheeler, then take a side trip to murder'em, then come back to here. You got to stop him. He gone lose his soul, dat what he gone do."

"Why would they poison Savage?"

"He ain't told you? Best you get him to do that, Cop'en. But you got to stop him from something evil."

"I promise you he won't commit cold-blooded murder while I'm with him."

"Dat's all I ask. You a good man. You keep our friend from the dark place."

Skinner stood, reached out and shook my hand.

"I miss old Smash. Too bad he had to drown along with the candy lady. He was my friend."

"Yes, I miss him, too."

Hebrone and I walked the two blocks back to the truck.

"Skinner fill you in on my evil intentions?"

"Said you had a little revenge on your mind. When were you going to tell me about it?"

"We'll talk when we get to the house."

"Yes we will."

• • •

We sat on the deck of the little cottage overlooking the water. A sixty foot fishing vessel passed by within yards of us. It was known as a "Party" boat, taking paid customers out to the reef for five hours of bottom fishing. The ticket price included rods and bait and deckhands to remove the fish off the hook for you. The boat anchored on the reef and it could be a miserable experience for a landlubber as the open ocean swells caused it to roll constantly.

The sun was low on the horizon. However, we could not see it from the deck, which was fortunate, as I was in no mood to honor the Key West custom of standing and clapping as "Old Sol" sank into the sea. Hebrone served gin over crushed ice and fresh lime. I did not push him on Savage's death. He would get to it in his own time.

"I figured we turn in early, get up at four a.m. and slip the lines at first light. We will run straight across the Gulf to Port Lavaca. Should take a little over three days."

"There's not enough fuel to go nonstop."

"We have an extra two-hundred gallons in fifty gallon drums, lashed forward."

Doing some quick figuring, I found we might still come up short, and I said so.

"The man that bought the boat will bring out fuel to us if we need it. He'll be standing by on the radio."

"If this was an airplane---"

"But it's not an airplane, Leicester."

He only called me by my last name when he was angry. I let it slide.

"You really sell the Wheeler?"

"Yes. Savage was the last straw. It was hard enough after Joanne died. But this---it's too much."

Joanne Fourche was Hebrone's live-in girlfriend. They were together for six years. She died from ovarian cancer.

"Maybe you should wait six months, and then make a decision."

"The decision is made. I've hired on with an aircraft delivery company. They want me to live near the home office. It's landlocked and there will be no time for the boat."

"What delivery company?"

"It's a startup. They have contracts to deliver big airplanes all over the globe. I get a piece of the action. It was too good to turn down."

"Why did you not talk this over with me before you made such a big jump?"

"Didn't need your input."

He did not tell me the name of the company and I did not ask again. It would be easy enough to find out later.

"So what about this couple who poisoned Savage?"

"They are young, late twenties. Daddy's money, both of'em been spoiled since birth. Always had their way. The girl's parents are in the oil business, the boy's, an investment conglomeration. Their wedding present was a seventy foot Bertram yacht, complete with Captain and Steward. A Falcon jet flies them from Texas to the boat, wherever they choose to go. One of the places was a berth next to ours. The girl took offense to Savage. You know how that old wolf loved to howl when the moon was full. Seems nobody had ever said no to her before. Things escalated. I just never saw it coming, her poisoning Savage."

"How'd you find out?"

"Their boat Captain. He said the woman did it, and the husband knew about it and encouraged her."

"What did she use?"

"Antifreeze."

"Ah, God."

"Yeah."

"Did you come to the boat and find Savage?"

"No. I was away for two days. The boat Captain called a local vet when he discovered what they'd done. The vet couldn't save Savage."

"Where did you bury him?"

"At sea. That old wolf spent his whole life onboard the Wheeler. I went out into the Gulf Stream, committed his body to the deep."

"What about this couple? What are your plans?"

The cruelty and resolution showed in his eyes as clearly as when the muzzle of a gun aims at one's forehead.

"Those two people go through life incurious about anything, whether history or science or the well-being of any other human. They are like some subspecies, interested only in what's in front of them at the moment. They need to be taught a lesson. Revenge is a great satisfier."

I sat my drink on the table, looked toward the west, the sky was still glowing from the sunset. Sometime it may be required of man to simply accept fate, to bear his cross. Every situation is distinguished by its uniqueness, and there is only one right answer to the problem posed by the situation at hand. In this case did a double murder exacted for revenge over the killing of a wolf equal justice?

As if he knew what I was thinking, Hebrone sat his drink down on the table rather hard. "Leicester, there is a moral aspect to nature as well as a material aspect, and in this case, it is my duty to link the material to the moral. Anyone, including you, who disagrees is deep in the mire of folly."

"How long have we known each other, Hebrone?"

"Get to your point."

"I'm aware that you've killed a lot of people, but I've never seen you murder anyone."

"That's what you think? That I'm going to murder those two spoiled brats?"

"Skinner thinks you are in an evil state of mind. I know about your black moods."

"The barkeep may be right."

"Is he?"

"Tell me, Captain Leicester, what would you do?"

"I'd wait six months before I sold my boat."

"The two who killed Savage---?"

"What you and the wolf experienced, an animal to a man, no power on earth can take from you. However, human life, under any circumstance, never ceases to have meaning, and this infinite meaning of life includes suffering and dying, privation and death, though not necessarily at your hands."

"The two---?"

"I think you need to make them feel responsible."

"You ever kick a dog for pissing on your leg, Leicester? You think the dog understands why you kicked him? Just about as much as those two rich shits could be made to feel responsible for poisoning Savage."

"So your solution is cold-blooded murder?"

"I have given this a lot of thought, and no, murder is not a consideration. It disappoints me that Skinner would think I'd do that. It hurts me to the core that you would think it. My past will always haunt me. To never be completely trusted, even by your closest friends, is a terrible burden to bear."

"I never believed that you would---"

Hebrone held up his hand to stop me.

"That you even had to ask was enough."

"What do you want me to do, say I'm sorry?"

"It would help."

"Okay, I'm sorry for thinking you would kill two stupid rich kids for poisoning Savage. Hell, I'd consider it if I were in your shoes."

Hebrone laughed.

"All right, Jay. Apology accepted."

"You do have to admit, your reputation precedes you. I disagree with Jean-Paul Sartre, who wrote that *'man invents himself'*. I think the meaning of our existence is not invented by ourselves, but rather detected."

"That's exactly what I'm counting on."

"What does that mean?"

"The rich kids learning of my reputation, knowing that I may come after them and the horrible things that could happen. The seeds are being planted even as we speak."

"I'll be damned. Now I see your plan. Tell me..."

"Their boat Captain started by telling them who I was, my

background. He also told the boy's father what had occurred. The man called me and offered to assist in anyway that he could. Seems he has been wishing to teach both of them some respect for other people for a long time. He was truly distraught at what they had done with the poisoning. When he heard I couldn't live on the Wheeler any more, and that it was up for sale, he bought it---for three times what it was worth."

"So we're going to make a mock assault on the young couple. Make them think they are going to die a horrible death, with full cooperation of the boy's father. Brilliant. I can't wait for the details."

"Both sets of parents are in on it. The boy's father called his daughter-in-law's parents and they are on board, one hundred percent."

"I am included in this little scheme of yours, aren't I?"

"It's why I invited you along."

"We need to tell Skinner."

"When we get back. We may even have to have a little fun with him. He takes life too seriously."

"Let's turn in. If you are going to get me up at four a.m., I need some sleep."

Sometime later, I lay in bed listening to my stomach growl. We had not eaten dinner. I looked up at the play of light on the ceiling. It was the moon reflecting in part from the water twenty yards away. It made strange but steady movements, changing, as the moon moved in its orbit and the tide and wind ebbed and flowed. I thought about Smash. He would love to have been on this adventure. I liked the man and missed him. There was always a kind of distance between us, but there's nobody, except maybe Hebrone, I trusted more, and nobody I admired more. We were different, but close. I knew he was on my side, no matter what. I didn't always understand the man, and I often disagreed with him, but I guess that's the mark of a friend. You make up your mind about a person in the beginning and then stick in there no matter what.

From the files of Dr. James Couche:

"I make the following declaration. In 1934 at the Scripps Institute Annex, in San Diego, California, Dr. Milbank Johnson, M.D., who was then president of the Medical Association of Los Angeles, conducted a clinic using the Rife Frequency Instrument to treat cancer. One patient, an elderly cattle rancher presented with end stage stomach cancer; he was a bag of bones and too weak to move on his own. Upon examining the man, I put my hand on the cavity where his stomach was underneath and I could feel his backbone. The stomach was just one solid mass, just about what I could cover with my hand. I thought that there was nothing to be done for this man. However, in the course of time over six weeks to two months, to my astonishment, he completely recovered."

Chapter Four

The smell of fresh coffee woke me from a deep, restful sleep, no dreams, no sweats. An old German saying came to mind: *"A good conscience is the best pillow."* My old, well-traveled "GMT Master" Rolex glowed 4:00 a.m.

Taking a quick shower, I entered the small kitchen to find Hebrone had prepared a huge breakfast.

"We forgot to eat last night. Have a hardy meal. It may be your last one for several days."

. . .

The two engines on the Wheeler rumbled softly as we eased out of the harbor behind two charter boats heading for the Gulf Stream. I silently wished them good fishing. The December weather was a sailor's delight. The skies were clear, the winds calm, and the salt air not only smelled wonderful, but was clean and bracing.

We took up a heading of due west and held that for seventy miles until we were past the Dry Tortugas Islands, home of Fort Jefferson, now a National Park and one of the most beautiful places on the planet. It was, during the Civil War, used as a prison and held the controversial Dr. Samuel Mudd, who was imprisoned on the island when he set Booth's leg after he killed Lincoln. The island has no water and is accessible only by boat or seaplane. I once spent a week here, stormbound by a fierce winter gale. Though we ran short of water, there was plenty of beer and soda and the fish were abundant. The islands, which have a fascinating history and gorgeous beaches, were discovered in 1513 by Ponce de Leon, who named them Tortugas (which means turtle in Spanish) after the great number of green sea turtles found in the waters.

As soon as we cleared the islands, we took up a heading of North West, direct for Port Lavaca. The nausea I usually experience the first day at sea was quickly passing and by early evening, my sea legs had returned. I began to revel at the ocean.

Captain Opshinsky decided on a watch schedule of four hours on and four off. For a two man crew, I agreed, though on this first day we both were on the flying bridge and enjoying being at sea.

Late that afternoon, I volunteered to take the first watch, and suggested Hebrone go and stir up some grub. He did not answer. When I looked at him, tears were streaming down his face.

"I don't know if I can go below. That old wolf won't be there to lay his head in my lap and look up at me with those baleful eyes, asking why Joanne isn't with us."

"I understand," I said, wondering how he'd managed to provision the boat for this voyage.

We were quiet, watching the gentle waves of the Gulf of Mexico. There is no need to be ashamed of tears, for they bear witness that man has the greatest of courage, the courage to suffer. In a strong and violent man like Hebrone, this show of emotion might seem out of character, but not to me, for I knew the man. To live is to suffer; to survive is to find meaning in the suffering. If there is a purpose to life at all, there must be a purpose to suffering and in dying. But no man can tell another what this purpose is. Each must find out for himself, and must accept the responsibility that his answer prescribes. If he succeeds he will continue to grow in spite of all indignities. Hebrone is moving on, going to work for an aircraft delivery company. It's his motivation to continue to live. It is a peculiarity of man that he can only live by looking to the future. Nietzsche wrote: *"He who has a why to live can bear with almost any how."*

"I'll go below and make a couple of Ham Sams. You want a beer?"

"Yes and thanks. Give me a little time, I'll be fine."

"I know you will. Mustard or mayo on the sandwich?"

"There's a jar of 'Miss Molly's' salsa in the cooler. Spread some of that on the ham."

We ate the sandwiches, drank the beer, and watched the sun set in the water. At the moment, life just couldn't get any better.

"I'm going to shut the port engine down. We'll run with this configuration until daylight, then both engines during the day, and shut the starboard engine down tomorrow night. That should save some fuel."

"Fine by me, it's your boat. Or was."

Hebrone looked at me with a rather strange expression, but I meant nothing by the comment.

"I'm going below. See you at midnight."

Hebrone saluted me, and as I climbed down the companionway ladder, I heard the port engine stop running. That is always a sound that frightens me, too much aviation fuel running through my veins.

Lying in the starboard bunk, I could not sleep. The rumble and vibration of the one engine had an uncanny sound, like a cry for help sent out in commiseration for the unhappy load which it was asked to carry. There was a feeling of weariness in my bones. At what age does one become old, I wondered. No one is ever old at sea, but they grow up very fast. I grew up rapidly on the farm in Osyka, Mississippi, and was never as old as I was at twenty-one.

Giving up on sleep, I made a fresh pot of coffee, poured two cups, and started up to the flying bridge. The time was eleven forty-five p.m. Hebrone was not at the wheel. Fear began to set in. What had happened? Then I spotted him forward, up near the bow, and gave a big sigh of relief. Giving the fog horn a short burst caused Hebrone to turn and, seeing me, returned to where I'd taken over the steering.

Handing him the coffee, I said, "What were you doing?"

"Checking some gear. You're early, but thanks for the java."

"Anything I need to know about the boat?"

"Keep an eye on the temperature. That engine tends to run a little hot. If it does, back off the RPMs for a few minutes and it'll cool down. You get any rest?"

"No, just got older. You see any other ships?"

"Maybe a submarine, but no ships."

"Really, a submarine?"

"That's what I'm telling myself it was. A bright light, going south to north, ten to fifteen knots, just below the surface."

"Had to be a sub."

"Yeah. I'll see you in four hours."

Settling in to steering the seventy-five year old Wheeler, a twin-engine blue water sportfisherman built in New York, on her course to Port Lavaca, Texas, a coastal town south and west of Houston, I had an unencumbered view into a clear sky, and the full moon cast a pearl glow on the water, the boat, and me. Where the moon did not penetrate, there was nothing, blackness, a liquid wash of empty space. Sometimes, when we were flying, we would look out the cockpit windows and gaze at the stars and see patterns there, feel kinship with those twinkling, gaseous spheres racing farther away from us at the speed of light, and register wonder, admiration, awe, a kind of joy, and forget, for the moment, the stupidities and brutalities of our lot. But tonight, the brightness of the moon caused the stars to seem washed out, hazy, like a cheap painting on black velvet. A phosphorous wake trailed behind the boat, and then disappeared, leaving no trace of our existence.

We motored on through the night, two loners destined for our fates, whatever that might be. I have determined that a loner is a better observer of the world around him, rather than thinking of what to say to someone. Life is too much of a struggle, but that is the nature of things.

Even within our physical bodies a conflict for supremacy is going on. The bacteria in our bloodstream are waging a constant war against alien germs. The red corpuscles fight the white corpuscles constantly in an effort to maintain life within the body. A battle rages within our minds. It is in man's nature to respond to the lewd, salacious, and the vile. We struggle against the darkness of this world. Darkness hates the light. I'm happy being a loner, only having to deal with my own darkness. I have also come to the conclusion that the surface appearance of things are not to be trusted, that the world is a more dangerous place than I thought.

False dawn started to break across the ocean. High up, a contrail was visible, the moon outlining the silver sphere of an airliner in the clear sky. I sent it a mental message, "Now, little bird with the cast iron tail, fly carefully. The air all around you is not always silky smooth with a gentle tailwind. Sometimes it will roar, and then you will know that it is infinite and that there is nothing more terrible than infinity."

At four a.m. Hebrone had not showed. Leaving the boat to steer itself, I'd seen neither ship nor undersea UFO; I went below to check on him. Finding him lying in his bunk, gently snoring, I poured a cup of coffee and eased back up to the flying bridge, letting him sleep. I was not tired, and the dawn easing over the calm sea is an experience one gets to enjoy only on rare occasions.

Two hours later, giant columns of cloud appeared marching across the landmass to the north. Soon golden shafts of sunlight began to angle between them, as if someone had lit a fire in the temple of heaven. We would probably have some weather tonight.

Hebrone appeared, offering fresh coffee.

"Why didn't you wake me?"

"You were resting."

"Let's get that port engine running."

I did not feel sleepy, and remained on the flying bridge sipping the coffee and enjoying the morning. Hebrone started the port engine, returning the boat to its normal self, the starboard engine seeming to give a sigh of relief.

"Looks like we may be in for a blow."

Hebrone looked toward the north at the building towers of cumulus clouds. "At least there's no hurricane lurking about, although cold fronts this time of the year can kick up some rough stuff."

"I'll check those fuel drums; see that they're lashed securely."

"There is some extra line in the chain locker, if you need more," he offered.

With the sun above the horizon, the wind picked up to about ten knots out of the northwest and the seas started to run a little heavier, about two feet. The Wheeler was in her element, cutting through the water with ease, rising and falling with the waves like a playful dolphin.

"It was good to see the 'Shade-man,'" Hebrone said, when I returned from checking the fuel drums.

"Shade-man?"

"J.D., the radiologist, reads the shades and shadows of the X-rays."

"Ah, you have a sense of humor this morning."

"Is he still obsessing over that 'radio wave machine' and the injustice of the American Medical Association?"

"It's still on his mind. He's retired, now, and has the Citation and his little farm to keep him occupied."

"His girlfriend's not too bad. Rather icy, though."

"She's a doctor, runs a clinic up in Philadelphia. They seem to get along fine. I met her for the first time yesterday. She'd been talking to Shack and Rose about me, so you know what her thoughts were."

"I can imagine. How are they doing, Shack and Rose?"

"Rose is still Rose, *Alis Volat Propiis*, (she flies with her own wings). She is starting to show her age, but I can't see any hint of her slowing down. As for Shack, I think he's finally decided that the herd owns the cattleman rather than vice versa."

"That Latin quote is the State of Oregon's motto. It was on the stern of a boat docked across from us in Key West. I woke to that saying every morning, finally had to look it up."

"You would."

"So what are your thoughts on this 'Wave' machine that J.D. thinks cures cancer?"

"It's called a Rife Frequency Instrument. It's a simple machine that uses an electromagnetic frequency generator to send the wave throughout the body to kill cancer cells."

"How can it kill a cancer cell and not a healthy one?"

"From what I've read, Rife unwittingly discovered the mortal oscillatory rate (MOR)—the electromagnetic frequency at which a specific organism is destroyed. Because every cell vibrates at a specific and unique frequency, identifying that frequency, then increasing its amplitude causes structural stresses that distort and eventually destroy the organism. Using this technique, one can destroy a virus without disturbing or harming surrounding tissues."

"Reminds me of a helicopter in 'ground resonance.' It keeps vibrating until it finally flies apart."

"Yes, that's a good analogy."

Hebrone adjusted the RPMs on the port engine. "Tell me about Rife."

"In a nutshell, Raymond Royal Rife, who died in 1971, was a medical visionary. I guess he could be called the father of bioelectric medicine. He developed technology that is used today in the fields of biochemistry, ballistics, optics, radiochemistry, and aviation. He designed several medical instruments, including the heterodyning ultraviolet microscope, the micro dissector, and the micromanipulator. But he is best known for creating a microscope that could see virus-sized organisms. His 'Universal Microscope' had 6,000 parts and could magnify an object 60,000 times its size. More importantly, it allowed him to view LIVE viruses. Even today's most sophisticated electron microscopes cannot do this."

Hebrone laughed. "You sound like a damn textbook on Rife."

"I've listened to J.D. rave about this man until he's etched in my memory. Besides, the whole thing is kind of interesting."

"I don't understand. If this Frequency Machine works so well, why was it suppressed by the medical establishment?"

"That is a long and complex story that would take hours to tell. Think ego, money, and timing. You should know that Rife's first machine was invented in the 20s, improved through the 50s, until it was infallible and simple to operate. It was tested by many doctors in southern California, where Rife had his company, with great results. Then a patient, who was from Chicago, received treatment, was cured of facial cancer, and returned to the windy city and sang praises of Rife and his machine. Eventually the head of the American Medical Association, and sole stockholder, a doctor whose name I do not remember, heard about the machine, went to San Diego and attempted to buy the company. Rife refused to sell, and the doctor began a campaign to discredit him. You have to remember, a lot of fraud existed back then. There was someone on every street corner who had an 'Electrical Box' hooked up with wires claiming to cure any ills found in the human body."

"I remember in Saigon, those were for sale everywhere. We bought one, opened it up only to find that none of the wires were connected to anything. Big scam."

"Exactly. Then, to make matters worse, one of Rife's engineers sued the company demanding more shares, claiming he was the one who discovered the frequencies used to kill the different organisms. The engineer lost the court case, but ruined the company and Rife financially. All the profits of the company went to pay for huge legal fees. Abruptly, for reasons never determined, the San Diego Medical Society proclaimed any doctor using a Rife Machine would lose their license to practice medicine. One would think that order originated from the AMA."

"So that was the end of Rife."

"No. In 1950, Rife and a new employee named Crane, began to build more machines and hired a salesman, Marsh. Sales were brisk. The AMA, ever vigilant, sent an undercover agent to buy one of the machines and tape recorded both Crane and Marsh making medical claims about the instrument. They were arrested for practicing medicine without a license and all the machines were seized. They spent three years in jail. I think Rife's discoveries were suppressed because the AMA was protecting its pocket book. Number one, the pharmaceutical companies had 'chemotherapy' to push for profit, number two, the American Cancer Society was a big money public relations fraud, and number three, the FDA was owned by the cancer monopolies."

"Where was the media in all this?"

"Silent, silent, silent."

"Wasn't J.D. going to take some kind of action to force the AMA to accept the Rife Machine for the elimination of disease organisms?"

"He was, and that could be dangerous, even today."

"Too much money involved."

"People do crazy things when it comes to the almighty dollar. Just look at Bernie Madoff. He made Charles Ponzi look like a small time thief."

"Yeah, I'm surprised somebody didn't whack Madoff. J.D. better be careful if he starts trying to rally the troops."

"I don't know what his plans are. He would be well-advised to tread lightly, enjoy retirement."

"Whatever happened to Rife?"

"He got old and tired of the fight. He finally signed over the ownership of the microscope and frequency instrument to Crane who continued the fight to bring a cancer cure to the general public. He didn't have the management or political skills to get qualified scientists, businessmen, financiers and attorneys to overcome the defenders of the medical orthodoxy. Following Rife's death, a company was formed to revitalize his work in accordance with modern scientific methods. It is proceeding cautiously to evaluate and test a number of electronic instruments."

"J.D. must have had some personal experience with the machine, or he wouldn't be so passionate about it."

"He mentioned a couple of friends who were cured, one of prostate cancer, the other of breast cancer. He read their scans, saw first hand the success."

"Kennedy once said, *'It is from numberless diverse acts of courage and belief that human history is shaped.'* Maybe J.D. can break that wall of silence and bring a cancer cure to the world."

Was I hearing right? Hebrone Opshinsky quoting Kennedy? The man has trouble completing an entire sentence.

Standing up and stretching, I said, "I'm going below to get some rest."

"Yeah, we may be in for a long night if this weather keeps kicking up."

From the files of Dr. Thomas Burger, San Diego, California, 1935:

"*I had a Mexican boy, nine years of age, who presented with osteomyelitis of the leg. His attending doctors had treated him at the Mercy Hospital. They scraped the bone every week. It was agonizing to the child. He wore a splint and was on crutches. With the bandage and splint still on he was given treatment with the Rife Frequency Instrument. In less than two weeks the wound was completely healed and he took off his splints and threw them away. He is a big powerful man now and has no recurrence of his osteomyelitis. He is completely cured. There were many cases such as this.*"

Chapter Five

Waking from a rather pleasant dream, I remembered reading somewhere that we should take our dreams seriously because we are not intelligent enough to create them. The movement of the boat was more pronounced, which meant that the seas were increasing as the approaching cold front got closer. I stuck my head out of the companionway hatch and could hear the wind whistling in the rigging above the sound of the engines, a dull aeolian hum like that of a propeller on an airplane.

Relieving Hebrone at the wheel, I noticed he'd lowered the thick plastic panels that enclose the flying bridge and keeps out the wind, rain, and sea spray.

"Seas are running about ten feet out of the north west. We're heading straight into them, which makes it easier steering. It's going to be a fun day. See you in four hours."

With that he disappeared below. I was glad he'd gotten over or was at least coping with the loss of the woman and the wolf. He'd pulled the power back on both engines to make it easier on the boat. I left the RPMs at the current setting and settled in for a long day.

Hebrone not living on the Wheeler or by the sea would seem strange, for that had been his life for all the years that I had known him. But as with youth, sentience, and continence, everything ends.

The strong wind did not approach with any subtlety. Suddenly it was blowing over forty knots and it came from directly ahead. Hebrone and I had been in many winds before, and so there was no concern. The seas built more slowly than the wind and soon they were of a size to test the behavior of the Wheeler in what could be termed rough waters. Occasional spray made a ripping sound across the plastic panels on the flying bridge. I was dry and there was never a pound from the hull. She rose to meet each sea most gracefully, her roll was easy, and so without whip I had no difficulty standing without holding on. Indeed, the Wheeler had been built well and from a sound design.

The weather was continuing to deteriorate. The sky was dark, almost black and scud was running at mast height. This squall line was proving to be a nasty lady filled with lightning and hail. Now in the roaring cauldron, I started to sing some idiotic ditty about a sleepy lagoon and a tropical moon. Then, without warning, both engines came down with a terrible fit of coughing and slowed until they were barely ticking over. I feared we would swing broadside to the breaking waves. The right crest could roll us over. As quickly as they slowed, both engines resumed normal operation.

In seconds, I was joined by Hebrone on the fly bridge.

"Sorry about the engines. I was transferring some fuel."

"You could have warned me."

He shrugged, but said nothing.

It began to rain much harder. Water spewed against the plastic as if someone were using a fire hose. There was considerable lightning. We reached a crest just as a prolonged flashing occurred and I was appalled to see the entire horizon was formed by a wall of water perhaps a hundred feet ahead. A rogue wave, I thought. Then everything became black. We waited for the crash and it came. The plastic gave way and luminescent streams of salt water slopped all around us, but the Wheeler had made it through without damage.

Hebrone grinned. "It may be time to go down to the wheelhouse."

"Well, if you insist. I do find it rather pleasant up here with the wind in my face, though."

In the comfort of the wheelhouse, we traded off every two hours as the steering was arduous. The little Wheeler held her own. The waves were hills obliterating everything beyond themselves. They were by far the greatest waves I had ever seen and so very long from crest to crest that our motion ascending or descending each one was wonderfully smooth.

So it went throughout the night.

It was a furious dawn and we thought that it would never come. If anything, it was blowing harder. Time and again it seemed certain that we would be overwhelmed and capsize. We were so very small.

The storm continued throughout the day. Not once did the Wheeler falter. We both had been concerned, driven to fear at times and were exhausted. We remembered how it is always so when deep fright and nervous fatigue arise together.

The storm abated late in the afternoon. The passing of this wind and wave hell had left us in such a state of dazed euphoria that we were ready to believe that both boat and our lives were charmed.

In calm seas, we now motored through an area with hundreds of drilling rigs, all seeking that "black gold." It had been years since I'd been in this part of the Gulf, and I was stunned at the number of rigs, supply-boat traffic, and helicopters passing overhead almost constantly. We needed to be vigilant so as not to run into one of the structures or boat traffic. I was glad we passed through in daylight, for it would be scary at night.

Finally, at the end of the third day, we arrived at Cavello Pass and crossed the bar into Port Lavaca with a half hour of fuel remaining in the tanks. I had visited this place a couple of times before and, though a busy area, it always struck me as being drab. Where Key West somehow gave the impression that June lasted all year, this part of the Texas coast reminded me, even in the winter, of long hot summers, of harsh storms—local squalls to hurricanes—that rotted baseboards, splintered lattice work, of relentless winds that howled for days, scoured paint, and rusted gutters white with sea salt. Even the people looked wind blown and scoured, or so it seemed to me as we docked the Wheeler stern first in a slip at the marina.

A young boy no more than twelve years old stood on the pier and watched us with large brown eyes. He was barefoot and balanced himself, stork-like, with one galled foot on top of the other. They were dirty feet and had not seen a pair of shoes for a long time. Behind him, I watched a cat carry a still-alive rat across the dock. Its head swayed up and down in desperation. It was a movement without hope.

"You be the boat out of Key West?" The boy asked, remaining in his one-legged stance.

"We be," I answered, running a spring line and tying it off on a cleat. "How would you know that my fine young friend?"

"I ain't yo friend. Mr. Ardmore said to tell you yo car be here in a minute."

"Our car?"

Hebrone stepped down into the cockpit. "Ardmore is the one bought the boat, the father-in-law of the girl that poisoned Savage."

The boy, overhearing what Hebrone said, moved over close to the stern, resumed his one-legged stance.

"You be the man come to kill Miss Lucy? She a nasty lady, that missy. Thinks she better'en all us folk. Treat me like a slave-boy. I ain't no slave. I be Mr. Ardmore's chief of boat operations. He a fine man, Mr. Ardmore. Treats me well. Hired me after my Papa was lost in the hurricane."

"How you know what I'm here to do?" Hebrone said, with a scowl on his face.

"Mr. Ardmore, he told me about Miss Lucy killing ya dog. I'm sorry for yo loss. I got a dog. He up yonder lying under dat bench. Somebody kill my dog, I'd kill'em too."

"Why would Mr. Ardmore tell you I'm coming to harm Miss Lucy?"

"'Cause he tell me everything. Like he told me about dis boat. He say it an old boat and I'm in charge of keeping it shipshape, though it look like you been doing a pretty good job. Guess it be a mess down below after y'all come through dat storm."

"How you know we been through a storm?"

"My business to know what all goes on in the waters of the Gulf. Have to keep my boats safe and clean."

"How many boats are in your charge?"

"Three. Four now this one show up. I be an important man to Mr. Ardmore."

A white limousine, almost as long as the Wheeler, pulled up close to where we were docked.

"There yo car. Can I help wid de bags?"

"We can handle them, but thanks. What's your name?"

"My name be Boo."

"Well, Boo, I think my old boat is in good hands. Take good care of her. And Boo, don't say anything to anyone else about Miss Lucy and me, or why I'm here."

"What Mr. Ardmore tell me never go no further."

"You mentioned it to us, Boo. What if you'd been mistaken about who we were?"

The boy scratched his chin and frowned, nodded his head as if understanding.

We left him in deep thought and walked toward the limo.

"Mr. Opshinsky, I've been instructed to drive you and your deckhand to Houston, to a hotel. Mr. Ardmore will contact you there."

The driver opened the door, took our bags and put them in the trunk.

"Deckhand?" I said, folding myself into the plush leather seat.

Hebrone smiled. "Driver, would you stop by an auto parts store somewhere along the way."

"Certainly, Sir," the man said, shutting the door. "A parts house."

As we headed away from the marina, Hebrone picked up a phone built into a side panel. Talking to the driver, he said, "Do you have Lucy Ardmore on board often?" "Would you know if she owns any animals?" "A cat." "Thank you."

"You going to tell me what's running through your mind? Parts house, Lucy Ardmore's cat?"

"Antifreeze."

"You are going to buy antifreeze at the auto parts store. Please tell me no harm will come to the cat."

Hebrone turned and looked at me. He was not smiling. "No harm will come to the cat, but Miss Lucy won't know that."

"But you were going to buy the antifreeze before you knew if the woman owned any animals...?"

"Yes, rich shits like her always have animals to control. If not, maybe she'd enjoy a glass of antifreeze."

He did not look at me when he said that, but out the tinted window at the winter Texas landscape.

We settled in for the two hour drive to Houston.

I looked over the inside of the limo. One could get used to this form of transportation.

We stopped on the outskirts of Victoria, Texas, just before getting on Interstate 69 and Hebrone bought a gallon of anti-freeze in a bright yellow plastic jug. Whatever his plan, he would tell me at the appropriate time—if he had a plan. I wasn't sure that in his own mind he didn't contemplate killing the woman. From my perspective, he would not commit murder, though he was certainly capable. His relationship with that wolf was something special. Never have I seen two beings bond the way that they did. Hebrone made me promise, on more than one occasion, to take Savage if anything happened to him. What worried me most was that Hebrone knew a hundred ways to make the woman's death look like an accident, if he so desired.

"I'm not going to kill her, Jay."

"Are you psychic now? You think you can read my thoughts?"

"I know you too well. It's written all over your face."

"Didn't we have this conversation in Key West?"

"We did, and you had the same look on that handsome mug of yours."

"At least you think your deckhand is handsome."

. . .

The hotel was a brand new twenty story building half of which was luxury condos, the other half extended-stay suites. The name Ardmore was everywhere. The limo driver escorted us up to the 18th floor on a private elevator. There was no check-in desk.

"I am assigned to you 24/7 for as long as you need me." He handed Hebrone a card. "Those numbers will reach me anytime. Be advised that Bill, Jr. and Lucy Ardmore live in the condo on the top floor. Mr. Ardmore will be in touch. Good-day, gentlemen."

The suite was designed for the ultra rich. It was nice, but I didn't belong in these surroundings—never would. I didn't feel comfortable. My comfort zone was a cottage in the woods, a cramped cockpit of an airplane, at the wheel of a well-built boat, not in some millionaire's playpen that didn't look lived in and never would, furniture that didn't appear comfortable and probably wasn't. The view from the balcony was magnificent, though. It overlooked Houston Hobby airport and the city skyline. A glass of cognac and a good cigar would make things better.

Before I could find the liquor cabinet, the phone rang. Hebrone answered it and few words were exchanged. Hanging up, he looked at me. "The man wants to join us for dinner. He's having it sent up to the suite, will be here in half an hour."

"Is it black tie? I forgot my tuxedo, but then deckhands don't have to wear them, do they?"

"Funny. Look, I want to do what I'm going to do and get out of here tomorrow."

"What exactly are you going to do?"

"Let's meet with Ardmore. After that we'll know."

The doorbell chimed exactly thirty minutes later. Bill Ardmore, Sr. and the food arrived together. Two young women in white coats and blue skirts set up the table. Ardmore introduced himself. He was a tall, grey-haired man of at least seventy years of age who looked forty. He was a poster-boy for proof that longevity is wholly a function of membership in the "Lucky DNA Club." A warm, friendly man whose smile showed teeth that sent some dentist's child through college. He had green eyes that sparkled with intelligence.

"Mr. Opshinsky, I've seen the Wheeler. It is a wonderful boat that you have put your heart and soul into."

"This is Jay Leicester. He sailed from Key West with me and will assist in teaching your son and daughter-in-law some of life's lessons."

He shook my hand.

"We met Boo, your chief of boat operations. I'm curious, why did you tell him of our objective?"

Ardmore didn't seem to mind the question, which was good, because I really didn't care.

"Ah, little Boo, he likes to feel important. He's a lovely boy who's had a bit of bad luck. I'm teaching him integrity and trust. I would adopt him, but it would be rather awkward at my age. I've arranged for his future and education. The courts have appointed me as his guardian. His poor mother is a crack addict and prostitute. His father drowned at sea in some weather in one of my boats."

The man said prostitute and crack addict like he knew something about either one. I wondered.

"Dinner is served, gentlemen." He waved a long arm at the table.

A fine dinner it was, sirloin steaks, baked potato, salad, and a bottle of 2006 Chateau Lafitte Rothschild that was way too young to drink, but still luscious. The two young women hovered over us with such practiced professionalism one almost didn't know they were present.

When dinner was over, the entire meal was whisked away and the women disappeared. I don't remember them speaking a word the entire time.

There was a short but intense discussion about plans concerning Bill, Jr. and his wife, Lucy, with emphasis on the wife. No harm was to come to either of them, and a company aircraft waited to fly us back to our destinations.

With that, Ardmore excused himself, thanking Hebrone for understanding about the "children," and that if he ever decided he wanted the Wheeler back, it would be available.

After he left, I found a cabinet behind a small wet bar that was stocked with expensive liquors and brandies.

"Hebrone, you think this may be Ardmore's private suite?"

Looking around, he nodded. "Yeah, I'd say so."

Selecting an XO cognac, I poured a snifter, offering a glass to Hebrone. He declined. I brought my own cigar, never travel without them. They are handmade by Ernesto P. Carrillo in Little Havana in Miami.

Out on the balcony, I cut the end off the cigar and realized there was no way to light it. Inside, under the bar, I found a box of Arango Statesman, sulfur free cigar matches—perfect. Back outside, I lit the fifty-four ring, long filler cigar and savored the taste of the aged Cuban-seed tobacco. Few things are better than a fine cigar and a rare cognac.

Hebrone joined me, sipping a foreign-made beer that I'd never heard of nor seen before. I was not a beer drinker.

"I'm going to place a note from Savage on the antifreeze and leave it inside the 'children's' condo when I steal the cat."

"You're going to remove their cat? Why?"

"Tomorrow, before we leave, the cat will be returned along with a note from Savage."

"A note saying...?"

"That he hopes the feline enjoyed the sweet, sticky taste of the antifreeze as much as he did."

"You are not going to feed any of that stuff to the cat."

"No, but Lucy Ardmore won't know that fact."

"So what part am I supposed to play in this little scheme to frighten the 'children?'"

"Write the notes. Your penmanship is better than mine."

At four a.m. Hebrone left with the gallon of antifreeze and the note I'd written, and headed up to the condo of Bill, Jr. and Lucy Ardmore. The note said:

I am Savage, the one you fed this liquid. I am watching you. Be very careful.

I did not ask how Hebrone planned to gain entry, nor knew the floor plan of the condo, or where the cat slept. I could only assume Senior furnished all the information to him.

One hour later, Hebrone returned with a beautiful brown, gold, and black striped Calico cat.

"Let's get a couple of hours sleep. I'll return the cat in person, with a note attached to its collar, then we'll be off to the airport."

"You are going to let them see you?"

"Will be most effective, don't you think?"

Scratching my chin, I looked at Hebrone. "I think it's brilliant."

From the files of Dr. Harry Goodman, an eye specialist,
Santa Fe Hospital: 1936

Patient, Mrs. Julia M. Gowdy presented with cancer and senile cataracts with little vision in either eye. After treatment with the Rife Frequency Instrument for a month, her vision has improved 29% in one eye and 10% in the other. She is now cancer free and can read her phone book without difficulty. We have now treated three other cancer patients and all are completely recovered.

Chapter Six

The corporate jet lifted off the runway from Houston Hobby airport and turned eastward climbing into a clear, crisp winter sky. To the north, Houston Intercontinental airport glimmered in the morning sun with its never ending stream of airliners lined up to land. Settling into the plush seat, I began to relax as we continued our unrestricted climb to cruising altitude. Flying always puts me in a liminal state, a transition between two worlds.

Looking around at the interior of the cabin, I was impressed. This was the Dassault Falcon 7X, a French-built large-cabin, long range business jet first introduced to the public in 2005 at the Paris Airshow. I had watched its development because its nearest competitor was the Gulfstream G550, an aircraft, in my opinion, that could not be bested. I was wrong. The 7X is the first fully fly-by-wire business jet (no mechanical connections to the control surfaces) with three Pratt & Whitney engines that produce 6,402 lb thrust each at takeoff. With room for 14 passengers, the nonstop range is almost 6,000 nm. In today's dollars, one can own the Dassault Falcon 7X for a mere fifty-million.

Glancing over at Hebrone, I waved my arm around the spacious cabin. "Not bad. Your boy Ardmore is worth more than I imagined."

Without smiling, he said, "There are two ways of being rich—have a lot, or want very little. I once had an old Montagnard village chieftain in Vietnam tell me that if there was anything I wanted, to come to him and he would show me how to get along without it."

The lone cabin attendant, a woman in her forties who wore no wedding rings, came back and asked if we needed anything. We told her we were good. She returned to the front to be with the crew, one or both who might be unmarried, and thereby carry on that age old tradition of flirting. I remembered many such encounters during the twenty-five years that I flew the line. But then memory is always more vivid than life. In memory there are no clocks, leaving time to the life span of the universe. The memory of our lives always comes as unbidden as the night.

"So tell me Miss Lucy's reaction when you handed her the cat?"

"Fear. It is always fun to see fear in the eyes of the spoiled brat or the bully when they suddenly realize that they do not control the world."

"Did she read the note attached to the collar?"

"Yes. For a moment she stood, slack-jawed, gaping, uncomprehending. Then she cursed at me. Hers was a full-throated, almost lunatic fury, sharpened by the well-educated voice that carried it."

"What'd she look like?"

"The word to describe her would be telegenic. She was dark tanned and beautiful, even at that hour of the morning. Her eyes seemed to carry the very wrath of a scorned female in them. It's how I remembered her on board the yacht in Key West. She is a vain and selfish woman dedicated to her own pleasure and interest with enough of daddy's money to pursue them. She thinks quickly, but not deeply, although she has moments of perception that gave her the aura of sharpness she doesn't deserve. She had me fooled for a while."

"What did you say to her?"

"Not a word. I looked her directly in the eyes for perhaps five seconds, turned and walked away."

"Outstanding. God, I wish I'd been there."

The cabin attendant came and bent over Hebrone. "Mr. Opshinsky, the Captain would like a word with you when you have a moment."

Hebrone followed her back to the cockpit.

I had asked to ride to Key West to drop Hebrone off, then to be flown back to Meridian. I wanted to say goodbye to him on the island and I wanted more time aboard the Falcon 7X, maybe even get a chance to look over the cockpit instrumentation. This airplane had the new Honeywell Primus EPIC "Enhanced Avionics System" (EASy), that I had never seen in operation.

Hebrone returned, handed me a printout. It was from Bill Ardmore, Sr.:

Mission accomplished—no Bush intended
Job well done—things will be much improved
Lil Boo says will keep Wheeler shipshape
Thanks for everything

"He didn't say anything about the Deckhand's contribution or my penmanship?"

"Here's a printout addressed to you."

Mr. Leicester, have read your dossier
When next we purchase company aircraft
Would like you to handle transaction
Thanks for your help with the "children"

"I knew you'd benefit some way by coming on this trip with me. You always do."

"Thanks for the invite."

"Times they do change, don't they?"

"Yes, they do," I said, thinking I knew what he meant. No violence, nobody got killed. No revenge for the loss of his beloved wolf and the sale of the Wheeler sportfisherman.

Looking out the window, I saw only water, that vast expanse of the Gulf of Mexico, so calm and blue now in the noon sunlight. Hard to believe the change from a couple of days ago when it was a raging cauldron with the power to frighten the bravest of men.

We flew along, suspended between sky and earth, and I was amazed at the beauty. Flying, even as a passenger, stirred in me the feeling that I did not deserve it, but I accepted it, and lived by it, and I sought always to understand it. What deep pleasure I've derived from being aloft, how privileged I've been. We take everything for granted today. Even the launch of the space shuttle is, for the most part, ignored by the media.

The crew pulled the power back on all three engines; we were beginning our descent into Key West. It suddenly was extremely quiet in the cabin, and one felt as if riding on a magic carpet, albeit an expensive one. The touchdown on the runway was smooth and I envied the pilots their ability, as most all of my landings were controlled crashes.

The crew shutdown only the left engine, as we would not be long on the ground. I followed Hebrone off the airplane. He shook my hand, promised to be in touch as soon as he settled into the new job with the aircraft delivery company. I watched him walk to the FBO office. He suddenly stopped, turned and gave me a military salute, held it for a second, then turned and went inside. It was something he'd never done before, and I would remember that gesture for years to come.

Back aboard the Falcon, the Captain offered me the left seat, something much appreciated by this old aviator. I made a meager protest about never having flown this type of aircraft, but the crew said they were aware of my background and that it would be their pleasure to acquaint me with Dassault's latest edition.

The three big Pratt & Whitney turbofans quickly accelerated the nearly 60,000 pounds of airplane to rotate speed and I gently pulled back on the side stick control and we climbed away from the Florida Keys like a homesick angel. I marveled at the avionics on the flight deck. Designed by Honeywell, the system displays information on four 14.1-inch flat-panel screens. Most noticeable to me was that the EASy flight deck allows pilots to make "heads up" data entry using a cursor control device (CCD) kind of like a mouse on a computer. By limiting the time spent punching numbers into a flight management system, the chance for input errors is reduced.

The Captain said that the design of the Falcon 7X flight deck was the result of extensive input from pilots, aviation authorities and safety experts. It was designed to simplify flight management tasks, improve crew coordination, and provide unsurpassed situational awareness at all times.

There were a lot of benefits to the system, but the one that impressed me the most was that the crew would be able to extract maximum aircraft performance in instances such as wind shear encounters or a collision avoidance maneuver, without overstressing the aircraft or stalling.

All too soon we were on short final at the Meridian, Mississippi airport. My time aboard the Dassault Falcon 7X had been a real pleasure, even though my landing was somewhat frightening. We parked at the FBO owned by an old friend, Earl Sanders. I thanked the crew for allowing me to fly the "bird" and told them there was no need to shut down the engines, I'd just jump off and run.

Inside the FBO, Earl stood behind the counter with his wife, Annie.

"I might have known that was you. Fly into my operation in a brand new corporate jet and do not have the courtesy to buy a few gallons of fuel."

"Hello to you, Mr. Sanders, Mrs. Sanders. How about flying me up to the Union International airport in one of those little airplanes you own that are tied down on the ramp earning no revenue. I'll even pay for the gas."

"I guess the next thing you'll want is for me to fly you around the country hunting for J.D. Ballard, at my expense, no doubt."

"Why would I do that?"

"Oh, you haven't heard? J.D. went missing a couple of days ago."

"What do you mean, went missing? Was he flying?"

"Yes, he landed here, fueled up, said he was going to a meeting in

Aspen, Colorado. It was his first trip to that airport. He knew I'd been there many times and wanted to pick my brain on the area. Seems he never showed for the meeting. I'm sorry, Jay, I thought you knew."

"No, I haven't heard. He flew me to Key West a week ago. I've been out of touch. You can give me all the details on the way."

We flew to Union in a Cessna 206, the finest single engine airplane ever built, second only to it would be the Piper Cherokee Six. One is a high-wing design, the other a low-wing, pick your preference. Whatever cargo you can load into either aircraft, it will haul with no problem.

Earl Sanders is in his mid-sixties, six feet tall with not a speck of grey in his curly black hair. A former "All-American" running back in college, he looked as if he could still dress out and play today. He flew as a copilot for Eastern Airlines, and after they went belly up, Earl opened a Fixed Base Operation at the Meridian, Mississippi airport. The FBO has been a financial success, and we have been friends since college. We played football against each other and share fond memories of our youth, not to mention our love of all things aeronautical.

I looked at him with envy for I, too, have reached mid-life. An age where I've done a lot and when looking back, can see it all. I see what I've done and can't imagine doing as much in years to come. If they came.

Earl allowed me to fly his 206, for he knew that I would be disappointed if he didn't. As soon as we were airborne, I pointed the nose toward Union, turned to him and said, "Talk to me."

"J.D.'s girlfriend, Nancy Wiseman, the doctor from up at Philadelphia, called me, asked if J.D. had fueled with us, wanted to know what time he departed. She said he never made it to the meeting in Aspen. She was making inquiries with the FAA (Federal Aviation Administration) to see about flight plans, departure times, etc. Seems the weather was down in the mountains and he landed at Denver for fuel and to wait for clearing of the weather. That's the last anyone heard from him.

I looked down at the winter land that had been wet, but now it was dry and rainless and had been for weeks. A tractor hauling hay trailed dust. What was green and lush a couple of months ago had lost its verdancy and was now desiccated and the memory of one made no difference to the experience of the other.

"Did he takeoff from Denver and try to make it into Aspen?"

"I don't know. Talk to Wiseman. He may have turned up by now. If you need anything, I'll be glad to help."

Earl dropped me off at the Union airport and I watched him takeoff and head back to Meridian. I checked on my airplane, a bi-wing Stearman kept in a hangar next to J.D.'s. All was well and the Citation was gone.

A note was left on the windshield of my truck.

Please call me at once!
Nancy Wiseman

It was dated four days ago.

I drove to Rose English's house to retrieve B.W., my cat.

"You did not call like you promised. If you had, I could've informed you about J.D. Nancy is frantic—call her."

"Yes, mother."

"How is Hebrone? What was his problem?"

"Someone poisoned his wolf. After he lost his girlfriend, then Savage, he couldn't bear to stay aboard the boat."

"I always knew the man had a soul, in spite of all the killing in his life. Where's he gonna live now?"

"I'm not sure. He's going to let me know, but you can bet it won't be anywhere near the water."

"Why anyone would want to live on a boat is beyond my comprehension. The thing is always moving and wet, not to mention the fact it might sink."

"Spoken like a true landlubber cattleman."

"Woman. I'm a cattlewoman."

"You've also been talking to Nancy Wiseman about me. I wish you wouldn't do that."

"You are an interesting man. Why not talk about you? Besides, when your name came up, Nancy had not hooked up with J.D. I was simply looking out for you. All your life you've been one good woman shy of true happiness."

"Looking out for my love life? How about Susannah Ward?"

"That was just fun."

My cat ran into the room. I picked him up and we both looked at Rose. She was an aging woman who appeared to take the process in stride. Grey streaks ran through her hair and tiny wrinkles were working their way toward her eyes and mouth. She had a round, hard face with the dark eyebrows of the matron who is still alive and appreciates it. She seemed a woman who liked her own skin. In my experience, this was a rare thing.

"What do you know about J.D.?"

She reached over and scratched B.W. behind the ear. "Nancy said he didn't show for some meeting out of state. She was worried and wanted to talk with you."

"Have you checked on my cottage? Is it still standing?"

"It was this morning, however it desperately needs cleaning. Have you ever thought about hiring some domestic help?"

"I always thought that you…"

"I am not your cleaning lady, though God knows anyone could do a better job than you. There are things growing in your bathroom unknown to science."

"Let's go, B.W. This old woman is getting riled up, and you know how mean she can be."

Rose threw her head up in mock indignation and headed for the front door to let us out. I watched her walk like a deer in the forest. Sometimes she walked as well as a wolf or a big coyote when it is not hurried. She walked like the great predators, when they walked softly.

At the door, I said, "I love you, old woman."

"Piss off, Leicester, clean your bathroom, and call Nancy Wiseman."

"Yes, mother."

B.W. and I arrived at the cottage to a sunset of intemperate beauty. A gold and orange flush that refused to subside, its warmth caught among the leafless, shivering trees that ringed the small building like a living halo. But this was winter in the south and I knew it could quickly bring a soul-freezing cold that made one want to seek an ocean of warm water and anything to drink with alcohol in it.

It was good to be back at the cottage in the wildwoods, a place where I always feel at ease. Throwing my ditty bag on the bed, I noticed that the whole place was spotless. Bless her heart, Rose had cleaned in every nook and cranny.

Feeding the big cat a can of his favorite tuna, I knew it was time to call Nancy Wiseman. It was not a call I wanted to make.

In September 1936, Dr. Milbank Johnson wrote to
Dr. Gruner in Canada:

"*We have opened the third clinic in the Pasadena Home for the Aged. We see patients three mornings a week, Tuesday, Thursday and Saturday. Among them were cases of pulmonary tuberculosis, carcinoma, chronic varicose ulcers of the leg, and other cases of more or less definite infection origin. At times the results of treatment with the Rife Frequency Instrument are absolutely astounding, causing an instantaneous sterilization of the wounds, whether interior or exterior. Cure has been complete in all cases.*

Chapter Seven

Looking out the back door of the cottage, the haze of an exquisite twilight etched the tops of the tall oaks on the far hill, making them seem rock solid. It was the kind of evening that makes you feel that life is worth living.

Nancy Wiseman answered on the first ring.

"Oh, Jay. Thank God you're home. I need help. No one has heard from J.D. in five days."

"Earl Sanders told me this afternoon. You'll have to fill me in on the details."

"It's J.D.'s obsession with that damn radio frequency cancer cure. The people opposed to it are somehow involved, I am convinced."

"Really?"

"Yes. Can I come and see you? We can make plans on how to proceed."

"Right now? I just returned from a week's voyage at sea."

"I was on board when we flew you to Key West, remember? J.D. does not have the luxury of time, if he's still alive."

I gave her directions to the cottage, and then built a fire. The temperature wasn't cold, but it was cool enough for me. I've been known to turn on the air-conditioner just so I could build a fire. I opened a good merlot. B.W. lay on the hearth watching the flames as if gathering some intrinsic wisdom.

Soon I saw a reflection of car lights turn off the gravel road and move slowly along the terrace row leading to the cottage. I waited until she rang the doorbell.

"Nancy, please come in."

"Thank you. The fire is nice."

"Would you like a glass of wine? I have a merlot open."

"That would be wonderful. Oh, look at the cat."

"I'll put him in the back, if he bothers you."

"No, I love cats."

She reached to pet B.W., but he jumped off the hearth and ran to his querencia.

"It takes awhile with that boy. I assure you that if you ignore him, he'll be in your lap within the hour."

She took the wine and sat on the couch facing the fireplace. A truly handsome woman, she had a fine face and her eyes were not as hard as when we first met. Her black hair was pulled back tight into a ponytail. She wore a sweater and jeans with running shoes. I thought about her and J.D. and wondered what happens to people who love each other. They have whatever they have, and they are more fortunate than others. Then one of them will get an emptiness forever.

The fire settled in the grate, bringing a renewed brightness into the room. Nancy crossed her legs, tilted the wine glass and looked through the dark liquid at the flames. I decided to let her get to her concerns in her own time.

She took a sip of the wine, looked at me. "We live in a society full of narcissistic, shadowy people whose agendas course beneath the world of civilization and disrupt or contradict its professed values. Why should the simple pursuit of the ever more complex be so troubling?"

"Because at birth we are ejected from a secure linkage to a nutrient cosmos into a perilous world in which we are beset with painful opposites and driven by powers indifferent to our well-being."

The woman looked at me as if I were insane.

"Look, Nancy, I know J.D. was obsessed with this radio frequency cancer cure, but you're going to have to bring me up to speed with what has occurred."

"You're right. I'm just feeling responsible right now."

"Hell, we're all responsible for something."

"I encouraged him, maybe a little too much."

"Start at the beginning. Tell me what he was doing in Aspen and how or why you think any of this has to do with his obsession."

She closed her eyes, leaned back on the couch. Then her eyelids parted like dark wounds. "J.D. was to attend a medical conference. He was retired, but he liked to keep abreast of what was happening in his field of medicine and it gave him a reason to fly around the country and write the trips off as expenses. He'd had some threats warning him not to pursue the public airing of the oppression by the medical establishment concerning the cancer cure using that simple noninvasive radio frequency method."

"You encouraged him because you think this method has some merit?"

"I've read the research, studied the success rate of Royal Rife; saw what the AMA did to him. They destroyed him. I'm convinced, as much as J.D., that the resonance destruction of cancer cells is viable. There was a doctor in Australia who used this method for twenty-five years with amazing success. I've read his case histories. Much study is needed, research funding is critical. Modern technology must be utilized."

"The medical establishment wants it suppressed. Why? That does not make sense. It seems to me, as a layman, that any medical professional would want this knowledge, this ability to cure a horrible disease."

"It would take hours to relate all the reasons the medical community wants this suppressed. Not all of them, mind you, only the ones involved in cancer treatment."

"Then it's all about money and power."

"Isn't everything?"

"There has to be one person or a small controlling group that's behind all this. Do you know who?"

"No."

"All this aside, our main focus right now is to find J.D. He landed in Denver due to bad weather at Aspen. Fill me in from there."

"He was to attend a three-day radiological conference, however he had planned to stay a couple extra days and get in some skiing. He'd rented a condo at Snowmass; it's a resort west of the airport on Snowmass Mountain."

"I'm familiar with it. I owned a timeshare there for a few years, right next to Lucille Ball. We met several times. She had a thing going with a well-known comedian and I baby sat her grandchildren on occasions."

The slight grin on her face resembled the illusion of a smile you sometimes see, if the muscles clinch right, on the face of a corpse.

"Name dropping does not become you, Mr. Leicester."

My face reddened.

"If that's what you think I was doing, you were wrong."

"Have it your way. J.D. was to call me when he checked in at the condo. I was concerned because it was his first time flying into Aspen, and he was doing it solo. So, when he didn't call, I phoned Snowmass. He never checked in. Aspen Flight Center, the FBO on the field, said his plane wasn't there. I then called Centennial Airport at Denver and they said the Citation was on their ramp and that it took on fuel the same day J.D. was supposed to land at Aspen. The weather had been bad across the area and several aircraft had diverted to other airports. This morning when I called, the woman said the Citation was no longer on their ramp."

"Did she say when he departed?"

"She asked around, but no one knew. I want to hire you. Find out what's happened to J.D. I'll pay your going rate."

"You are insulting me, doctor. I realize we don't know each other very well, and only because of that will I forgive you. J.D. Ballard and I have been friends for a long time. If something's happened to him, I'll find out what and who's responsible."

"I meant no disrespect, I only..."

She was a woman comfortable with the formulas of scientific law, but lost in the clouds when it came to engaging the storm forces of the emotions.

"It's okay, as long as we understand each other. I will not do this for you, or for some perceived cancer cure, nor to expose some money grubbing, power hungry group of doctors. I will find out what happened to J.D. because he's my friend."

She stroked the inside of her thigh with an index finger whose nail polish was the dark shade of venous blood.

"What are you going to do?"

"I have some contacts in air traffic control. We know he flew to Denver. If the Citation departed from there, even VFR with no flight plan, it can be tracked. We'd be out of luck prior to nine-eleven, however now nothing moves without someone watching."

"If you find the airplane, what then?"

"I'll have to go there. Maybe someone would remember who flew it in, who met the flight."

"I wish I could go with you. The clinic…" She smiled. She was a willowy woman who looked good in jeans and sweater. Her smile distorted the olive thinness of her face, one side tardy and limited in its ascent.

"I understand. I like to work alone. It's easier for me that way, besides, I tend to get under people's skin rather quickly."

"Yes," she said, getting up from the couch and handing me her wine glass. "So I'm told. You will keep me informed daily, I hope?"

"Count on it, doctor."

Walking her to her car, she turned, "I like your little place in the woods."

"Thank you. So do I. Don't worry, we'll find J.D. He's probably somewhere enjoying the snow."

"I'll be waiting for your call."

Back inside, B.W. was lying again on the hearth.

"You didn't care for her, old boy? That's unusual for you not to socialize with the women. They say your ilk is a good judge of character.

You don't think the lady doctor had anything to do with our old friend, J.D. going missing, do you?"

The big cat eyed me, looked back at the flames.

J.D. Ballard had few enemies. He was a radiologist, what kind of enemies could he make? There were only two possibilities; the people wanting to keep a simple and cheap cancer cure from ruining a multi-billion dollar industry, or a jealous girlfriend. Did Nancy Wiseman fit that bill? She and J.D. hadn't been together that long, a year or so. I knew nothing about her. There were two people I know who could shed some light on the doctor—Rose English and Shack Runnels. They served on a cattleman's board with her.

Tonight I was too tired to deal with this. In the morning I'd make some calls, find out where the Cessna Citation was located, delve into Nancy Wiseman, and learn all I could about killing cancer cells using radio waves and those people or organizations that have a hand in repressing treatments for this killer disease.

I fed B.W., made a roast beef sandwich, sat in front of the fire and finished the bottle of merlot. Not in the mood for cognac and a cigar, I walked out in the front yard of the cottage and looked at the sky. The stars seemed to be trepanning tiny holes in my skull to ease the pressure of my own life. Going to the porch, I sat in the cypress glider and thought of the remembered dead. How frail is the force that holds one on earth. How fragile the essence called life.

Leaning over and putting my head in my hands, I thought about the mystery of life, then remembered what Robert Frost wrote, *"We sit in a circle and suppose, while the secret sits in the middle and knows."*

It was time to go to bed.

· · ·

"Shack Runnels, how you doing?"

"Different day, same shit."

This was the cattleman whose land joined Rose's. He was born in this county, raised up hard, worked even harder and had become a wealthy land owner and cattle grower. He was one of those people who seemed to belong to the landscape, much like one would think of the local sheriff, county newspaper, hospital, mayor, or the school system. Shack was a stolid and stoical part of the environ. He was also a man not to be trifled with. There are legendary tales of men who made that mistake.

It was him and Rose who took me under their wings and allowed me to ameliorate into these woods without getting myself killed.

"Spent a few days with Hebrone. He said to tell you hello."

"Yeah, I heard you went sailing. What's going on with the 'grunt'?"

"Somebody poisoned his wolf."

"Who?"

"Young rich bitch who objected to the howling at the full moon. Fed him antifreeze."

"Jesus. I assume the woman and anyone around her is now dead."

It was better to let Shack think what he wanted about revenge. He and Hebrone were friends and had been through some deadly times together—all my doing—so it was better to leave him to his own assumptions.

"Hebrone couldn't live aboard the Wheeler after that. Sold it to someone in Houston. I went with him to deliver it."

"I can understand that. His girlfriend died on the boat, now the wolf. Yeah, I probably couldn't stay there either."

"What can you tell me about Nancy Wiseman, the DO from Philadelphia?"

"Why? You sniffing around her? I'm pretty sure she's hooked up with someone."

"She is, and that someone is J.D. Ballard, a retired radiologist. He's come up missing."

"Ballard, he's the one has that small jet hangared next to your little put-put out at the airport? I've never met the man. You think she had something to do with his disappearance?"

"I don't know, Shack. My involvement started last night. I'm trying to get a handle on all the players."

"Why would you think I'd know anything about the doctor?"

"You serve on a board with her, and if it's a female anywhere within your eyesight, you know all about her."

"I am now, and have always been, faithful to my wife. I simply appreciate the beauty of what God has placed on this earth."

"Can you tell me about Nancy Wiseman?"

"She's the finest doctor in these parts. I would trust her—and do—with any member of my family. She's tough, honest, very smart, and I'd vouch for her under any circumstances."

"That's powerful, coming from you. So you don't think she'd whack her boyfriend as a result of some perceived jealous rage?"

"Nor for any other reason. Put that in the bank, Jay. She's good people."

"That's what I needed to hear. Is Rose going to tell me the same thing?"

"Yes."

"Okay, thanks."

"So what happened to the boyfriend, this Ballard fellow?"

"He was flying out to Aspen, Colorado, for a meeting. He never made it."

"Flew his little jet into a mountain?"

"I don't think that happened. The girlfriend has to be cleared first. He was involved in something else that could get him in trouble. I'll look into that next."

"All right, let me know if I can help."

. . .

"I think Nancy Wiseman killed J.D., flew his airplane to Denver and came home. She used this fight he was having with the AMA as a red herring to throw everyone off the track. It's plausible."

"Then you are an idiot," Rose said. I could imagine her face getting red, the voice sounding angry. "Give me a motive. No, you can't do it because you don't have one."

"Maybe she caught him with another woman, or he dumped her."

"So what. They aren't married, besides she can have her pick of men. She's wealthy, she's still got her looks, and has a good future. Why would she risk all this to commit murder? It makes no sense."

"Women are strange creatures."

"And men aren't? Give me one thing, anything, in defense of your sex."

"We'd have been fine, except God gave us a penis."

I love picking on Rose. There was fire coming out of her nose and I was glad we were talking on the phone.

"You're barking up the wrong tree, and you know it. I think you just want to eliminate Nancy, and then find out what really happened to J.D."

"Shack vouched for her."

"So that's exactly what you were doing. Why didn't you just say so?"

"Wouldn't have been nearly as much fun. At the moment, though, we don't know anything has happened to J.D. He simply didn't show up where he was supposed to. There are many explanations possible."

"You will find out."

"I will find out."

"Jay…"

"What?"

"Sometimes you are an SOB."

"Bye Rose."

After hanging up, I called the number for an old friend who was now head of the Houston Air Route Traffic Control Center. He agreed to see what he could find out for me. I gave him the Cessna's "N" number, the approximate dates and route of flight. If it was in their computer system, he could access it. He promised to call me back this afternoon.

With nothing else to do, I called the FBO on Centennial Airport in Denver and asked to speak to the Line Supervisor. By shear luck he remembered the Citation for two reasons, the "N" number, N1JD, was his son's initials, and because a man flew the airplane in alone. However when it departed the next day, a female was in the left seat accompanied by two men. While not unusual, it seemed odd to him. When asked if shown a photo of the woman could he recognize her, he thought that he could, but that he didn't get a good look at the two men. The woman had blond hair, but it appeared to be a wig, a bad one, at that. The weather was cold and all three were bundled up, so he didn't get a good look at their build, only that the woman was as tall as the men. I promised to be there within a couple of days with a photo for him to look at.

As soon as I hung up, my friend from Houston Center phoned.

"Denver Center has your Citation landing at Aspen yesterday afternoon at three o'clock. Departed Salt Lake City and flew direct to Aspen. That's all I could get."

"Thanks, I owe you one."

This was getting to be more complicated, but could have a simple explanation. Maybe J.D. changed his itinerary and simply didn't inform Nancy.

A call to Aspen Air Center confirmed the Citation was on their ramp, however Snowmass Village had no Dr. J.D. Ballard registered, though they did show he never used last weeks reservation. That was a little odd.

Now all I had to do was locate a photo of Dr. Nancy Wiseman, find a way to get to Centennial Airport in Denver, then over to Aspen. But first, I must see if Rose would take B.W. and look after the Cottage.

From the files of Dr. Robert Stafford, June, 1957.

An 82 year old female patient named Mrs. Byess presented with end-stage cancer and a life expectancy of 2 to 3 weeks. She was treated for 3-5 minutes every other day with the Rife Frequency Instrument. Within two weeks she began to recover. She eventually got out of bed, was walking around and made plans to go home. Unfortunately, she fell and broke her hip and died a week later. However, an autopsy found no cancer in her body at time of death.

Chapter Eight

A call to Earl Sanders at the Meridian airport proved to be fruitless. All his airplanes were flying and none were heading west that I could hitch a ride aboard. The weather was too cold, Colorado too far, and my Stearman too slow for me to fly myself. That left only the airlines. A check on the internet showed Southwest Airlines had a through flight to Denver that left Jackson at one p.m. with a stop in Dallas. If you fly the airlines in the south, all routes lead to either Dallas or Atlanta. From there you can go anywhere in the world. I booked the flight, printed out my own boarding pass and called Rose.

"Can you keep B.W. for a few days? Where can I get a photo of Nancy Wiseman within the hour? I'm leaving the cottage in a few minutes, can I bring you anything?"

"Yes," she said. "Try to bring me some sign of good breeding, a proper bloodline, any small courtesies, and a much greater respect for your elders."

"I'm not a bovine, and I have excellent breeding."

She hung up. God, I love that woman.

Throwing my ditty bag in the truck, I slammed the door and started out the drive from the cottage. It seemed to be a theme in my life; tossing bags in a vehicle and leaving these woods. At the tree line stood an old fifty-foot magnolia. The past summer had proven good for the tree for it had bloomed late. The flowers looked as though a hundred angels with white wings had gathered there awaiting God's orders.

Rose handed me a photo of the board members of the Philadelphia Cattleman's Association taken last year. One could easily recognize Nancy Wiseman. It would have to do.

"How long will you be gone?"

"I'm not sure. J.D.'s airplane is on the ground in Aspen. He stopped over in Denver, and then the Citation flew to Salt Lake. I'll start there, work my way to the resort."

"Are you going to tell Nancy?"

"No. I want to look around first. J.D. may simply be taking some alone time. I'll know in a couple of days."

"Be safe, Jay."

. . .

The Boeing 737 reached the top of its climb and accelerated to cruise speed. Twenty minutes out of Jackson the crew pulled the power back to flight idle and started a slow descent into the Dallas area. Save that fuel. They have it down to a pure science, every dollar counts, and it is most obvious in the number of seats crammed into the cabin. The only way to describe it is sardines in a can, and this flight to Dallas was full. Six seats abreast in a fuselage originally designed for four. I had a middle seat with a twenty year old college girl, who forgot to shower this morning, and an 80 year old man who clicked his dentures the entire flight. I was glad when we landed in Dallas and all the passengers deplaned. There was an hour layover, and then I would reboard the same airplane for the leg to Denver. I spent the time at the Hertz rental counter making a reservation for a car upon my arrival.

To my delight, the passenger load was light on the Denver leg and I had no seatmates. Even the flight attendant was overly friendly. She was in her mid-thirties with a short hairdo. She was blond, with little makeup, and had wrinkle lines from too much sun. Her petite figure seemed shapeless under her loose uniform. It was her eyes that told the story. They were happy eyes that showed she had not been hurt too badly by love or the world and that she still had a lust for life. Had it been under different circumstances we might have gotten together, as she had a two day layover and let me know that she was available.

It was cold when we landed in Denver. Cold enough to put Hell back in business. I had not dressed for the climate, but did bring a coat. I would have to endure. The heater in the rental worked well enough and I headed out of the new Denver International Airport, whose architecture I admire, though some don't, and headed for the Centennial Airport.

The line supervisor, whose name was Redmond, was tall and lanky, with a leathery face drawn taut by many cold winters servicing airplanes on windswept ramps. His smile was capped and flashy. Only small wrinkles appeared at the corner of his eyes—eyes that had a certain curious manner about them. They were blue and bordering on manic.

I handed him the photograph of the Cattleman's Association board members. He looked closely at it. "I'd say this is not the woman who flew the Citation out of here. Even if you put a blond wig on her, she's older than the one I saw. Sorry."

"The airplane showed up on the ramp at Aspen. It's there now. Seems it left here and flew to Salt Lake. That mean anything to you?"

"No. I wish I could be of more help."

"You didn't get a good enough look at the men to give me any description?"

"Nothing jumps out at me. They were two middle-aged men dressed for the cold. One of them did sit in the copilot's seat, if that's any help?"

"Can I get a copy of the fuel ticket?"

"Sure."

The fuel was paid with J.D.'s credit card and it looked like his signature. This trip to Denver seemed like a dead end.

"So, Mr. Leicester, what's this all about?"

"The owner of the Citation is a friend. He didn't show up for a meeting, and no one's heard from him for over a week."

"You going to Aspen?"

"According to the FBO there, the airplane's on their ramp. Maybe I can find out something."

"I have a friend who runs the operation. If it'll help, I'll give him a call."

"I'd appreciate it."

"If you're planning on driving, you are out of luck. The passes are closed due to ice and heavy snow. Word is it will be several days and you'll need chains on the tires."

"I'm in a rental."

"If you want, I can check around. Someone may be going over and have an empty seat."

"Outstanding. Thank you."

"It won't be today, though. Aspen has a curfew, and it's only an hour until that time. Where you staying?"

"I don't have a room."

"There's a motel a couple of blocks away. Come on, I'll call them and get you crew rates. When you check in, let me know, and I'll phone if I find an empty seat."

Parking in the lot at the motel, I saw that the place had an aura of quiet desperation, and the idea of staying overnight depressed me. But I didn't have a lot of choices. I was stuck.

After checking in, I felt a little better. There was a restaurant and bar that advertised prime beef and fine wines. Leaving my room number for Redmond with the FBO at the airport, I took a quick shower and phoned Rose.

"Nancy Wiseman has called here twice hunting you."

"The line supervisor couldn't identify her from the photograph as the woman who flew J.D.'s airplane from Denver. I'm going to try and get to Aspen tomorrow. If no one can point to the doctor, I'll call her."

"I just don't understand why you think she'd have anything to do with J.D. disappearing?"

"I'm just looking at the facts, Rose, and eliminating the innocent.

You haven't been to Denver lately, have you? The lineman looked long and hard at you in the photo, although I think it was simply lust in his eyes."

"I'm getting awful tired of you, Leicester," she snarled like a treed bobcat.

Why does everyone call me by my last name when they're angry?

Laughing, I say, "Put Nancy off until I can look around Aspen. I don't think she's involved, but I want to be sure."

"Will you at least call me when you decide?"

"Yes, Rosie. Goodbye."

I hung up before she could say anything. She hates the name, Rosie.

Almost instantly the phone rang. I thought it may be her, but it was Redmond.

"One of our tenants is flying his Baron to Aspen at seven in the morning to pick up some people. He's going over empty and said he'd enjoy the company."

"That's great. Where do I meet him?"

"Come to the FBO office. I'll introduce you. Don't be late."

"Thanks, Redmond. If you'll stop by the motel, I'll buy you dinner."

"Maybe a rain check. The wife's expecting me home tonight."

Hunger began to gnaw at me, so I decided to see if in fact the motel restaurant served up Prime Beef.

The bar was dark with maybe a dozen tables and three booths. Only a few customers were there. Surprisingly, classical music wafted softly from overhead speakers. I have always felt that music is an inexplicable awakener of the dark engines of our immortal souls, especially when I hear Willie Nelson and Ray Charles sing a duet titled, *Seven Spanish Angels*.

I took a seat at the bar and ordered a glass of Chardonnay.

"How's the food in the restaurant?" I asked the tender.

"If you like strip sirloin, there's none better."

"What about the wine list?"

He handed me a book almost an inch thick.

"California and Italy. Don't ask me why, but there are several decent bottles from good years at reasonable prices. If you know anything about wine."

I took no offense at his remark, sipped the white wine and looked around the bar.

I spotted her sitting in a corner booth. She hung her head over a glass of wine, the long hair resembling a nun's Habit. Trouble: women alone in a bar are either alcoholic, working, or desperate in one of hundreds of ways. If one is smart, they are better left alone.

"What's her story?"

The barkeep looked over at the woman.

"She's been here for four or five days. Extremely shy, always alone. A few men and a couple of women have tried to move in, but she's turned them all away. If you're looking for companionship, I've got a couple of numbers, reasonable rates.

"Thanks, but no. I was simply curious."

Just as I said that, she slid out of the booth and walked up to the bar right next to me and set her wine glass down.

"Could I have another glass of Chardonnay, please?"

"Me too, barkeep, and put the lady's on my tab."

She turned to me. "I can pay for my own drink."

It was a soft, demur voice, in no way sarcastic. I watched her close for any sign of dissembling.

"I wasn't hitting on you, young lady. Just offering a little southern hospitality."

She was tall, beautifully built, and had porcelain skin. Even in the dim light, her hair was shiny like a colt. She looked healthy and broad shouldered. She had eyes a deep shade of brown that suggested melted chocolate. I am convinced that chocolate is the pathway to salvation. Her only flaw was a row of protruding upper teeth, which seemed to be attempting to smile, while the lower set did its best to hold them back.

"Where in the south?" she asked, throwing her head to one side, causing the long hair to move like the mane of a horse.

"Mississippi."

"I was born in Fairhope, Alabama."

"Ah, Fairhope, the home of the Grand Hotel and Henry Stuart, the Poet of Tolstoy Park and his little round house. Why are you in a motel in Denver in the middle of the winter?"

"You are familiar with the 'weaver of rugs?' I grew up a couple of blocks from the little domed house made of concrete blocks. It's still there, preserved, in the parking lot of a bank. I'm supposed to start a new job with a resort up in the mountains; Snowmass Development Corporation. I've been trying to get there for five days, but the weather has been too bad to drive. With the ski season in full swing, all the airlines are booked solid. I'm afraid I may lose the job if I can't get there pretty quick."

"Well, Miss…?"

"Richmond, Beverly Richmond."

"Miss Richmond, this may be your lucky day."

I told her about flying over in the morning and that she was welcome to ride along. She could leave her car at the airport and retrieve it when the weather improved.

He face immediately lit up, as if my unexpected presence was further evidence that the world was a marvelous place, that it offered genuine miracles on a daily basis.

"Beverly, I'm going to have dinner in the restaurant and I hate to eat alone. Would you join me?"

"That would be nice."

She was the shyest person I've ever known. She was not shy from ignorance, nor from being ill at ease, nor from any defect. She was shy, as certain animals are, such as the coyote when away from the pack. She had a strange, rare smile which surfaced from a deep, dark pit within her soul.

The bartender was right, the sirloin was outstanding accompanied by an Italian Barolo from a good year. To my surprise Beverly ate all of her steak and had high praise for the big, tannic wine, though she knew little about the subject. Her brown eyes stared with sensual expressions, knowing something, never smiling except with dark secret.

She wanted to know about me, what I did, why I was here. Leaving out the part about J.D. missing, I told her about my life in aviation, opening up a consulting business, living in a cabin in the woods, and simply offered that I was going to Aspen to retrieve an airplane.

The young woman was pleasant company, even in her shyness. If one overlooked the flaws with the mouth, she was truly a beautiful woman. Her smile would start from her soul and come frankly and wonderfully to the surface. She had a fine face, perfect nose, kind, gay, truthful chocolate eyes.

She suddenly looked at me and said, "This is fun. I have not had any fun in a long time."

"Yes, fun. I have found that you have fun only when you are in love."

She hung her head. "Yes, only when you are in love."

I suspected someone had hurt her severely, but I was not about to pry.

After dinner, I escorted her to her room. I followed her along the hallway—firm hips squeezed into tight jeans. I liked her confident walk. I liked her slim body and long legs, hair draping over square shoulders.

We reached her motel room door. "You want to come in for a drink? Or whatever might appeal to you?"

This surprised invitation was offered with such shyness that I could not refuse.

We sat in small chairs around a small round table holding onto drinks until we had to put them down. There were subtle things with her eyes. It was hard to tell if it was real or only my imagination.

She began to talk easily to me. She was pure sex appeal. Her voice had husky and familiar sounds, like one of the most seductive forms that lovemaking can take. Her eyes became misty, smiling, but a little sad. "You want to go to bed?"

"Beverly, nothing would give me greater pleasure, but no. It would be a mistake—for both of us. I'd better go."

She saw me to the door. "Thank you for not taking advantage of the loneliness."

"I'll meet you in the lobby at 6:30 in the morning."

Standing in the empty hallway, it came to me that there is a sense of achievement and assurance that results from victory over temptation that cannot come to one otherwise.

In my room, I turn out the lights and climb into bed, entering a darkness that seems more than dark, living a life that feels much the same way.

Case History of Dr. John Bolt

FEMALE—Diagnosis and History: Adenosquamous cell carcinoma of the mouth together with secondaries in both sides of the neck which was treated with surgery. Patient then presented with recurrence in the floor of the mouth and two other sites—including lymph nodes. Treatment started immediately with Radiowave Therapy. Nine years and ten months later the patient had no evidence of the carcinoma in the mouth. The patient also developed breast cancer which was also treated by Dr. Bolt. After treatment no evidence of activity from either cancer was detectable and laboratory analysis some two and a half years later indicated that no cancer was present.

Chapter Nine

Beverly was waiting when I arrived in the lobby. She followed me to Centennial Airport in a rusted Toyota sedan that looked older than its driver. Everything she owned seemed packed into the small car. To my delight, she took only one large suitcase when we parked.

Redmond and a tall, thin, distinguished man with thick glasses and a mustache stood in the lobby of the FBO. He was introduced as Dr. Victor Frank. We shook hands and I said, "This is Beverly Richmond. She works for Snowmass Development Corporation. The roads are closed and she needs to get to work. Hope you don't mind an extra passenger?"

Redmond looked at me rather strangely, but Dr. Frank said, "Certainly not," and shook Beverly's hand. "I own a condo there, at the bottom of Fanny Hill."

The Beech Baron had been towed to the front of the FBO. It was an older B-58 model that appeared to have just emerged from the factory. Redmond put Beverly and her bag in the club seats behind the pilots and locked the doors. I walked around the plane admiring the sleek lines of one of the finest twin-engine recips (Piston engines driving propellers) ever built.

"You have kept her up very well, doctor."

"Thank you. I understand you are a retired airline pilot. Would you like to fly this morning?"

"I would be delighted. What's the weather like at Aspen?"

"CAVU. (Clear air and visibility unlimited) A little turbulence over the windward side of the mountains, but should be no problem."

As we buckled our seatbelts, I asked, "What kind of doctor?"

"Pathologist. *Mortui Vivos Docent*, the dead teach the living." He laughed. "There is an old saying about doctors: The psychiatrist knows everything and does nothing. The surgeon knows nothing and does everything. The dermatologist knows nothing and does nothing. The pathologist knows everything, but is always a day late."

I laughed with him.

We departed westbound and climbed toward the Rocky Mountains. It was a flyer's day and the Baron performed wonderfully. I elected to hand-fly the plane and managed to over control in the roll axis until I got the feel of things. Turning the yaw dampener on helped. We leveled at fourteen thousand feet, as high as we could go without breathing oxygen, and set cruise power on the two three-hundred horsepower engines.

It was exciting going across the mountains—those enormous snow-covered mountains—and the endless valleys and lakes, the rivers and streams and small towns snuggled against steep cliffs. The Rockies are beautiful. I watched the morning light glint off the polished wings of the airplane, tethered not to the earth, but to the soul of the airman. I think the soul would surely float, like a child's kite, as far as the winds of chance might take it. How peaceful this world, the aviator's world, and silent, save for the smooth purr of the engines and the wings in the wind.

A woman I once spent some time with asked me to define flying. Louis Armstrong when asked to describe jazz said that those who have to have it explained to them will never know. So it is with flight.

Looking in the back seat to see how Beverly was making it, I found her fast asleep. Below, Leadville appeared, covered with a deep layer of snow; further to the south, Twin Lakes lay like two huge eyes in a dark hole. Soon we crossed a ridge and saw Aspen nestled in the long valley with steep cliffs on either side. Even in good weather pilots need to be alert when landing here, many crashes have occurred on approach to this single runway, one I had the displeasure to witness.

The tower cleared us to land and we did so without incident. We taxied to the FBO and shut down the engines. After unloading Beverly and her bag, I thanked Dr. Frank for the ride, and went inside to rent a car.

Dr. Frank's passengers were waiting and as I signed for the rental, he started his engines and taxied away. Walking to the door, I watched him depart and silently wished him Godspeed and a safe flight.

J.D.'s Cessna Citation was parked on the ramp. I wanted to get Beverly up to Snowmass, find a place to stay, then come back to the FBO and start the search for J.D. I planned to begin with Redmond's friend who ran the operation.

The drive up to Snowmass was familiar. The roads were clear of snow and I was amazed at the development going on in the area. There was only one home along the drive up the mountain when last I was here. Now there were dozens. They took away from the wildness of years ago.

We parked in the lot of Snowmass Development and I went inside with Beverly. The company handled the rentals for all properties on the mountain and I inquired as to any vacancies. There were two sections joining the village proper that resembled a motel and maybe there was some cancellation. There was not, however the young man checked the Holiday Inn near the airport and found that there was one room available. He let me talk to the innkeeper and I gave her my credit card to hold the room.

"You are lucky, Mr. Leicester. That's probably the only room this side of Denver for the next two months," the man said.

"Lucky, yes. You have accommodations for Miss Richmond, I presume?"

"We have a dorm to house new employees until they go through orientation. After that, housing will be arranged here, at the village."

"Well, Beverly, I guess this is goodbye. It's been a pleasure. I hope this job works out for you."

She hugged my neck. "Thank you for what you've done. Maybe we will see each other again."

I headed back down the mountain.

It had been fifteen years since I'd stayed at the Aspen Holiday Inn. When it was built, it claimed a Five-Star French restaurant, and it truly was Five Star. It was in this small restaurant with individual rooms for privacy that I would taste two foods for the first time; lightly battered and fried Brussels sprouts sprinkled with sea salt, and escargot placed in individual shells with a thick garlic sauce. And these were just the appetizers. The rest of that meal was even more stupendous; all washed down with first growth French wines.

The motel seemed not to have changed, though to my sad disappointment, the French restaurant was gone. The lobby was bustling with skiers, some just off the slopes, and others on their way out. At the big fireplace in the lobby a young woman sat with her leg propped up on a cushion, sporting a fresh, white cast, her skiing done for the season. However several young men were paying her close attention. The place and the people seemed full of energy. I suddenly felt old, an exile in my time, full of a systemic desuetude and drifting toward irrelevance. When one loses the "youthful energy" in us something is lost forever.

Looking around at the people, they appeared blue-collar, egalitarian, and patriotic. It was the America of Whitman, Faulkner, Hemingway, Sherwood Anderson, James Agee, Fitzgerald, an improbable coalescence of contradictions that had become Homeric without them realizing an importance to the world.

My room, though Spartan, was clean and warm and afforded a view of the mountains to the west. The sun glistening off the snow-packed peaks was an artists rendering of light and shadow. There was no balcony and the windows were sealed shut. After unpacking my ditty bag, which contained a change of clothes and some toiletries, I went in search of food.

I followed a waitress—broad hips squeezed into tight jeans—through the crowded restaurant to a table. She handed me a menu and left me to the view out the picture window. To the south was the tall mountain that got in the way of Aspen Airways' Convair 240 one winter night. They were attempting a go-around in bad weather and did not make it. There were 38 passengers aboard.

A young, linebacker-sized woman with sunken cheeks blushed with rouge, a heart-shaped mouth made girlish with lipstick, and wide, dark eyes that moved with tactical precision from diner to diner while taking my order, said, "You alone?"

"I'm alone."

"Too bad, you're a good-looking guy."

"A hungry one, too."

The food was served. I shook a liberal dose of McElheny's Tabasco sauce over everything. Sometimes hot sauce was the only way I knew I was still alive.

Eating the burger and fries, I watched two women sitting across from me who were wide and generously weighted in the legs and hips. They were animated and every few minutes one would say in a loud voice, "I have to pee. God, I have to pee." The last thing I heard leaving the table was, "I have to pee. God, I have to pee."

I knew these two women. They were sisters; Oholah and Oholibah. It was time to head to the airport.

. . .

He was a tall man, with a ravaged face of great breeding, merry blue eyes, and the long, loose-coupled body of an Alaskan caribou. He appeared an eerie clone of an airplane mechanic I knew years ago in Mississippi.

We shook hands. He introduced himself as George Barrows.

"Redmond called, said you were inquiring about the Citation on the ramp."

"You have a place we can go and talk?"

"Sure, come back to my office."

It was a small space, arranged for work, not comfort. A desk, two chairs, and a file cabinet comprised the furnishings, with a narrow window overlooking the ramp to the north. J.D.'s Citation was visible at the far end. With the exception of two aircraft brake assemblies welded together to form bookends, there was no other aviation ephemera visible.

"George, my friend who owns that Citation—I pointed out the window—was due to attend a medical conference here in Aspen last week. He never made it, though his airplane did. No one's heard from him. We know he landed in Denver due to weather here in Aspen. We learned the Citation left Denver, flew to Salt Lake, then to here. Anything you can help me with will be appreciated."

"You a cop?"

"No."

"Have you called the cops?"

"Not yet."

"What do you do?"

It was a fair question. Redmond must have told him nothing about me.

"I'm a retired airline pilot and have an aviation consulting business. I sold J.D. Ballard, my missing friend, the Citation."

He leaned back in his chair, put his feet up on the desk, and lay both hands in his lap. Tilting his head back, he looked at the low ceiling, seeming to ponder what I'd told him. Then he looked me directly in the eyes.

"Your Citation landed here two days ago. I personally guided the plane to parking. A woman was in the Captain's seat with a male copilot. Two men were passengers. A limo drove out on the ramp; two of the men helped the other off and into the car. He looked in bad shape, couldn't hold his head up or walk. I assumed he was inebriated. The woman locked up the Citation, said they would be here for a week and would phone in a fuel order later."

"Four aboard. You're sure?"

"Yes."

"They left Denver with only three."

"Maybe they picked up someone in Salt Lake?"

"Maybe."

"Here's what I suggest, let me arrange a meet with the local sheriff, he's a friend. You can run down the limo, check the hotels, hospitals. Of course, if they are staying in a private home, there'll be no way to know. We'll keep alert for any movement with the Citation, fuel orders, and departure times. If you have any ATC connections, you might want to keep in touch with them. If there's any movement with the airplane, they'll have a record."

"ATC was how I knew the Citation was here. If that airplane starts to move from this ramp, I want to know."

"It's a promise."

Barrows stood, extended a hand. "Where you staying?"

"Holiday Inn."

"I'll let you know when we can meet with the sheriff."

"You ex-law enforcement?"

"Auxiliary deputy. Kind of a hobby."

"Thanks, George."

As I started out the door, he said, "You want to take a peek inside the airplane? I have a key."

"Let's go." Why didn't I think of that?

Like the key to any Ford tractor, any Cessna key will work on a door lock. It has often made me ponder why even put locks on them if any key will work?

Barrows handed me a pair of work gloves.

"In case fingerprints are important later."

He took his hobby seriously.

Looking around inside the Citation revealed little out of the ordinary. There were the usual empty Styrofoam coffee cups in the trash can, but no one smoked or ate in the cabin. I turned on the battery switch and activated the flight management system. Someone had erased the data for the last flights.

Barrows shook his head. "Not much here."

Then it dawned on me, the Rife Frequency Generator was not aboard. J.D. went nowhere without it. Whoever flew this airplane into Aspen took it with them when they left.

"I'll be at the Holiday Inn."

. . .

Sitting in my room, the late evening view to the west was magnificent. The sky was golden, the mountains bound not by earthly borders, but by the arbitrary definitions of light and shadow. "Where are you, J.D?" I said aloud. "Has this supposed cancer cure by some frequency generator caused you harm? Or death?"

F. Scott Fitzgerald wrote that *the cleverly expressed opposite of any generally accepted idea is worth a fortune to somebody.* Had J.D., by threatening to go public with the suppression of the cancer cure, activated some sinister plot to kill him?

The phone beside the bed rang. It was an ugly-sounding noise.

"Leicester."

"Ten o'clock in the morning. I'll pick you up at the motel, and we'll meet with the sheriff at his office in Aspen."

"Okay, I'll be waiting in the lobby. Thanks, Barrows."

With little to do the rest of the afternoon, I decided to drive up to Snowmass Village, and walk the main street. There was a restaurant/bar at the very end where skiers could ski right up to the deck, take off their skis, and clomp around in their ski boots, grab a beer, have a bite. It was a perfect spot for people watching, and the food was first rate.

It was almost dark when I parked in the lot just below the village. There was an open-air ice skating rink there and it was full of skaters. The temperature was rapidly closing in on the freezing level and I was struggling to breath, having forgotten the altitude was almost nine thousand feet. Halfway down the village street was a huge sunken fireplace. A hole with wooden benches around the perimeter about three feet below street level circled a gas fed fire with lava rocks. Not only was it warm, but romantic late at night with a soft snowfall, a good bottle of wine, and a happy companion. I sat on the bench and warmed for awhile—totally alone.

Two other couples joined me on the benches. It was time for me to go.

At the end of the street, I walked upon the deck of the restaurant. A few late skiers were getting into their cups, dressed for the cold, warmed by the alcohol and oblivious to the Eden-like scenery surrounding them. Inside, the waiters were in between the daytime crowd and the evening dinning. A beautiful young woman with long blond hair, dressed in ski apparel, played an upright piano accompanied by several couples dressed similarly and all sporting the windblown tans of sun and snow.

The lighting was dim and candles glowed on tables. Seating myself, I picked a table on the south end of the restaurant beside a big picture window overlooking Fanny Hill, the ski slope for children and beginners and people like me who could barely stand on the things. Several teenagers were sliding down the hill on disks resembling the lids of garbage cans, though they were actually called space sleds and looked like fun.

A young man came over. "Sorry, we're setting up for the night crowd. What can I get you?"

"A wine list and a menu. I think I'll dine with you tonight."

"You picked a good day. The chef is preparing tenderloins to die for. I'll be back with the wine list."

The wines were mostly French and California from good years, but reflected resort prices. There was a Chateau Lafitte from a horrible year in France for this harvest, however I knew the wine was drinking quite well, and it was reasonably priced.

He poured the wine. "This was not a good year, if it's undrinkable, let me know."

Honesty—a rarity today.

The Lafitte was much better than expected and I offered a glass to the waiter.

"This is good. People have been sending it back. Next time, I'll sample it."

The tenderloin and claret went well together and I started to relax. The restaurant was filling with teenagers and college kids. This was their "hangout" while mom and dad dined at the Red Onion and the Copper Kettle in downtown Aspen.

Two hours later the wine bottle was empty, I was fully relaxed and my brain was turning to love. The college girls were looking older, or I was thinking I was younger. It is a sad thing, but alcohol always makes me feel rich and invisible.

"Waiter, give those two ladies at the bar a drink and put it on my tab."

"Certainly, sir," he said without inflection.

The two young women looked at me, then at each other and giggled. It was time for me to head down the mountain. At the door, I turned and saw her, hair hanging over her drink, the nun's habit, sitting alone at a table. Beverly. No, I said to myself, no. Go down the mountain, you have a meeting with the Pitkin County Colorado sheriff in the morning.

Outside the air was cold and bracing, the thin jacket barely able to maintain body temperature. The narrow street was filled with people, laughing, embarking on an evening of fun in the Colorado Rockies. I was searching for a missing friend.

Case History of Dr. John Bolt

FEMALE—Diagnosis and History: Recurrent carcinoma in the left breast. Biopsy proved recurrent duct carcinoma in the left breast existed. Radiowave Therapy commenced immediately. After sixteen days of treatment the mass had halved in size. Repeated treatments over a period of years took place whereupon all her cancer antigens were measured and were found to be within normal limits. Examination ten years after her original treatment indicated no cancer was present.

Chapter Ten

The wine acted as a sedative. Sleep was sound and I don't think I turned over all night. I awoke happy, rested, and refreshed. I have never been sad one waking morning of my life. I have experienced anguish and sorrow, but never sadness.

After a quick shower and fresh clothes, I headed for the lobby to wait for Barrows. Complimentary coffee was self-serve and I poured a cup, longing for a dollop of honey. People were passing through, heading for the ski lifts. The two "sisters" who sat across from me at lunch yesterday came down for coffee. They were dressed in tight ski pants, after-ski boots, and were animated about shopping in downtown Aspen. I hoped there was a restroom near the stores.

George Barrows walked through the door, his lanky frame and severe face a study in toughness and determination. We could be friends, given the right circumstances.

"Any movement on the Citation?" I asked.

"Nothing," he said, shaking my hand. "You heard from the owner?"

"He still hasn't shown up. I'm afraid he was the one who was incapacitated you saw being helped from the airplane into the limo."

"I've been thinking about that. Why the side trip to Salt Lake? If someone wanted to do harm to your friend, why bring him here, to a place where he was expected?"

"Two good questions. I've no clue."

Barrows poured himself a cup of coffee.

"Have you checked the weather?"

"No, why?"

"Looks like you'll have some time to look for the answers. A big storm is due in tonight. Nothing will move in or out of here for several days. Three to four feet of snow is forecast, with high winds and below freezing temps."

"That's just wonderful."

"Let's go meet with the sheriff, he's not a man to be kept waiting."

The woman behind the desk wore a deputy's uniform and the intensity in her eyes and the tautness in her facial muscles belied the fact she had seen much of the rough side of our society, maybe too much. She wore heavy makeup that was cracked in some places making me think of a clay sculpture badly done. Recognizing Barrows, her face seemed to soften. She stood, slid both hands in the back pockets of her uniform pants and looked at me.

"He's waiting in his office, George," she said, never taking her eyes off me as if I was public enemy number one.

"Sadie, this is Jay Leicester. He's looking for a missing friend."

She nodded at me, kept her hands in her back pockets and said nothing.

"Sadie," I said. "Your middle name wouldn't be Rose, would it?"

"It is not. Why?"

"Just a guess."

However rugged George Barrows appeared, Sheriff Pete Freuchen, of Pitkin County, Colorado, was even more "mountain man." His hair was thin, dark, and slicked back across his scalp. The sharp nose, excited eyes, and pointed jaw gave him the appearance of a hawk. He was not a young man, I guessed early sixties, but his high cheek bones and fiery eyes radiated energy and oozed violence. Every physical feature of his was sharp. He seemed to possess superhuman strength and vitality. His chin, nose, ears, lips, even his shoulders appeared as though drawn by a sadistic cartoonist.

On his well-worn desk was an ashtray filled with Winston cigarette butts. When he spoke, his voice sounded like a cancer patient coughing up pieces of lung with every word.

He shook my hand, waved us to two chairs across from him. He lit a cigarette, looked at me. "George said you were from Mississippi. Met several of the sheriffs from there. One, named Waddell, from the coast. Invited me down for some bill fishing. Ever heard of him?"

"I've made his acquaintance." I did not go into detail about my friendship with William Waddell, sheriff of Harrison County, Mississippi.

"George said you had a friend go missing, think he may be in our area."

Barrows told me the sheriff could be trusted, so I related the whole story, stressing the point that J.D.'s involvement with the Rife Frequency generator and going public with the suppression by the medical establishment, could have resulted in some overzealous people to want him eliminated.

Freuchen carefully laid his cigarette in the over-full ashtray, put both gnarled hands on the top of the desk. "That is the dumbest thing I've heard in thirty years of law enforcement. No doctor or group of doctors in their right mind would want a cure for cancer suppressed. The American Cancer Society would be all over this---this frequency generator, in a heartbeat."

"Unless they couldn't acquire the patent, and the pharmaceutical companies involved in chemotherapy drug business, and the FDA, which is owned by the cancer monopolies, would lose tens of billions of dollars. Strong motive to shut up one man."

The sheriff lit another cigarette, put out the one smoldering in the ashtray. "This Rife machine work?"

"My friend's positive that it does. He's a medical doctor, a radiologist, and has seen the results. He's convinced himself and convinced me."

"When I get lung cancer, and I will from smoking all these cigarettes, it'd be nice to have one of those machines around to try out."

"You ever thought about quitting?"

"I'm sixty-three years old, been smoking since I was twelve. A little late, don't you think?"

I did not argue. There are some people who it does no good to point out obvious facts. I know. I have been one of those people.

Freuchen picked up the phone, punched a button. "Sadie, would you come in here." He looked at me. "All right, Leicester, let's see if we can find your missing doctor."

Sadie took all the information on J.D. and started the process of locating him. I was impressed at the thoroughness of the sheriff's department, and their willingness to involve other law enforcement agencies.

"Let Sadie know how to get in touch with you. We'll run this as a missing person, no mention of a conspiracy to silence your friend, at least not at the moment."

"Thanks, sheriff. Barrows and I will work the aviation end and if anything surfaces, we'll let you know."

When I stopped by Sadie's desk, she looked at me like I was some cur dog.

"You somebody important? I haven't seen Pete get so up in arms in years. I just want you to know you ain't got no clout with me, buster."

"My name is not buster, its Jay Leicester, and what did I do to piss you off, girlie?"

She laughed, looked at Barrows. "He's okay, George. Get him out of here."

In the car heading back to the motel, I asked, "What the heck was that all about with the deputy?"

Barrows laughed. "That's just Sadie being Sadie. She was raised in these mountains, in a cabin with no electricity, running water, a crude fireplace as the only heat. Her Pa was a prospector, dug for gold and silver all over this country. Her mom died of pneumonia when she was twelve. She took over the household chores while the old man roamed about looking for the mother lode. Sadie ran her own trap line, sold the pelts to a local trader."

"What became of the father?"

"He went out one day, never came back. No one's heard from him since. Probably died of exposure on the mountain or an animal got him. Sadie married a man who worked for the railroad, but he died a few years later from that old demon alcohol. After that, she made it as best she could, finally moving into Aspen. She's been with Freuchen for the past twenty years, a loyal servant to both him and the county. She's just a tough old bird and basically a good person."

"Freuchen and her an item?"

"I never asked."

"Understood."

We pulled up in front of the Holiday Inn.

"Thanks for the help with the sheriff. If nothing turns up on my friend, I'll fly the Citation back to Mississippi, after the storm clears. Any chance of getting it into a hangar?"

"None. We are good at thawing them out, though. Let me know the day before you depart, we'll have her ready to go. If I were you, I'd gather up some supplies, anything you'll need for a couple of days. If this storm is as bad as predicted, everything is going to shut down."

"It's been a while since I've weathered a storm in the high-country. Thanks for the advice."

Barrows reached across and shook my hand.

"You have my number," he said, his grip like iron.

On the way inside, I noticed the sky was thickening, but sunshine still broke through the clouds in spots and the wind was not blowing with any velocity. It was hard to believe a major snowstorm was bearing down on this area of the Rocky Mountains. One of my old Captains, who flew this country for Frontier Airlines, related to me how in the early days of the DC-3s, they would navigate through these storms with little instrumentation, using their wits, knowledge of the terrain, and aeronautical skill. Theirs was the days of the true airmen, not the button-pushing, video game playing pilots being graduated from AB-Initio flight schools of today, who rely on automation for everything from takeoff to touchdown.

At the front desk, I inquired as to what the motel planned in case of power outages during the impending storm. I was assured that there was a working generator, enough food to feed a full house for a week, and that if I needed anything, to let them know and it would be supplied. Heading to my room, I felt much better, though being snowbound for several days with a motel full of strangers did not appeal to me.

A note in a white envelope was taped to my door covering the electronic key slot. I ripped it off and went inside. Nothing seemed disturbed, but then I didn't have much to disturb. The note, written in ink, was neatly printed on Holiday Inn stationary.

> *You sir, need to mind your own business.*
> *Dr. Ballard is safe. His future health depends on several things,*
> *Including how fast you return to Mississippi.*
> *Consider this a threat, a warning, or whatever you wish,*
> *But know this, it is serious.*

I immediately called Sheriff Freuchen. Sadie said he'd gone for the day. When told about the threat, she said she'd be there in a few minutes to pick it up and get the motel's surveillance tapes. Maybe they could identify who placed the note on my door.

Out my window the clouds were getting much thicker, the wind was picking up, and it had started to sleet and snow. The storm front was approaching. I read the note again. Someone, for whatever reason, held J.D. How it had happened, who was responsible, or what their intentions were, at the moment, was only speculation. What was not speculation is that these unknown people were intelligent and knew about me and why I was in Aspen. The question that begged an answer was, who are they, and how could they possibly know about me. Could this really be medical professionals, sworn to *"first do no harm,"* involved in suppressing a cancer cure fueled by profit, and kidnapping of a colleague? This would be a stretch, even for a fiction writer.

There was a knock on the door. "Trap line Sadie," help had arrived.

Looking through the keyhole, my jaw dropped. It was not Deputy Sadie, but Doctor Nancy Wiseman standing there looking impatient. I opened the door.

"Nancy—what, how?"

"I got the last flight out of Denver. It was rough, worse ride of my life, everyone was throwing up. We almost didn't make it. Are you going to invite me in?"

"Come in. Why are you here? How did you know where to find me?"

"Rose informed me. I saw J.D.'s Citation when we landed. Some man named Barrows told me you were staying at this hotel, said something strange about me not being the female pilot, and that you would explain."

"But why are you here? What about your clinic?"

"The clinic is being covered by a friend, another DO from Meridian who owed me a favor, until I return. I was too worried about J.D. to sit around and do nothing, so here I am."

Nancy threw her bag on the bed. She appeared disheveled, haggard. Her long, black hair was uncombed and matted. Her thin face and tired eyes made her appear a little older than I remembered.

"Have you learned anything about J.D.?"

Motioning to a chair at the small round table, I said, "He didn't make it to Aspen, as you know. He landed at Centennial Airport in Denver. A ramp supervisor there provided assistance and, when I learned that the airplane did, in fact, finally arrive in Aspen, helped me get here. The Citation departed Denver with a woman flying, male copilot and one male passenger. Seems there was a side trip to Salt Lake City, where an extra passenger boarded. Barrows, the man you met at the Aspen FBO observed the people deplane when it landed. However he didn't know J.D. and couldn't identify him from my description. One of the men seemed incapacitated and had to be helped from the airplane into the limo that met them. I think that person was J.D."

A gust of wind rattled the window and sleet beat against the glass. The storm was arriving with full force. Nancy ran her fingers through her hair, thought about what I'd said.

"What did this Barrows person mean about me not being the pilot?"

"I brought a photo of you. I had to be sure."

She looked hard at me, and then surprised me by saying, "Fair enough. Are you convinced, now?"

"Yes." I shoved the warning note across the table. "This was taped to my door a few minutes ago. Don't touch it, a deputy is on the way to pick it up and run it through forensics."

She bent over the table and read the note.

There was a knock on the door.

Deputy Sadie pushed her way into the room. When she spotted Nancy, she stopped cold. "My God, you've already found someone to keep you warm during the storm. Hell, you could've asked me, I might have been available."

"Deputy Sadie, meet Doctor Nancy Wiseman. She and the missing Doctor J.D. Ballard are—friends."

"That mean you're sleeping with the man, doctor?"

"Yes, it does, if it's any of your business."

Sadie laughed, walked across the room and offered her hand to Nancy.

"Nothing personal, doctor, I just need to know who all the usual suspects are. Did you touch that note?"

"I did not."

"Good, then your prints should not be on it." She put the note and envelope into a clear plastic evidence bag, sealed it up. Looking at me she said, "The motel security is removing the video of the hallway. I'll look at it back at the sheriff's office." Then to Nancy, "I'm not going to see you on it, am I Doctor Wiseman?"

"Only once, and that would be about a half hour ago when I arrived."

"Where are you staying? I'm sure we'll want to interview you later."

Nancy looked perplexed. "I don't know. I haven't made reservations anywhere."

"Oh boy, looks like you may have a roommate, Leicester."

Nancy looked at me with a question mark.

"There are no accommodations in the area. All rooms are booked. I got the last one this side of Denver."

Sadie went to the door. "I'll let you know if there's anything on the video. You two stay warm." She laughed and closed the door behind her.

"I don't like that woman."

"She comes across as a little gruff, kind of reminds me of Rose. People seem to respect her. She was raised in these mountains, had a rather harsh upbringing."

The lights flickered, but did not go out. Wind shook the windows.

"I need a shower."

"Help yourself. We really need to find you some place to stay."

"What's wrong with here?"

"If you haven't noticed, there's only one bed."

"So?"

"It would be rather awkward, don't you think?"

"Why?"

"Well, you and J.D...."

"My God, you're thinking about sex. Haven't you ever slept in the same bed with a woman without having sex with her?"

"Not that I can recall, well maybe once, but that was in Mexico."

"I can assure you, it won't bother me in the least."

"Okay, suit yourself, but I've been told that I snore."

"So do I. I'm going to take a shower."

While she was in the bathroom, J.D. and the fact that he may be incapacitated, entered my thoughts. If the people we were dealing with are medical professionals, and I use that term loosely, they would have the expertise and access to drugs. How they were able to administer them was another question. I knew a young woman who was kept drugged for five or six days to keep her from identifying her tormentors.

She was kept on prozac and Ritalin and placedon and zephyrill, drugs that were antipsychotic, anti-anxiety, antidepression, or the "anti-the-side-effects-of-the-other drugs" drugs. I think she ended up with a six-drug cocktail. She was kept, not exactly sleeping but not exactly awake. When I found her, there was a flicker of recognition, but she would quickly slide away under a molecular coverlet, like an ember dimming under ashes. My attempts to talk to her were pretty much unsuccessful. During recovery she told the doctors she hallucinated every imaginable thing—Jesus, Elvis, Hitler, dildoes, rats, chocolate ice cream, cockroaches, having anal sex with Bill Clinton, which she said didn't really hurt because his penis was so small.

The drugs had thinned out the essence of being human. She said she seemed too insubstantial to even hold light, to be at all luminescent, not able to cast a shadow. The vitality of the human had been diluted. Her brain was a neurochemical theme park. It was appalling.

What would I do if this was happening to J.D.? A rage began to build in me, but unlike Hebrone, I had some control over it, though there was a feeling of being vulnerable and lost, isolated and alone. Maybe Doctor Nancy Wiseman showing up was not such a bad thing, maybe she could keep me from committing black murder.

Case History of Dr. John Bolt

MALE—Diagnosis and History: Carcinoma of the prostate. Adenocarcinoma was confirmed at biopsy. The patient was treated with Radiowave Therapy. Over six years and seven months the patient's prostatic specific antigen remained in normal limits. At that examination no symptoms of the disease were present and ten years after his initial therapy no signs existed.

Chapter Eleven

Nancy emerged from the shower looking much refreshed. She had changed into different clothes, jeans, a heavy sweater, and after-ski boots. Her long, black hair hung in damp strands.

She'd made a lengthy, arduous journey to help look for her lover. I began to admire her, but with some caution, for within her she seemed to carry a portion of darkness, like the impending storm raging outside the window. She exuded a dreadfulness and the fragrance of confrontation that seemingly comes natural to her.

"Storm's getting worse," she said, drying her hair with a towel, holding her head first to one side, then the other, as if somehow that would quicken the process. "I could use something to eat. How's the food here?"

Before I could answer, the phone rang. It was Deputy Sadie.

"Barrows stopped by; we looked at the surveillance video. He recognized the person who taped the note to your door as the woman who flew the missing man's airplane into Aspen. It is definitely not Doctor Wiseman. That should be good news for you, Leicester, especially since you're sleeping with the good doctor."

"I am not sleeping...how long before we hear from forensics on the note?"

"It has to go to Denver. The weather will delay things for several days. Relax, enjoy your new roommate. We'll let you know if anything turns up on your friend."

Hanging up the phone, I looked at Nancy.

"Let me guess, the deputy?"

"Yes, the woman who flew J.D.'s Citation from Denver, to Salt Lake, to here, is the same one who taped the note to my door."

· · ·

The phone rang, again.

Jerking the receiver out of its cradle, I said, "Leicester."

"By calling the police, you just got your friend killed."

The line went dead. It was a male voice. They were watching. Sleet peppered the window like birdshot.

I immediately phoned Deputy Sadie, informed her of the call.

"They are on to you. Hell, they could be staying in the room next door. We'll run down the guest registry, see if any names stand out. In the meantime, you and the Doc be careful."

"Thanks, Sadie."

Nancy looked concerned. "Do you think they'd go so far as to harm J.D.?"

"I have no idea who 'they' are, but yes, I think J.D. is in harm's way. Do I think these people are medical doctors? No, but I believe the ones they hired to shut J.D. up are capable of killing him."

"What are we going to do?"

"We're going to eat in the dining room, let these people know intimidation won't work on us."

"Should we get police protection?"

"They're not out to silence us, and they may not recognize us on sight. So I don't think we're in any immediate danger."

She threw the wet towel across a chair, tied her still damp hair into a ponytail.

"Let's go eat."

The restaurant was crowded. The storm brought everyone in off the slopes early. It was an eclectic, noisy, fun-loving group. At a far table,

I spotted sisters, Oholah and Oholibah. There was a short wait to get seated and the same waitress, who served me lunch yesterday, appeared at our table. She looked haggard, tired, but her wide, dark eyes still darted from diner to diner.

"Ah, I see you are not alone tonight," she said with a smile, handing us menus. "We're running out of the specials, but the steaks are great."

Nancy looked at me with a slight smile.

"Bring a wine list and give us a minute with the menu."

"I'll do it. Be back in a few."

Two men sat over by the south window. They seemed to be in deep conversation, but kept looking in our direction. My paranoia was growing by the minute. I pointed them out to Nancy.

"They were aboard the plane with me from Denver this afternoon. Both flirted, but it got so rough they finally turned green and shut up."

"Maybe that explains their interest."

"Or they are involved and followed me from Denver?"

"Let's not let our imagination run amok."

"Yes, let's not," she said, with a smirk.

The waitress returned with the wine list. We both ordered rib eyes, rare, and I selected a bottle of Heitz, Martha's Vineyard from a decent vintage. The noise had grown to such a crescendo as to almost drown out normal conversation. The steaks were perfect, the wine even better. Enjoyment of the dining experience was tempered by the din, and the fact that somewhere nearby someone may be keeping careful tabs on the both of us.

I signed the check and we headed back to the room. As we passed through the lobby, the huge fireplace was roaring with a warm blaze. We stopped and watched for a few minutes.

"You want a nightcap?" I asked.

"A cognac would be nice," Nancy said, pointing at the hearth. "We could sit by the fire, try and pick out our enemies."

"Find us a good seat while I go to the bar."

When I returned, Nancy was nowhere to be seen. Then, coming

from the area of the restrooms, I spotted her. Relief flowed over me like a fine summer rain.

We sipped the cognac and I longed for a cigar but, alas, they were in the room. The fire blazed and churned, swirled and threw sparks as the raging wind blew fiercely outside. Through the front door of the motel, we could see the snow blowing horizontally. It was a nasty storm and I was thankful to be in a safe, warm place, sipping fine cognac with pleasant company. I only wished the circumstances were different.

"This is nice," Nancy said, sipping her drink. "The storm's scary, though."

"Winter in the mountains, nothing like it," I said, raising my glass to her. "The weather will be over in a day or two and everything will be covered with beautiful fresh snow."

Staring into the fire, my mind wandered to J.D. and his predicament, a serious situation of his own doing. Maybe not his fault, but certainly caused by his own scientific conviction that a cancer cure was being suppressed by greed. When I was young and without artifice or guile, my world seemed safe and without tragic events before I really knew how tragic life could be. Once it happened, I learned that the consequences of tragedy could not be avoided. I finally softened into the ascetic's acknowledgement of the illusory nature of life. I became, as J.D. surely had, a true believer of the rude awakening.

Nancy stirred in the seat beside me, smiled, turned back to stare at the fire. I took a sip of the cognac, wishing again for one of my Charlemagne cigars.

I thought of Deputy Sadie running a winter trap line which seemed tragic in a way. A young girl alone in the wild, unprotected in dangerous country, with even more dangerous and hungry animals roaming about. To spend the night far from help if illness or accident or attack occurred was a tremendous risk and extremely brave. For her, it was all there was. It was hard and cold and scary, and I'm sure she'd do it again, if it was all there was.

When I was nine years old, I picked cotton on my grandfather's eight hundred acre farm, down from ten thousand acres owned by my great grandfather. Unlike Sadie, I never picked alone. (Back then my grandfather had "help" in the fields.) Picking time came as summer was waning. In the early morning it was cold; dew soaked the fields and made the bolls slick. The burs, needle-like stickers on nut-like shells would slice a finger, or worse, stab under a fingernail. They would break off and if you didn't dig them out they would get infected. By noon it would be blazing hot. Snakes, the bad ones, like copperheads and rattlers hid in the stalks. Wasps and yellow jackets would boil out of holes in the black dirt. Old men would put a saliva-soaked wad of Prince Albert tobacco on the sting to ease the pain. The cotton would stink of poison, a smell that would stay for weeks in clothes. You could even smell it in the bales in the warehouse. Sometimes the cotton was so tall you didn't have to bend over to pick. I was paid a penny a pound. But, unlike Sadie, I didn't have wolves and bears competing with me for the cotton.

"You thinking about J.D.?"

"Actually I was thinking about Deputy Sadie and picking cotton."

"Okay," she said with a look much like Rose would give me when she thought I was a little crazy.

A couple about my age sat down across from us on a matching two-place couch.

"How long do these storms usually last?" The man asked, looking at each of us.

"Unfamiliar with the weather patterns in the Rockies, are you?" I asked, suddenly wary.

"We usually ski Vermont."

"Are you from there?"

"Burlington."

"Are you familiar with Vermont?" the woman asked.

She was mid-forties with long forearms and her hands were knitted in her lap, showing slim fingers with clear polish on manicured nails. Her voice was cold, and in the firelight her eyes were smoky and dull. Two words came to mind: Ice Queen.

"I've skied Stowe."

"That's not far from our home," the man said.

"Yes, but Stowe is so passé," the woman spoke up. She was attractive and would have been striking if it wasn't for the frown and sterile, cold manner.

"I'm John," the man said, reaching across the table to shake hands. "This is my wife, Ashtoreth. We've been here a couple of weeks. Our flight was supposed to leave tomorrow, but the airline says the storm will shut things down for a couple of days."

"Ballard, J.D. Ballard. This is my wife, Nancy."

Nancy jerked around, looked at me, but said nothing.

"J.D. Ballard, really? I attended a conference in Atlanta last year with a radiologist named J.D. Ballard. He was supposed to be here in Aspen this year. I was looking forward to meeting with him again, but he never showed."

Shrugging my shoulders, I made no comment.

"If I may ask, what line of work are you in?"

"Aviation. You?"

"My wife and I both are radiologists. We were here for a conference, decided to get in an extra week of skiing. That is a real coincidence, you having the same name as our colleague."

"Well, they say life is a series of random intersections that conform to a statistical pattern, so coincidence is inevitable. It's only when multiple coincidences create their own patterns that I become wary."

"Is that an aviation '-ism?" the woman asked, in a tone that made you want to slap her.

"You could say that."

"What do you do, Nancy?" John asked. "Are you a stay at home wife?"

"Actually, I'm a pilot. I help J.D. in his business."

"My wife and I both have our pilots license, but we only fly for recreation."

"Do you have your own airplane?" I asked.

"We bought one of the Cessna Mustangs, but we wouldn't think of flying it into the mountains. We're not that experienced."

"Are you both type-rated in the Mustang?"

"Yes, we owned an older model Citation 500 for a couple of years. We were happy with Cessna's support, so when we wanted to upgrade, we stayed with them."

"I knew a man who lived across the lake from Burlington, an artist. He had a farm near a small town called Au Sable Forks. What's the name of the huge body of water? I keep forgetting."

The man turned his head and looked at me, as if he could see better out of one eye, or thought I was putting him on.

"You mean Lake Champlain."

"Yes, never can remember that name."

"Your friend wouldn't be the artist Rockwell Kent?"

"You know of Kent?"

"Everyone in that part of the world knows of him. Ash and I have several of his prints and some of his books. You don't seem old enough to have been friends with him. He died in 1971."

I noticed he'd shortened his wife's name. "Is that some kind of accusation?"

"No, just a statement of fact."

"Does the word, Asgaard mean anything to you?"

"It was the name of Kent's farm, it's Nordic, means 'Farm of the Gods.' What's going on? I don't understand."

I looked at Nancy, she nodded.

"We wanted to be sure you were who you say you are."

"Why?"

"My name is not Ballard, it's Jay Leicester, and this is Dr. Nancy Wiseman, J.D.'s significant other. He was supposed to attend the radiology conference, but turned up missing. We are here to find out what happened. We've been threatened, advised to return to Mississippi. A woman, matching your wife's description flew J.D.'s Citation from Denver to Salt Lake to Aspen. It's parked on the ramp at the Aspen

FBO, as we speak. That same woman left a note on my door with the threat. Forensics is going over it for DNA and prints. So, you see our predicament."

The man sat back in his seat, his wife turned and looked at him.

"That damn cancer cure," he said, leaning forward again. "We knew it would get him in trouble. We talked to him extensively about the frequency generator in Atlanta. We did our own research, and were supposed to meet him last week. He was always too vocal about it."

"You both are convinced it works?"

"We are. Even more so since M.D. Anderson cancer center was awarded two million dollars for research on a similar project."

"Yes," Nancy said. "The Kanzius machine. Gold and carbon are the metals being used. Tiny bits of the metal are placed into the patient's tumor and radio waves are used to rapidly heat them, killing the cancer cells, leaving healthy cells unaffected."

"That's correct," Ash said. "Sadly Kanzius died last year, but the research carries on. He wasn't a medical professional, you know; he was trying to cure his own leukemia."

Nancy nodded. "I saw the *60 Minutes* segments on him. J.D. works on the theory that different frequencies in themselves can destroy cancer cells without the need for injecting the metals into the tumor."

"The Rife method," John said. "It's plausible. Is there any way Ash and I can be of help?"

"Let us know if you happen to see J.D. We think he may be in the area, possibly held in a private home, maybe drugged. We can only speculate what they plan to do with him."

Ashtoreth—Ash, spoke up. "It's pretty obvious if whoever is behind this has him hostage, they can't let him go, they'll have to kill him."

It was a fact I'd thought about, but didn't want to admit.

"You've contacted local law enforcement. Do they have any leads?"

"They are looking at motel security video, seeking information on a limo that met J.D.'s airplane at the airport, doing the forensics on the note with the threat, running names of guests. Checking real estate brokers on private homes rented out during the ski season."

"Who knew he was attending this medical conference?" John asked.

It was a good question. I looked at Nancy.

"As far as I know, I'm the only one that knew," she said. "You two were planning to meet him here, so you knew."

"You think he was abducted in Denver, before he got to Aspen?"

"That's what we are assuming at the moment."

"This is so bizarre," Ash said. "Can you believe this could happen in today's society? Maybe in the thirties or forties, but this is 2010."

Why the time frame she mentioned was relevant, I had no idea, but she was correct about one thing, it was bizarre.

She suddenly stood up. "If you will excuse me, I have to visit the ladies room."

I watched her walk toward where I knew the restrooms were located, where I'd seen Nancy emerge.

John leaned forward. "Do you really know about Rockwell Kent or was that something you read about and knew he lived in upstate New York?"

"I go back a long way with Kent. Dan Burne Jones, the author of *The Prints of Rockwell Kent, a Catalogue Raisonne* was a friend of mine, and through him I acquired several of his prints and all of the books he published." I did not go into detail about working a case in the state of Maine involving an entire collection of Kent's work, the head of the Chicago Mafia, and an art dealer from New Orleans who murdered her brother for profit. It was a moment in my life where I met true evil and found true friendship. I learned much. Now was not the time to talk about it, especially with a stranger.

"We bought some of Kent's sailing prints; *The Lookout, Hail and Farewell, Bowspirit, Home Port, and Fair wind.* They are wonderful works."

"Yes, they are." I did not tell him of the prints in my collection, it would seem like bragging, although there is one that is my favorite and of which I am most proud: *Godspeed.* It was one of a set of twelve used in a national advertising campaign for the American Car and Foundry Company that ran from 1930 through 1931. It depicts an angel hovering over a sailboat far at sea. A comforting thought to any who have sailed.

"You practice in Mississippi, Nancy?"

"I have a family clinic. What's your last name?"

"I'm sorry, Natenberg. My wife and I both work for a local hospital in Burlington. We met J.D. in Atlanta and found his outspokenness about the frequency generator intriguing. Our first thoughts were that suppression of a cancer cure, even in the 1930s, was impossible. Scientists would have known about it. It couldn't be covered up. Well, our research showed that the truth is the cure for cancer was covered up. The naiveté of cancer researchers as well as scientists in related fields persists today, in the 21st Century."

"John, you have to agree that it has to be a small body of influential people who would lose untold wealth if this simple noninvasive cure were to become known worldwide."

He looked at me, nodded. "I do agree, and we must realize most doctors and researchers are not people who fight political battles. They crumble when challenged by determined political powers. If J.D. were to get national media attention with his theory, then how courageous will the rest of us be, or for that matter, the American Free Press?"

Two couples came in through the front door of the motel. Cold, gusty wind blew across the lobby fanning the flames in the fireplace, sending cold shivers over all of us.

"Here comes your wife."

John stood. She sat beside him, a blank expression on her face. I looked at my watch; she'd been gone twenty minutes.

· · ·

The electricity went off. It was eerily silent, the only light from the fire. For five minutes there was no sound. It was as if the world had ceased to exist. Then the generator kicked in and the lights came back, though dimmer, and sound returned.

"This storm is bad," John said. "I think we'll go on to the room. I'd like to talk some more with both of you about this. Please, if we can be of any help with locating your friend, let us know. Maybe we can meet for breakfast. We're in room 213. Give us a call."

We all stood, shook hands, and they walked away.

"That was coincidental, don't you think?" Nancy asked, sitting back down.

"Maybe too much so. We'll get their info to Sheriff Freuchen. He can check them out. You want another cognac?"

"Sure."

The bartender poured the cognac. With the winter storm raging there was, surprisingly, few people in the bar.

"A woman called a few minutes ago asking about you."

"How do you know me?" I asked, suddenly alert.

"She said you were sitting in front of the fireplace with an older woman. I have a good view of the lobby and fireplace from here." He pointed. I followed his finger and could see Nancy sitting in front of the fire. "She's not that much older than you."

"She'll be pleased to hear that. What did this person want to know about me?"

"Asked if I knew you, what room you were staying in, said she was interested in making contact. We get this kind of thing all the time. A lot of famous people stay here. Are you somebody famous?"

"It's your lucky day, I am not famous. So what did you tell the caller?"

"Nothing. Even if I'd known you, I wouldn't give out that kind of information."

"You are a wise man, Tender." I signed the check, peeled off a twenty, laid it on the bar. "Name's Leicester, let me know if anyone else asks about me."

"I know who you are. It's on the computer, from when you signed for the last drinks. Have a good night, Mr. Leicester."

We watched the fire and sipped the cognac.

"Someone called the bar and asked about me. They knew we were sitting by the fire. Bartender gave out no information."

"Male or female?"

"Woman. Said she wanted to make contact with me."

"Handsome man like you, doesn't surprise me. What did she think, that I was your mother?"

"Didn't mention you."

"How nice."

A young couple joined us, sitting in the place recently occupied by John and Ashtoreth Natenberg. They were oblivious to the world around them. We watched the pawing and kissing until I wanted to scream, "Go to your room, for God's sake."

Nancy and I walked down the long corridor to our door. Another note was attached in the same place. Inside, I carefully opened it. Nancy read over my shoulder.

We are not amateurs.
You and the woman doctor need to know your
friend has been moved out of the area.
Go back to Mississippi.

"They didn't move him in this weather," Nancy said. "I'd bet the note was placed by Mrs. Natenberg."

"A good bet," I said, dialing the sheriff's office.

A harried-sounding deputy answered.

"Is Freuchen there?"

"The sheriff is busy. There is a storm raging, electricity is out all over the area. Do you have an emergency?"

"My name's Leicester. Have the sheriff call me. He knows what it's about."

I hung up. Wind rattled the window. It felt like the whole building shook.

"The woman—Ash—was gone twenty minutes. Plenty of time to tape the note on the door."

Nancy sat on the side of the bed taking off her boots. "She fits the description, but my gut feeling tells me otherwise. There is nothing we can do tonight. I sleep on this side of the bed."

"Good, because I'm accustomed to the other side."

Nancy went into the bathroom. I undressed and got under the covers. This was probably the most awkward position I've ever been in my life.

She came out, dressed in some kind of tight-fitting sleep ware, switched off the lights, got into bed.

"Goodnight, Leicester."

"Night, Wiseman."

Case History of Dr. Warren Kobs

MALE—Diagnosis of transitional cell cancer of the bladder which was removed surgically. The patient then had x-ray therapy of the pelvis. When the patient presented to Dr. Kobs he had recurrent bladder cancer, the base of the pelvis and multiple secondaries throughout the skeleton. Multiple Radiowave Therapy treatments of the patient were undertaken with the effect that a complete resolution of all symptoms was observed. A bone scan taken three and a half years after the last treatment revealed healing to all the sites of the previous cancer.

Chapter Twelve

Four beasts rose from the churning sea. The first was a lion, and had eagle's wings. It flew to the beach, shed its wings and stood on the wet sand like a man. Suddenly another beast, a bear, rose from the sea, and had three ribs in its mouth between its teeth. It stood beside the lion. Then I looked, and there was another, like a leopard, which had four wings of a bird on its back. It flew and stood beside the other two. Then a fourth beast, dreadful and terrible rose from the sea, and I did not know its species. It had huge iron teeth and ten horns. It devoured, broke into pieces, and trampled underfoot the other three beasts. I watched the horns and there was another horn, a little one, coming up among them, and it pulled out the other horns. Then, in this horn were eyes like the eyes of a man, and a mouth formed and spoke pompous words. A fiery flame poured forth from its mouth and it came toward me and I was afraid.

. . .

I woke cold, shivering. The heat was off and outside the storm was at its peak. Snow piled against the window, and there was an inch of ice on the glass inside the room. Fumbling for the phone, I called the front desk and was informed the generator was shut down at midnight and was due to come back online at six a.m. My watch read, 5:45. Nancy was wrapped in the covers and still sound asleep. I dressed quietly and headed for the lobby. Surely there was coffee somewhere in this frigid motel.

There was coffee and a breakfast buffet was being laid out in the dining room. A generator, especially for the kitchen, hummed in the background.

The Natenbergs were nowhere in sight. I did not want to run into them this morning. Taking two large coffees, I headed back to the room.

Nancy was dressed, and stood looking out the window at the raging storm. She smiled when spying the coffee.

"You are a gentleman after all, Mr. Leicester. Thank you. I have never seen ice on the inside of a window before, have you?"

"Many times. We used to get it on the inside of DC-3s when flying in the mountains. It would be so cold that our breath would freeze on the glass. Same principle here."

"I am aware of the process, but thank you for reminding me."

The motel generator kicked on and heat began to blow into the room. It would be nice to take a hot shower.

. . .

The phone rang.

"Leicester, Pete Freuchen. You called?"

"Hello, Sheriff. The storm causing you a lot of problems?"

"We've had worse. It'll be gone tomorrow. What's up?"

"Two things. We got another note with a threat, it also said they were moving Ballard out of the area."

"They won't be going anywhere for awhile. All the passes are closed, airport, trains. We're shut down. What was the other thing?"

"We were befriended by a couple last night, said they were doctors attending the Radiologist conference and knew Ballard. It's a possibility the woman might be the one putting the threats on our door and they both fly airplanes similar to the one Ballard owns."

"Give me the info on them, and Leicester, who is 'We?'"

"I'm sorry, I thought Sadie would have told you. Ballard's significant other flew in on the last flight out of Denver yesterday. She's the one got me involved to start with."

"You know she's clean?"

"Pretty sure."

"I'll run a check. Where is she staying? There are no rooms available, must be a private home."

"She's staying with me, here at the motel."

There was a long silence.

"As soon as we get caught up, I'll send someone to pick up the note and get another look at the video."

"Look Sheriff, I know this may appear strange, but it is what it is. There's nothing between this woman and me. She had nowhere else to stay. Talk to your deputy, she met her."

"Okay, Leicester. Sit tight. We'll do what we can."

Looking at Nancy, I said, "I'm gonna get a quick shower."

"The Sheriff believes we are up to something evil?"

"Put yourself in his place, what would you think?"

The water in the shower was not hot, but warm enough to relax muscles that begged for exercise. I dressed in the bathroom and emerged to find Deputy Sadie and Nancy sitting at the small table talking like old friends.

"The Sheriff caught me on the radio, I was nearby. The couple who was to meet your friend, what room did you say they were in?"

"213."

"Okay. Bad news on the motel surveillance video, when the electricity went off, it was lost. Maybe we can get something off the second note. These two are John and Ash Natenberg?"

"Ashtoreth, the husband called her Ash."

"Tell me why you are suspicious of them."

"I'm not suspicious, just looking at the facts. They met J.D. in Atlanta at a medical conference, both claim to be Radiologists. He talked at length about a cancer cure being suppressed by the AMA and others. They were to meet him in Aspen to discuss it further. Both admitted they fly the same type of airplane that J.D. owns. It could have been them that flew the Citation from Denver to here. If George Barrows could get a look at them…"

"I'll work on making that happen. If they are staying here, it shouldn't be a big problem."

Nancy spoke up. "They wanted to have breakfast with us. Why don't you call them, and then get this Barrows person to come and take a look?"

"Good idea. What about the roads, are they passable? Can Barrows get here?"

Deputy Sadie tapped a ballpoint pen on her writing pad. "I wouldn't bet on it, but George is used to this country. If we can get in touch with him, we'll know what his situation is."

"Then call him up, Sadie," Nancy said.

She tried Barrows at home from the motel phone. There was no answer. She tried his cell, still no luck.

"Knowing George, he probably made it to the airport." She looked up the number of the FBO. "How did you get to work?" There was a pause. "Okay, can you make it to the Holiday Inn? Leicester has a couple he thinks may be the ones who flew the airplane into Aspen with their friend aboard. He wants you to take a look at them. They'll be in the dining room." She hung up.

"So, what did he say?" I asked.

"He'll be here within the hour. Nothing is moving at the airport. The tower is closed till noon."

I went over and dialed room 213. John Natenberg answered on the first ring. We agreed to meet in the dining room in half an hour.

Standing and adjusting her gun belt, Sadie said, "I'll wait for George at the front door. We'll come in and have breakfast like nothing is out of the ordinary. If it's a positive I.D., I'll take them into custody and bring them to the Sheriff's Office and have a little chat."

"You won't need to call for backup?"

She laughed. "I think I can handle the situation. There are only two of them."

Looking at her, I thought that she was probably capable of arresting two people.

John and Ashtoreth Natenberg were right on time. We went through the buffet line together. It was all fruit and bran muffins for them, bacon, eggs, and biscuits for me. Nancy followed the Natenbergs with the healthy diet. I never planned to live forever.

"No word from Dr. Ballard?" John asked.

"We got another threatening note tacked on our door last night while we sat with you in front of the fire in the lobby," I said, then looked at Ash. "You were gone to the bathroom a long time, it wasn't you that put the note on the door, was it Ashtoreth?" I said it in a joking manner. She took it that way.

"I confess, I'm the one did it. We are holding Dr. Ballard in our room, keeping him drugged until we can figure a way to dispose of him."

She looked directly at me and, though being factitious, the eyes were cold, evil, and absolutely believable: the Ice Queen.

George Barrows and Deputy Sadie went through the breakfast buffet. I was pleased to see both piled food on their plates. There was not a piece of fruit or bran muffin visible. Sitting at a table nearby, they showed no interest in us.

"Ah, Mr. Leicester, there's a deputy; you can have me arrested now for kidnapping."

"Very well, if you insist."

To everyone's surprise, I got up and went to their table.

"Well, what do you think, George?"

"Neither one. I've never seen them before, and the woman is definitely not the pilot who flew the Citation."

"Thanks. I appreciate your help. When's the airport expected to reopen?"

"By mid-afternoon. The runway's clear and the front should pass through in a couple of hours. You planning on leaving today?"

"No, maybe tomorrow or the next."

I winked at Sadie and went back to my seat.

Nearing our table, I observed the three medical professionals. In unison they looked up at me and I was reminded of what Gilda Radner—God rest her soul—said about doctors: *Doctors are whippersnappers in ironed white coats who spy up your rectums and look down you throats and press you and poke you with sterilized tools and stab at solutions that pacify fools. I used to revere them and do what they said till I learned what they learned on was already dead.*

As I sat down, Ash said, "Well, did you turn me in for kidnapping and mayhem?"

"Actually, I did, but not in the way that you think."

John looked at me. "What does that mean?"

"We set this meeting up. The man with the deputy runs the FBO at the airport. He observed the people who flew J.D.'s Citation in and watched them drive away in a limo. The Captain flying the plane looks a lot like Ash, and the woman who put the threats on our door resembles her. We wanted him to get a good look at both of you. We had to be sure."

"You son of a…"

"It's alright, John." His wife reached over and touched his arm. "I think it's pretty smart. We probably would have done the same thing."

The Ice Queen surprised me. I had her pegged to be the one who would be offended.

"This is the second time, Leicester," John said, with more irritation than anger. "You satisfied, now?"

"Yes, I am convinced."

He stood. "Come on, Ash, these people are starting to bore me."

They left, leaving me with the check.

. . .

"That went well," Nancy said, throwing her napkin on the table.

"I don't blame them. What I don't understand is why they wanted to meet with J.D. again, a year later, to talk about the cancer cure."

George and Sadie came over and joined us.

"We gave it a shot," Sadie said.

"There was a resemblance, but they are not the ones." George reiterated.

"What happens now?" Nancy asked.

Sadie answered. "The storm is beginning to ease. We should be able to get the threats to Denver for forensics to go over. We're running the names here at the hotel, checking with limo companies and real-estate agencies. Maybe something will break."

"I need to get back to the airport. People will want their airplanes deiced to get out after the storm. You want that Citation dug out?"

"Not today. We believe J.D. is still in Aspen. Sadie and law enforcement need more time. As soon as we know, I'll call you."

"Good luck, Leicester. I hope you find your man and that he's okay."

George and Deputy Sadie left together.

"You want some more coffee, Dr. Wiseman?"

"What I want is to find J.D. Ballard."

We walked out to the lobby. The fire was roaring in the massive fireplace. People were milling about, the young unable to contain their joy at the three feet of new snow and eager to find their way to the ski-lifts. The older and wiser were less enthusiastic, knowing the extra physical exertion involved in making it up the mountain and back down. Several people were worried about the airlines running. Their time in this winter paradise was up and they needed to get home.

Not knowing J.D.'s fate was pulling at both Nancy and me. The cat and mouse game made me feel trapped. I also knew that when you are the mouse you don't have much to say about it to the cat.

Nancy shivered before the fire. I looked at her. She was magnificent in her way; brilliant and true as steel. She was attractive, productive, and independent, but she was also carrying emotional baggage wrapped around Ballard. I realized if it were me in J.D.'s shoes, there wouldn't be a Nancy Wiseman carrying mental weight because of me. I doubt if anyone would even be looking. Maybe Rose, or Shack. But it was J.D. with the hook in his mouth, not me. He had the unfortunate luck to have drawn the ire of wealthy enemies who had the where-with-all to hire the kind of people that I associate with that shadowy trade. False names and passports were standard. They were relentless, focused, and detached where violence was concerned. They were adrenaline-driven, devoutly disciplined, and had a public persona that was affable and unremarkable. In short, dangerous. Their flaw is that they are obsessive by nature and are commonly the victim of their own cyclic thought patterns. Their brain functions like a compass needle, swinging inevitably back to whatever or whoever it is they are trying to avoid.

"The wind's quit blowing, let's go outside. I've never seen such deep snow," Nancy said, tugging at my elbow.

We walked out to the north side of the main building. The clouds obscured the mountains and everything was grey and gloomy. Even the snow had a pale sad hue, or maybe it was simply an illusion brought on by our situation.

"People drive in this stuff?"

"Sure, there's no ice underneath. The snow has little effect if one has the proper tires or chains. It's not like in the south where we get the ice storms and little snow. On rare occasions it happens here, and then it is bad."

"Are we going to just sit around and do nothing while the local sheriff looks for J.D.?"

"If you have any suggestions, I'm listening."

She looked at me with a stare that said many things, the one I sensed the most was my utter uselessness.

"You have the proper tires on your rental? Maybe we could ride around and at least look for J.D."

"Or we could see if anyone has checked out and get you your own room."

Nancy kicked at the snow and headed back inside.

The unmistakable sound of a low-flying helicopter caught my attention. I scanned the overcast. It passed directly overhead, headed to the north. The hospital and the Ski-Rescue both used helicopters. I did not envy the pilots who not only had to launch in almost any weather conditions, but must contend with rocks in the clouds and the density altitude of the mountains. Where we stood was seven thousand feet above sea level.

Helicopters have come a long way in design and instrumentation since I flew them. The machine I learned to fly had a hundred and fifty universal joints that must be working in concert at all times or disaster could strike. Me banging it around on the airport concrete didn't help.

Nancy went straight to the front desk and found there had been several checkouts and that a room would be available for her by two o'clock.

She looked at me. "There, now can we go ride around and look for J.D.?"

"We can try."

Case History of Dr. A. I. Simmons

FEMALE—The patient had Hodgkin's disease in the left neck node and an enlarged thymus in the chest. The patient had had chemotherapy however the residual disease was still present. The patient was given four courses of Radiowave Therapy. One year after the last treatment the patient was well without disease.

Chapter Thirteen

After moving Nancy to her own room, which was on the same floor as mine, we went to dig out the rental car that was virtually buried under three feet of snow. It took some effort. The engine needed ten minutes to reach operating temperature. Soon we were warm and comfortable and made our way out of the parking lot onto the highway which was salted and plowed and in surprisingly good shape considering the storm and freezing cold.

Since this was her first trip to the area, I headed south into town. Aspen is an old mining village with some unique buildings snuggled at the base of the mountain with the same name. I was fortunate to know the area before the rich and famous discovered it and turned it into a glitzy shopping center no one, except the ultra wealthy, could afford to visit.

I've sat in a bar where skiers could literally ski off the mountain and glide onto a barstool. They could listen to the *Nitty-Gritty Dirt Band* sing *Mr. Bo Jangles* live for the lunch crowd. John Denver, just starting his singing career, would perform for diners in log cabins after they were pulled up the mountain aboard a six mule-team sleigh. Times were simpler then.

I pointed out the Copper Kettle, a five star restaurant, where I spent an amusing two hours at dinner with an unassuming Carl Reiner. The Red Onion, owned by the Smothers brothers, who would perform regularly there when not on the road. This was before their TV show that ultimately led to their meteoric rise and fall.

We drove south to the hospital where orthopedic surgeons made fortunes during the ski season fixing spiral fractures of the leg that occurred as often as the common cold. Then we headed back north, toward Snowmass. I thought she would enjoy seeing the little mountain village.

Nancy kept looking out the car window as if J.D. would suddenly appear walking down a snow-covered street and wave at us. As we passed the Holiday Inn, it appeared to be bustling, the storm now gone. A few miles further we passed the airport, where things were unusually quiet, and further still, we turned off the highway and headed west up the mountain. This road had not been plowed and it was slow going. Cars were coming down and everyone was being careful. Halfway up, we ran into an accident; a car slid into an embankment rounding a curve a little too fast. Several people had stopped to help and we were able to ease around the not too serious fender bender and continue on.

"You spent a lot of time in Aspen?" Nancy asked.

"Yes, but as I told you, the condo was at Snowmass and I spent most of my time on the mountain. Except for going down to dine at the Red Onion or Copper Kettle, there was no need to go into Aspen. Snowmass Village had everything one could want. I was there for almost two years."

"How nice." There was no sarcasm in the statement.

We parked in the lot next to the ice rink. There were no skaters due to the three feet of snow. We walked down the village street that was a picture postcard. Christmas lights were strung, decorations up, and people skied down the middle of the street. Nancy looked in the windows of the shops, the combination grocery store/deli emitting wonderful aromas. She spotted the fire pit with the benches in the middle of the street and asked what it was and I explained. She smiled like a young girl and said it sounded romantic.

At the end of the street, we climbed up the wooden steps to the deck and went into the restaurant that was packed with skiers. The clomp of ski boots, loud talk and laughter, the clink and clamor of dishes and glasses, and the smells of fresh mountain air and food added up to the ambience of a true village ski bar.

A waiter came by carrying a tray of Bloody Marys. "Seat yourself if you can find a table."

We stood looking over the youthful crowd, searching for an empty seat. I spotted her sitting alone, next to a window on the south side of the restaurant. She saw me at the same time, jumped up and ran to where I stood and hugged my neck, her innate shyness seeming to have vanished.

"Hello, Beverly. How goes the training?"

Her chocolate eyes and fine face with the perfect nose suddenly turned sad.

"I am so lonesome. To see a familiar face is uplifting. Come sit with me."

"Would you introduce me, Jay?"

"Beverly, this is Doctor Nancy Wiseman."

"Oh, I'm so sorry, I didn't know you were with someone."

"It's okay," Nancy assured her. "We are not a 'couple.' We are working together on a mutual project."

We followed Beverly to the table. She wore tight ski pants that looked good on her slim body and coltish legs. She had on a bulky sweater and her long shiny hair flowed over her shoulders.

"Beverly is from Fairhope, Alabama, a good old southern girl. She's working for the Snowmass Development Corporation."

"How do you two know each other?" Nancy asked.

"We met in Denver. I was able to give her a ride over to Aspen."

"Yes," Beverly said. "The passes across the mountain were closed and my car was not equipped for snow. I'd been stuck in a motel room for five days trying to get here to start a new job."

"I'm sure Mr. Leicester was glad to help." Nancy looked at me with an accusing smile.

"What kind of doctor are you?" Beverly asked.

"I practice family medicine in a town a short distance from where Mr. Leicester resides."

"I wish I'd been smart enough. I would love to have gone into medicine. I watched my mother die of breast cancer and I felt powerless to help her. I think it would be nice to help people."

Nancy softened her tone. "Sometimes, even with the latest in medical technology, we can't defeat death. We can only offer solace and relief from pain. We all die, Beverly, sometimes it's hard to accept that."

"How's the training going?" I asked, hoping to change the subject.

"I'm breezing through. Not much to it actually, just getting familiar with the company's way of doing things. It's amazing how booked up this place stays, two years in advance is the norm."

"Are there condos for sale?" Nancy asked.

"They are building more, but all that the company owned is gone, and even the new ones are already sold. Attrition makes some available, that's what they call it, attrition. I think it means someone dies or has financial trouble and has to sell. We have a waiting list on those."

"Business seems good. There should be a future for you here."

"I hope so."

We ordered lunch and made small talk until Beverly had to return to her training class.

"Mr. Leicester is in room 114 at the Holiday Inn. Call him if you start to get lonely or depressed. He is a good listener. It's always nice to have someone to talk with, especially in unfamiliar surroundings and during the Christmas season."

I stood when she started to leave.

Beverly reached up and kissed me on the cheek, whispered in my ear, "I'll call you."

She smelled like soap and hair conditioner; a clean refreshing aroma.

After Beverly left, we had coffee and watched the people moving in and out of the restaurant. Through the window, we could see beginner ski classes were in progress taught by tanned, windblown, healthy looking young men and women who worked for tips so they could have access to the slopes in their free time. They came from all over the world to Aspen; mostly college kids looking for adventure, love, and the best skiing in the world.

I awaited Nancy's onslaught concerning Beverly and my perceived reputation, but none came. Instead, she remained silent, watching the changing view out the window. Maybe she was thinking about J.D. At the moment we were no closer to knowing his fate than we were before leaving Mississippi. Our only hope was for law enforcement to come up with something on the threatening notes, the limo service, or get a break on housing, some place where J.D. could be held. It dawned on me that whoever kidnapped him would have to come after Nancy and me, that is, if they thought we would continue with what J.D. was doing to expose the suppression of the cancer cure. All I knew at the moment was that they could not have left the Aspen area. It would be at least sometime tomorrow before anyone could get out by car. They would not chance going by airline, and private aircraft, they had to know, was being watched.

"You ready?" she asked.

"What?"

"Are you ready to leave this beautiful little picturesque village, Mr. Leicester, go and look for J.D.?"

"Yes, let's do that."

We eased carefully back down the mountain. The car accident had been cleared away, but the snow was still deep and the road was slippery in places. The thick overcast sky seemed to be getting lighter and the wind had calmed.

Passing the north end of the airport, a Gulfstream flew low over our heads, climbing out of the narrow valley for blue skies and parts unknown.

"The tower must be up and running and the runway looks in good shape," I said. "Let's stop by the FBO and see how things are going with George Barrows."

"We can see how J.D.'s Citation fared with the snow storm."

"Good idea."

The lobby of the FBO was packed with people. The ramp had been plowed and several corporate jets were being deiced and preparing for departure. Barrows came through the front door looking a little harried.

"Leicester, hope you're not wanting to go out today?"

"No, we thought we'd come by and see how you're doing?"

"Good, I need a break. You two come on back to the office and we'll have some coffee."

He sat down heavily in his chair, pulled off his gloves, rubbed his eyes, and motioned to a coffee maker on a table against a far wall.

I poured the coffee and handed him and Nancy a cup. "Everybody wants to leave at once."

"Yes," he said, massaging the back of his neck. "That's always the case. We've called in all our people to help and we still get behind, though most of the owners are understanding and patient. A few of the pilots get irritated, but we know how to handle them."

"Well," I said, sipping the strong, black liquid. "If I had a fifty-million dollar jet sitting on the ramp, I might tend to get a little testy if told I had to wait."

Barrows grinned.

"I've briefed all our personnel to be on the lookout for the ones who flew the Citation in," he said. "So far, we've not heard from them."

"If you have a couple of spare brooms, Nancy and I will sweep the snow off the Citation."

"I have the brooms. Well, back to work. If anything turns up, I know where to get in touch."

Out at a service truck, Barrows handed us two brooms and each a pair of earplugs.

"It gets noisy; you don't want to damage your hearing."

At the Citation, we swept the wings, the horizontal tail surfaces, and as much of the top as we could reach. I pointed out a Cessna 206, a high wing, single-engine plane tied down on the ramp. Both wing struts and outer sections of the wings were bowed and bent from the weight of the snow. Major structural damage and expensive to repair, sad to see such neglect.

A Challenger 604 powered up in front of the FBO and we were glad for the ear protection. Nothing helped with the jet blast though, which reaches over a hundred and fifty miles per hour. It chilled us to the bone and the snow it stirred up was like being hit with tiny pin pricks.

We returned the brooms, waved goodbye to Barrows, and headed for the Holiday Inn.

We drove the short distance back to the motel. The clouds were breaking up and sunlight shafted down in spots like thin gossamer curtains, making the fresh snow glisten in elongated patterns on the ground like grains of sand on a beach.

"What now?" Nancy asked.

"We wait."

"For how long?"

"How long have you got? How long does J.D. have?"

She looked out the frosted window of the car, the ridge to the west shinning white, but did not answer.

"How long have you been in love with J.D?"

She jerked her head toward me, her dark hair curved around the lean face. The eyes had a mysterious quality that would intrigue most men. Staring at me, her face became distorted, and her eyes began to water like those of a woman out of sync with her own intelligence, a woman for whom loss was a given and in matters of love, ineptitude a way of life.

"Long enough to know it is mutual."

We parked in the lot, and I shut off the engine.

"Look, Nancy, something will break, maybe the notes will turn up something, or the sheriff will locate where he's being held. It's going to be alright."

"Don't patronize me, Leicester. I'm not some love-sick teenager. I'm worried about what J.D.'s going through."

Trying to figure out how this woman thinks is like attempting to put a cat in a bag; there was always an arm or leg left over, and at the end of it, claws.

"Let's go freshen up, rest for awhile, then we can go to the Sheriff's Office and see if there's any progress."

"Yes," she nodded. "At least that's something."

As we passed the front desk, the now familiar clerk waved me over. He had that earnest look of a man with serious matters on his mind. I've seen it enough to recognize that it was usually serious only to the one with the expression.

"Are you in some kind of trouble, Mr. Leicester?" he asked.

"I've always got trouble going on," I said, with a smile. "It's the nature of my life."

"The sheriff has called twice looking for you and stopped by here himself about an hour ago. He wanted access to your room."

"I'm sure you let him in."

"He's the sheriff."

"Of course, and he showed you his warrant?"

"Come on, Mr. Leicester, this is Aspen, not downtown LA."

"Okay, I'll give him a call and see what his 'trouble' is all about."

"Thanks for being understanding."

"You'll learn that those who do all the fussing have something to hide. Me, I'm clean as a whistle."

He laughed. "If you need anything, give me a call. And I mean anything."

I gave him a short salute and joined Nancy in front of the fire.

"What did the motel clerk want?"

"Wanted to know if I was interested in dating his sister."

"Rose English was right, you can be an asshole."

I waited by my door until Nancy entered her room. I wanted to be sure there was no threat taped over her key slot. She waved and disappeared inside.

I went around the room looking to see if Sheriff Freuchen had disturbed any of my personal belongings. He had not. Sitting for a moment looking out the window at the mountains to the west with their fresh dusting of winter snow, I wondered what he wanted, had he found out something, or found a body? Glancing over at the telephone beside the bed, I got up and walked over and picked up the receiver to call the Sheriff's Office. At that instance there was a knock on the door.

"Take a ride with me."

"Sure."

Case History of Dr. A.I. Simmons

FEMALE—The patient was given six to ten weeks to live prior to seeing Dr. Simmons. This patient had multiple lung secondary cancer and a primary osteogenic sarcoma in her lower left femur. The patient had had surgery and chemotherapy. The patient lived for over five years following treatment with Radiowave Therapy. In fact chest x-rays and CT scan subsequent to Dr. Simmons' treatment indicated no active cancer in her lungs or elsewhere in the body.

Chapter Fourteen

He was rake-thin, bones thrusting out through the skin of his face, eyes flickering yellow-green like ghost lights in a Mississippi swamp. Taller than I remembered, as tall as me, he radiated that edgy energy I remembered from our first meeting. I followed him down the hallway to the lobby. He wore green uniform pants and a heavy coat with *SHERIFF* written across the back in bright red letters, his boots were military style. The butt of a pistol bulged out the side of the coat. He was right-handed.

Sitting at the entrance to the motel lobby was a desert-camouflage Hummer, a real Hummer, with the wide stance, not some urban cowboy version. This one had the body style of a pickup and was adorned with Pitkin County Sheriff's Office decals and red and blue lights affixed to the top. Sheriff Pete Freuchen patrolled the roads of Pitkin County in style.

Sitting in the passenger's seat, I closed the door and watched Freuchen light a Winston cigarette.

"I've always wanted one of these vehicles, especially one rigged as a pickup. Never could afford it, though."

"This one was donated by an actor who wanted us to ride in four wheel drive comfort, and be able to get to his home if the weather was bad. A Ford Pickup would suit me, but it's not a bad machine, especially off-road."

"Yeah, it would fit just right on my little farm down in God's country."

"I talked to William Waddell, yesterday." He took a drag on the cigarette and watched my reaction. "Wanted to know if someone named Hebrone Opshinsky was with you. Seems you and Mr. Opshinsky are interesting people, to say the least."

"Opshinsky is not with me, and you have to take what W.W. says with a grain of salt. He has a vendetta against the man."

"Relax, Leicester, Waddell vouched for you. He did warn me that when you and your friend are together a lot of dead bodies seem to show up."

I made no reply.

Freuchen started the big diesel engine and drove toward Aspen. We came over a small rise and suddenly the sun broke through and illuminated the buildings of the town with a great scattering of light, and the cloud bank above the mountains to the west was edged with copper and gold.

"I ran that doctor, Nancy Wiseman, she's clean as a whistle, has a good reputation among the medical community. I could find no dirt on her."

"I don't know her very well. In fact I've known her less than a month and only met her face to face three times. I'm glad to know she's not some H.H. Holmes type character."

"Who's H.H. Holmes?"

"A prodigy of wickedness at the turn of the century in Chicago. A human demon, a being so unthinkable that no novelist would dare invent such a character. His real name was Herman Webster Mudgett. Posing as a medical doctor, he murdered a lot of people in gruesome fashion; a sick man. If you ever run across a book titled *The Devil in the White City* by Erik Larson, read it. People in your profession need to know that there are some truly evil things in this world."

"I've seen my share of the dark side, my friend, believe me. At any rate, your Doctor Wiseman doesn't appear to be an H.H. Holmes."

No, I thought to myself, outside of Hitler, few people are.

"The Natenberg's sheet came back as clean as Wiseman. No trouble with the law, their only fault seems to be a self-centered arrogance that rubs some people the wrong way."

"I got that from them, also. Young, smart, good-looking, and rich; maybe they earned their yuppie egoism."

Freuchen laughed. "Hell, son, you just described ninety-nine percent of the inhabitants of Pitkin County."

We drove on through Aspen, out by the hospital, climbed a ridge lined with expensive homes, then up to a small plateau, finally arriving at a gated drive with a deputy guarding the entrance. He waved us through.

"Why are we here, Freuchen?"

"We think this is where your friend, J.D. Ballard, was held."

"Was?"

"They're gone. We missed them by a couple of hours."

"Gone where? They can't drive through the passes, and the airport is being watched."

"Don't know. My people are going over the place, now."

We parked in front of a rustic log home with three or four out buildings. There was nothing ostentatious about the place. It had been recently built, but had the appearance of having been here for hundreds of years, some Frank Lloyd Wright creation seeming to emerge from the very rocks that surrounded it.

The main house was around five thousand square feet. It was small in comparison to other homes in the area. The décor was authentic western, nothing chrome, shiny, or glassy. Three smaller versions of the main house were spaced around the property. Whoever built this place put some thought into it.

"How'd you find out J.D. was here?"

"Limo service, then the real-estate agency. All the descriptions fit your bad guys. The driver was sure it was them. He picked them up at the private airplane and drove them here."

"So who rented the house?"

"A woman, paid cash. Name she gave doesn't exist, but fits the description of the pilot George said flew the plane into Aspen, and the one hung the notes on your motel room door."

I pointed to the rear of the house. "What's out back?"

"Couple of tennis courts, an Olympic-sized swimming pool, and a huge corral-like space for riding horses."

We walked by the pool and courts. There were tracks leading out to the corral.

"Your people been out here?"

"No."

In the middle of the open space, I saw the skid marks and the windblown snow.

"I know how they left Aspen."

Freuchen looked at me. "Helicopter?"

"Exactly. One flew over low this morning while we were in the motel parking lot. I assumed it to be from the hospital or Ski Rescue."

"But the weather was so bad."

"He was flying under the overcast, probably came in behind the storm and did some dangerous scud-running to get to the estate. Call George, see if by chance the helicopter landed for fuel."

Freuchen opened his tiny cell phone and punched in a number. He spoke to someone, and then closed the little flip-phone.

"Barrows is out on the ramp, but the girl said they did have a helicopter in early this morning. Come on, we'll drive to the airport."

Following Freuchen back through the log home, he barked orders at the deputies, told them where he'd be, and we headed for the Hummer. He had an aura about him, like he'd emerged from the deep woods only hours earlier, with a neck so red it could stop traffic. He seemed to still have animal blood on his hands from a recent kill and a desire to break and injure, his air of muscular confidence was fascinating to watch.

He lit a cigarette, cracked a window and blew the smoke out the opening.

"I did a little research on this cancer cure you talked about. I want to hear more, in fact, I want to know all you know."

"Why the big interest, now? You think lung cancer is in your future from the cigarettes, or is there something else?"

"Let's just say I have my reasons, and no, I do not have lung cancer, yet. I've spent most of my money on booze, boats, and women, the rest I just wasted. Maybe I can get involved in something worthwhile for the remaining years that I have left. I've known people who think that the future is so certain that they already speak of it as the past. I'm not that stupid."

I never figured Freuchen as a philosopher.

"In real life, Pete, we are all losers. We never get ahead of the game, and in the end, the game gets us."

"Yes, and I've always been such a smart, tough, miserable sonofabitch that anything less than reality was worthless crap."

I laughed. "You almost sound like my friend, Hebrone Opshinsky."

"Your friend and I may not be that much different. He was probably working one side of the mountain in '68 and I was on the other."

"I didn't know."

"Waddell said I should probably tell you."

"Why?"

"I don't know, Leicester. He just thought I should."

"Well, you men are all heroes to me. You were called and you served. This country needs to appreciate that fact."

"Thanks. It holds true more so today than ever before."

"'Nam was a mess, Pete, I don't have to tell you. However, it is the failure, not the success that we often remember, and the lesson it teaches is rarely a good one."

We rode on toward the airport in silence, each going back a long way to a war that cost much more than its worth.

Just before we turned into the airport, Freuchen said, "When we finish here, the cancer cure, I want to hear all you know."

"Okay."

George Barrows looked over the fuel ticket. "International Helicopters, out of Salt Lake, came in behind the front. Took on a load of fuel, we deiced the blades, and they left scud-running to the south. The only ones on board were the crew."

"Can I get the data off the fuel slip?"

"Sure, I'll make a copy for you. This have something to do with the missing doctor?"

Freuchen shifted from one foot to the other. "Looks like they landed behind an estate up on Traveler's Ridge, picked up the ones that leased the place. They fit the description of the people we're interested in."

"I'm sorry; I didn't put the two together."

"Neither did we, until Leicester, here, saw the landing site at the estate, and remembered seeing the helicopter fly overhead at the motel."

"You recall what kind of helicopter, George?"

"One of the new Agusta 139s. They have been around for a few years, but this one was fresh out of the factory, had less than two hundred hours, and still had that new smell."

"I'm familiar, Twin-turbine, five-blade main rotor with a range of between six hundred-fifty and seven hundred miles."

"Yes, this one had an eight passenger interior."

"A few years back, I was in Gunnison, Colorado, and they were doing icing tests on the 109. They loaned me a ground power cart. My batteries were low and it was below zero. I've followed the development of the company since then."

Freuchen looked at me. "You got all you need to track'em down?"

"I do."

"Then let's go. I don't want to spend the rest of what's left of the day listening to you and George discuss aviation." He smiled, the first time I'd seen him do so, then turned to his auxiliary deputy. "Good work, old man. Thanks for your help."

"Anytime," he said, putting on his gloves and heading back out on the icy ramp.

In the truck driving back to the motel, Freuchen kept glancing at me. I ignored him, figuring he'd get to it eventually.

"Waddell said you played football?"

"Some."

"What position?"

"Linebacker."

"You any good?"

"I called the Hall of Fame in Canton, Ohio, this morning to see if my bust was still there. They assured me that it was not and that there was no record of me ever being mentioned among the greats to have played the game."

"He said you played for the Colts."

"Baltimore Colts, not the team in Indiana, though Peyton Manning is a "football" player. I know his dad."

"I was a Bronco fan until John Elway retired. Don't follow them much now. You don't like to talk about playing the game?"

"Most people who ask me about football just want to say they met an NFL player. They have no clue about the physical side of the game. To hit someone and feel the fire from a pinched nerve shoot down the spine and into the hands and feet. Have never been rendered helpless by a helmet to the ribs and been left lying on the turf, suppressing the high-pitched screams and shrieks heard mostly from wounded soldiers on the battlefield. One can't fathom the pain and confusion of a reality-altering blow to the head, the kind that turns day into night and leaves one trying to account for hours of his life. Or the cracks of a broken leg or the searing tear of cartledge or ligament of a knee. Playing with injuries shot up with Novocain and doing irreparable damage that will haunt you the rest of your life. Breaking all ten fingers, some three or four times, taping them up and playing on, or looking for teeth lying somewhere on the muddy field."

"Yes," Freuchen said, looking at me with something that could be described as a half-grin. "I've seen and heard all that in combat; only I wasn't playing a game."

Point taken. There was nothing I could say.

"Talk to me about this cancer cure."

"I'm no expert on the subject. You want someone with knowledge about frequency generators, find J.D. Ballard."

"That may not be so easy. These people appear to be pros. They're using a classic tactic. Separate and isolate your target, then move in for the kill. Get them away from their comfort zone."

"If they only want to shut him up, maybe they won't torture or kill, merely try to intimidate him into silence."

"Would that work on your friend?"

"I don't know. He's smart enough not to get himself killed. He'll go along with them to save his life."

"I hope you're right."

We pulled in and parked in front of the entrance to the Holiday Inn. Freuchen shut off the engine.

"Why do you think the frequency generator is kept out of doctor's offices?"

"Doctors are only licensed to recommend treatments that are approved by the drug and medical monopoly. This machine will never be approved because health is not profitable, only treatments are. Radio frequency treatments are cheap."

"I want one of the machines."

"Why?"

"At heart, I am a scared and simple man."

"You can buy 'em. It's not illegal to sell them."

"I saw one advertised on the Internet. It's called Global Wellness, but Christ, Leicester, it claims to cure everything, over fifty diseases."

"Yeah, spells fraud in a loud voice. There was a time in our recent history when every street corner had someone with a box full of wires purporting to cure every human ailment. The only frequency generator I've seen in person was home-built by an aviation mechanic and only used three frequencies in sequence to treat most cancers. He was successful in treating himself, his wife, and a family friend of three different tumors all diagnosed by physicians. The cure was one hundred percent."

"You remember how the machine was built?"

"Sure. He bought a frequency generator at a local electronics store. They are used to calibrate a wide range of electronics and sell for around three or four hundred dollars. Hook up a couple of wires to metal plates, soak some cloth in saline, select the correct frequency, grab hold and let the current flow through the body; simple as that."

"You're pulling my leg, right?"

"No, Freuchen. I'll send you the details when I get back to Mississippi."

"I'm having trouble understanding how a radio frequency can kill a cancer cell. I read about something called an 'MOR.' Do you know what that means?"

"*Mortal Oscillatory Rate.* It seems every cell in the body will vibrate at a rate that, if fast enough, will kill it."

Freuchen scratched his chin. "I've seen Huey helicopters in 'Nam start vibrating when a bearing went out or a blade was damaged. The thing would disintegrate. Is it something like that?"

"Yes, and it seems cancer cells have a different oscillatory rate than normal cells. A scientist named Rife discovered the electrical resonance effect when stimulated by radio frequency energy. His experiments led to the exact vibration at which cancer cells implode, leaving healthy cells unaffected. It had something to do with a change in the electrical conductivity of malignant cells. I also understand that different tumors have *MORs* that respond to frequencies special to them. It's all medical, physics, and engineering, that's why you need to talk to someone a lot smarter than yours truly."

He laughed. "What are you going to do now?"

"Get a helicopter company to tell me who chartered their bird, and where it took the occupants."

"Good luck. What then?"

"Use J.D.'s Citation to run them down."

"I'll keep working on the estate out at Traveler's Ridge. Maybe they left something we can use. Keep in touch. Goodnight, Leicester."

Case History of Dr. A.Z. Beacham

MALE—The patient suffered tuberculosis in the upper left lung. The patient's biopsy confirmed that he had a small cell carcinoma in the right lower lobe with secondary spread of the nodes in the right hilum of the chest. The patient declined Chemotherapy. Radiotherapy was considered. After treatment by Dr. Beacham the patient was alive eight and a half years later with no clinical radiological evidence of the disease.

Chapter Fifteen

The desk clerk waved me over, fanning the air with pink message slips.

"Ah, Mr. Leicester, you have five urgent messages, all from women. The first day you were with us, it was only one, the next day, two, and today, five. Exponentially, if this trend continues, by the end of the week there will be a hundred, and soon all the women in Aspen will be calling for you." He smiled, showing a perfect set of gleaming white teeth, and handed me the notes.

Taking them, I said, "Yeah, I'm just a fun kind of guy. Thanks for taking the calls."

"That's my job. Oh, the doctor, she's called several times. Seemed concerned about you."

"Always nice to have someone worry for your safety." I waved the notes at him and headed for the room.

Sitting at the small table, I looked over the pink slips. There was one from Nancy that noted several calls, one each from Deputy Sadie, Ash Natenberg, Beverly Richmond, and one that simply said, "Come to Denver, stay at the same motel. We'll contact you."

I picked up the phone and called the front desk. "Tell me about the woman who left the message to come to Denver."

"I'm with a guest, I'll call you right back."

. . .

There was a loud knock on the door. Through the keyhole, I could see an irritated Nancy Wiseman. The phone rang as I opened the door.

"Come in, Nancy."

"Where have you …"

I held up a hand, and picked up the phone.

"The woman didn't say much, wouldn't leave a call-back number. She insisted I give you that exact message, made me repeat it. I'm sorry, that's all I could get."

"Any way for you to know where the call originated?"

"I'm afraid not."

"Okay, thanks."

Nancy sat down hard on the bed.

"What's that about?"

I handed her the note.

"This could be what we've been waiting for, Nancy. Maybe they want to give J.D. over to us. Or it could be a trap."

"Can't you get the police involved? If nothing else, as a back up."

"If they sense the cops are around they'll fade away like wispy river fog. I need to think about this."

"Where were you all afternoon? I tried several times to reach you. I was worried."

"Sheriff Freuchen came by and picked me up. They found where J.D. was being held, at an estate up on a ridge west of town. They missed him by a couple of hours. His captors flew him out by private helicopter."

"Was there any sign of him being hurt?"

"No, but they are still processing the scene. Maybe they can come up with some clue."

"It's obvious from this note that they went to Denver."

"Someone is there. We don't know if that's where J.D. is."

"True," she said, using her forefingers to rub her temples as if she had a headache.

"Give me some time to think this through, Nancy. I'll call you in the morning."

"You want to have dinner?"

"I'll order room service. I'd like to be alone. I want to track the helicopter down and do some thinking."

"I feel helpless," she mumbled, more to herself than me. Then: "You don't want me to stay and help in some way?"

"What I want for you to do is stay in your room and not answer the door for strangers until we can get out of here."

After Nancy left, I picked up the pink slips with the messages. There was no answer at the number Beverly Richmond left. Doctor Ashtoreth Natenberg and Deputy Sadie could wait until I dealt with the helicopter company.

Printed on the fuel ticket George Barrows copied for me was an 800 number for International Helicopters of Salt Lake City, Utah. Looking at my watch and noting the lateness of the time, I figured to get an answering service, however to my surprise, a man's voice came on the line and informed me that I had reached the main office and offered to help any way that he could.

"One of your company Agusta 139s flew from Salt Lake to Aspen, Colorado, landed, deiced, refueled, and then proceeded to a private estate where passengers boarded and were flown to an undetermined destination. We need to know who chartered the helicopter, how they paid, and where they took the passengers. There is a police investigation involved and this information is needed now."

"And your name is?"

"Leicester, Jay Leicester, Pitkin County, Colorado Sheriff's Office."

"I am not the person you need to speak with about this. If you will hold, I'll connect you to the Director of Operations. His name is Colonel Stan Papizan."

"Thank you."

A minute later, a voice said, "Stan Papizan, how can I help you?"

Repeating the request, I emphasized the urgency.

There was a short pause, then, "Mr. Leicester, I have no idea who you are, and the information you request would need a court order to be released. I'm sure you understand."

"Colonel Papizan, I'm going to give you the telephone number of the Pitkin County Sheriff's Office in Aspen, Colorado. You can call and give whoever answers the information, which may prevent a murder, or International Helicopters can deal with not only law enforcement, but the FAA. Seems your flying machine was in violation of IFR regulations by scud-running in a control zone, and I will testify to that fact as I observed the infraction personally. It flew not more than fifty feet over a densely populated area and then landed in a backyard to pick up passengers, which is also in violation of not only Federal Aviation Regulations, but State and County law as well. Revocation of the crew's pilot licenses, the company's Operating Certificate, and grounding of the helicopter, which I believe is a twelve million dollar investment, not to mention the loss of revenue to the company while the revocations are being adjudicated. What say you, Colonel Papizan?"

"Who are you?"

"Your worst nightmare, sir, if we can't get the information now, and a person dies as a result of you stonewalling for some perceived right of privacy."

"I'll call the sheriff's office within the hour."

"Thank you, Colonel. I thought maybe you'd see it my way."

After hanging up, I immediately phoned Freuchen's office, informed the deputy to expect the information from International Helicopters and to see that the sheriff got it as soon as possible. He said that he would see to it.

"By chance, Deputy Sadie wouldn't be there, would she?"

"No, it's her day off."

"What is her last name?"

"Plaxco."

"Thanks."

The phone rang as soon as I hung up.

"Hello, Jay, this is Ash Natenberg. Do you have a minute?"

"Sure, what's on your mind?"

"John wanted me to call and apologize for both our actions. We realize that sometimes we come across as arrogant and selfish people, but we are truly not like that, and we can understand your concern for Doctor Ballard. Has there been any word?"

"I accept your apology and no, nothing has surfaced concerning my friend, J.D."

"It seems we are unable to get a flight out for a couple more days. We'd like to invite you and Doctor Wiseman to dinner tomorrow night. Reservations are for eight o'clock at the Copper Kettle."

"Sounds like fun. I'll get with Nancy and let you know in the morning."

"That will be fine. Have a pleasant evening."

Standing and looking out the window at the dark, I could not help but question the motives of John and Ashtoreth Natenberg. Freuchen had checked them out, found nothing but still, they knew J.D., had planned to meet with him here, in Aspen. He turns up missing and they keep appearing in the picture. Them accidentally sitting with us in front of the fireplace in the lobby that first night seemed like too much of a coincidence. Yet what could be their motive?

I decided to take a quick shower and then order room service. Some of my best thinking has been done in a shower. Tonight, the water was hot, and the stinging spray felt wonderful, muscles relaxed and tension drained away. Sadie Plaxco, the wild mountain woman, eased into my thoughts. I wondered if she and Freuchen…but that was none of my business. She never remarried, and life among the ultra rich in a small Rocky Mountain village can get lonesome.

Drying off, I donned my last set of clean clothes and went to the phone to order some food. Just as I picked up the receiver there was a soft knock on the door. I hung up and went to see who it was.

"Beverly, what are you doing here?"

She wore similar tight ski pants and a bulky sweater that I remembered from the lunch at Snowmass Village. Her long shiny hair was up in a ponytail, which really didn't become her. She stood tall and broad shouldered and balanced easily on coltish legs. Looking at me demurely, the dim light from the hallway gilded the down on her cheeks. Her melted chocolate eyes reminded me again of the way to salvation.

"A group of us were going into Aspen for dinner, and I had them drop me off here."

"Come in."

She sat on the bed looking at her hands folded in her lap.

"I needed to talk to someone, needed some familiar company. If it's an imposition, I'll leave."

"What would you do?"

"Catch a cab into town, find my coworkers."

"Have you had dinner?" I asked.

"No."

"Why don't we go to the restaurant here in the motel, they serve some pretty good food."

"Sounds nice."

There was a loud pounding on the door. It made both of us jump.

The peephole revealed Deputy Sadie Plaxco dressed in civilian clothes. I opened the door.

"Leicester, want to have oral sex, then get something to eat?"

"Well, deputy, that sounds intriguing, however I do have other plans."

I opened the door wider, revealing Beverly sitting on the bed.

"Oh, my god, I am so embarrassed. Where'd you find this one, at a high school dance?"

"We met in Denver, she works for Snowmass Development, came down the mountain with some friends who were going to dinner."

"And just happened to end up in your room?"

"Sadie…"

"I'm being rude because I'm disappointed. Forget I was here, Leicester. Have a good evening."

"Sadie, if I hadn't had company…"

"Yeah, see ya Leicester."

Closing the door, I went back into the room.

"What was that all about?"

"A local Deputy Sheriff. There were some things we needed to get straight between us."

"Oh, it has to do with the airplane you're picking up?"

"You could say that, yes."

"Did you work it out?"

"Not necessarily."

. . .

We both ordered steak and salad and I selected an inexpensive California cabernet. The restaurant was full and noisy, but the food was good and the lighting dim enough that candles on the tables created an atmosphere of fine dining.

"Your friends going to stay in town long?"

Overnight. One of the company's condos downtown is vacant for a few days and they are going to dinner and the late show at the Red Onion, and then stay over. Everybody needs a break from the routine and indoctrination."

"You didn't want to join them?"

"I wanted to see you. Is that okay?"

"Yes, it's better than okay."

. . .

When I woke the next morning, Beverly was gone. I remembered her moving smoothly with my movements, like a honeysuckle vine wrapped onto a tall pine in a warm summer wind.

There was a note on her pillow:

I know I could never have you all the time,
But when I had you, I got all of you there was.
Love Bev.

The candle we brought from the restaurant had gone out, consumed itself all the way to the end, leaving lacy, wraithlike wings of white wax melted to the bedside table top. The temperature had dropped to a bitter cold overnight and the mountains to the west were glazed over with ice that gleamed like crystal. The sun was pale and distant and by the time I showered, its light was near blotted out by a high gray cloud layer.

I phoned George Barrows at the airport.

"Get the Citation ready to go. We'll be departing around noon."

Hanging up, I felt a sense of myself; I was sinking into a dark stream, diffusing into its crosscurrents.

• • •

After doing some thinking, I called Nancy. "I'm going to Denver. These people want me in Denver, that's where I'll be. We'll take J.D.'s Citation. I spoke to Barrows at the FBO; he'll have the plane ready by noon."

"The Natenbergs can't get a flight out of here; you want to take them with us? They could connect out of Denver to Vermont."

"Okay, you arrange it; I've got other calls to make."

"Fine. I may take the Citation on to Mississippi. I can't stay away from my practice much longer."

"We'll talk about it on the way. I'll meet you in the lobby at eleven-thirty."

• • •

It crossed my mind to call Beverly, see if she wanted to retrieve her car, but the passes were still closed due the storm and she couldn't get back to Aspen.

Sitting on the side of the bed, it occurred to me that Freuchen needed to know our plans and where to get in touch with me.

Deputy Sadie Plaxco answered the phone at the Sheriff's Department.

"I thought you were off today?"

"Came back in early. You were duly occupied, so I had nothing or no one to do. Didn't want to sit around watching a log fire by myself, that's no fun."

"Is Freuchen there?"

"Hold on a minute."

"Hello, Leicester, what's up?"

He agreed with the idea, said he'd call with any results from forensics and gave me a warning to be careful. It was good advice.

Case History of Dr. A.Z. Beacham

FEMALE—The patient presented with leiomyosarcoma. Her knee joint was seriously damaged. A knee reconstruction was essential. After two courses of Radiowave treatment with Dr. Beacham there was no evidence of malignancy. Two years after her first referral the patient was alive and well.

Chapter Sixteen

The Cessna Citation sat in the front door of the FBO. It had been deiced and appeared ready for flight. The weather at Denver was forecast for ten thousand feet overcast with unlimited visibility, winds were light and variable. John and Ashtoreth Natenberg rode with us from the motel and seemed to be appreciative of the offer for the ride. They showed up on time with only one bag each.

After turning in the rental car, I met with George Barrows, thanked him for all his help, and promised to mention him to Redmond at Centennial Airport.

Coming out of Barrows office, Nancy approached me with a serious look.

"Ash wants to crew with me to Denver, you have any problem with that?"

"None, I'll ride jump seat and keep an eye on you."

"I thought you'd object to an all female crew, especially since you've never flown with me, and you certainly don't know Ash's abilities."

"What I do know, is that you are type-rated in the Citation and current. J.D. said you were a good aviator, and besides, I've given check rides in this airplane to many different pilots."

"But women…?"

"I could care less what you have between your legs. What concerns me is if you can fly the plane."

She laughed. "You still surprise me, Leicester."

Off to the side, I noticed Ashtoreth eyeing Nancy and me. There was a slight smile on her face. She was a striking beauty and some of the "Ice Queen" mannerisms had melted. Given time, I could probably learn to like both of the Natenbergs.

We boarded the Citation, and I closed and locked the cabin door. The girls occupied the cockpit, John sat in one of the passenger seats, and I took the jump seat directly behind the pilots, ready for anything.

Ash ran the checklist like a pro and Nancy handled the small jet as well as any pilot I've flown with. The flight was uneventful and the landing at Centennial Airport impressed even me. We shutdown in front of the FBO, guided to a halt by none other than my old friend, Redmond.

Deplaning and walking around to the front of the plane, I said, "Ah, Mr. Redmond, George Barrows sends his regards. He was extremely helpful. I also want to thank you for arranging my flight over to Aspen with Dr. Frank, a good aviator and pleasant man."

Redmond shook my hand and looked at me rather strangely.

"Is this airplane going back out today?"

"It may be a quick turn or an overnight. I'll let you know in just a few minutes."

Nancy and the Natenbergs headed for the lobby.

"Can I see you in my office, Leicester?"

"Sure. Have them top the tanks and we'll make a decision on leaving or staying."

I followed the tall, lanky Ramp Service Supervisor into a small building that was typical of all line shacks at every airport in all the world. The smell of jet fuel, oil, stale work clothes and dirty gloves permeated the air. Redmond's leathery face with the wrinkles around the eyes wore a serious expression; their blue color did not seem manic today, but sad.

"Did you have any luck with finding your friend?" he asked, sitting on the edge of a desk.

"No, but we learned he was flown off a ridgeline in an International Helicopter's Agusta 139. I was hoping maybe they landed here for fuel."

He rubbed at an oil spot on the rough concrete floor with the toe of his boot.

"We've had no helicopters through here this week. You haven't heard about Victor Frank?"

"What about him?"

"An engine failed on the return trip. He crashed while attempting an emergency landing at Leadville. All aboard were lost."

It seemed that his fortune was not so good. Though we always choose the safest flight path, we are powerless to avoid the small treacheries of fate which comes at you cat-footed, tail swishing, and bloodthirsty

It made me sad; fate had once again reared its ugly head. I could not help but note that Doctor Frank, pathologist and Barron pilot was number forty-three of men with whom I have shared a cockpit whose wings are forever folded. The list keeps getting longer. I have always believed that to live to an old age, a pilot must define his limitations and stay within them. With constant practice, he can expand them, but prudence requires that he respect them. Even then fate will rise up and slap you down. Confucius said, *"The superior man, when resting in safety, does not forget that danger may come. When in a state of security, he does not forget the possibility of ruin. When all is orderly, he does not forget that disorder may come. Thus his person is not endangered, and his states and all their clans are preserved."* Confucius never met that old whore, Fate.

Back inside the lobby, Nancy had checked the weather and decided to continue on to Union, Mississippi, with the Citation. She needed to get back to her practice; the doctor filling in for her must leave tomorrow. I informed Redmond of the quick turn and helped Nancy prepare for departure. We had a quiet talk in private. I promised to keep her informed daily on the search for J.D., and helped her aboard the Citation, secured the cabin door, and watched her taxi away.

The Natenbergs had reservations on a flight out of Denver International tomorrow at six a.m. Telling them of the motel down the road, they decided to stay there. I called and reserved two rooms. My rental car was still in the parking lot of the FBO.

During the short drive to the motel, John said, "You seem kind of quiet, Jay. Something wrong? Or maybe there's something you're not telling us about Doctor Ballard?"

I looked at him; he was a truly handsome man, brown hair and rugged face. He was clean shaven with no scars or marks, a perfect nose with pearl-white, even teeth. He had the athletic build of a runner or football quarterback. One could put him and his wife together, a yuppie couple, both intelligent, medically trained with an aura of superior arrogance, maybe well-deserved. In later life they would probably emerge as good, down to earth people. Who knows?

"No, it's not about J.D. Ballard. I received some bad news concerning someone I knew briefly, a pathologist. He gave me a ride from Denver to Aspen in his Beech Barron. On the return flight he crashed and all aboard was lost.

"My God, I'm sorry. Do you know what happened?"

"They think he lost an engine and for whatever reason couldn't make the airport."

"The complacency of fools will destroy them," Natenberg said.

I snapped my head around. "Is that some stupid quote from somewhere?"

"Actually it's from the bible, Proverbs, I think. It wasn't meant to be personal. Just a fact one of my flight instructors told me one day and it stuck in my mind."

"You'd be wrong about Doctor Frank, he was a good aviator."

"Well, maybe the only real death we suffer is the things left undone; the dangerous things fear kept from us."

I stared at him. It was time to end this conversation.

The fates, ever screwing with me, gave us adjoining rooms. We agreed to meet for lunch in an hour.

The little red light was blinking on the phone beside the bed, a message from Redmond, wanting me to get in touch with him immediately.

"Some woman called asking about you, inquired about the Citation, even knew the "N" number. I gave her no information, just thought you'd want to know."

"She left no name, no call-back number?"

"Refused, said she'd try again later."

"Thanks, Redmond. I'm truly sorry about your friend, Doctor Frank, he was a nice man."

"Yes, thanks, Leicester."

. . .

Hanging up the phone, I sat on the side of the bed and thought about Victor Frank. We remember today that he died, we remember forever that he lived. Put most succinctly, we all owe life a death. Somewhere I remember Hemingway writing that, *"Any man's death diminishes me."* I agree, and felt diminished and a little depressed until something E.M. Foster said about death popped to mind. *"Those two who might best inform us (about that "undiscovered country"), the infant and the corpse, are notoriously silent on the matter."*

Going into the bathroom, I looked in the mirror and, like an insane man, began to talk to the reflection. "Alright you bad guys, Jay Leicester is in Denver. Show yourselves so we can settle this. Return my friend, J.D. Ballard, and let him continue to expose the suppression of a simple cure for cancer affordable for every person."

Smiling, I felt better, but the reflection in the mirror was certainly looking much older than I expected.

There was a knock on the adjoining door between the rooms.

"Jay, John and I are ready for lunch," Ash Natenberg said. "Is the food descent in this place? If not maybe we could go somewhere else, if you wish."

"Food's good, and they do a mean sirloin strip at night, plus the wine list is better than average."

"That's good, Jay. We thank you for getting us out of Aspen, Jay. It was thoughtful of you, Jay," she said leaning toward me.

She was using my name too much and invading my personal space and seemed completely phony. I didn't like the way this was going. But she smelled good and was a striking woman, but beauty always seduces us on the way to the truth.

Chewing on a greasy hamburger and even greasier French fries, I watched them pick at a wilted-looking salad and sipping hot tea.

"You need a ride to Denver International in the morning?"

John stabbed a little round tomato with a fork, looked at me. "We hired a limo service to pick us up. The flight departs at six a.m., so we need to get to the airport by four-thirty in order to make it through TSA lines. It would've been asking too much of you to take us at that time of the morning, besides, we can afford it."

"Yes, I'm sure you can." It came out more sarcastic than intended.

"Oh, I didn't mean that the way it sounded."

"Well, I would have gotten up at three-thirty and given you a ride, but I do appreciate you thinking of my welfare."

There was an awkward pause in the conversation.

Ash finally spoke up. "What are your plans now, about finding Doctor Ballard?"

"Whoever has him wanted me here. It's their move. I have some things I'm working on, but mostly, I'll just wait and see what occurs."

"Like what?" John asked.

"I'd rather not discuss it."

"We understand, and wish you good luck. We'll keep Doctor Ballard in our prayers."

"Yes, prayers are always nice."

After lunch we walked back to our rooms.

At the door, John said, "We're going to have an early dinner and want you to join us. Our treat, say six o'clock?"

"It would be my pleasure."

• • •

The blinking light: One message from Rose, wanting me to call her, and one from Sheriff Pete Freuchen.

I called Rose. "How's my cat?"

"Not nearly as mad at you as I am. You could at least phone me once in awhile. I have to hear from you through other people."

"Who?"

"Nancy Wiseman. She wanted you to know she'd landed safely and to call her with updates."

"Did she land in Union? That's a pretty short runway?"

"She didn't say. So what is going on, any word on J.D.?"

"Not really, he was in Aspen, but someone flew him out in a helicopter to god knows where. There was a side trip to Salt Lake City that I still can't figure out, and I was instructed to come to Denver by the bad guys. I'll wait here and see what transpires."

"You be careful and call Nancy."

"Yes, mother. Say hello to B.W. for me."

• • •

I placed a call to Aspen. Sheriff Pete Freuchen said the information from International Helicopters was a mirror image of what the real-estate people had on the person that rented the estate on Traveler's Ridge; middle-aged female, paid cash. The name and address she used didn't exist. The flight crew was told to land at the airport and await further instructions. They were either informed where to pick up the passengers or someone boarded the helicopter at the airport and forced them to go where ordered. Barrows didn't remember anyone meeting the crew, but couldn't be sure. International Helicopters had not heard from their pilots since landing at Aspen. Freuchen thought that they could be in as much danger as J.D. Ballard. So did I.

As soon as I hung up, the phone rang. It was Redmond from Centennial Airport.

"Turn on the television, go to channel 13, there's breaking news you need to see."

The serious young reporter read from a teleprompter. *"Two pilots from International Helicopters out of Salt Lake City, Utah, were discovered at noon today dead in the cockpit of their Agusta 139 helicopter on the ramp at Boulder, Colorado. Both men had been shot, execution-style, in the head with a large caliber weapon. A fuel service agent noticed the helicopter sitting at the far end of the ramp; it was not there the day before, and upon approaching the Agusta, found the pilots slumped in the cockpit. State Investigators, Sheriff's Department, local police, and the FAA are investigating. We hope to have live coverage at five."*

Turning off the TV, I called Pete Freuchen.

"You were right. If you know the sheriff at Boulder, you might want to give him a call. And Pete, keep my name out of it."

· · ·

Unbelievable! They would murder two innocent pilots simply because they could identify them and had knowledge where they were dropped off. Why prolong killing J.D.? Did they want to see who else would come looking, and then do away with them thinking to eliminate all proponents of the frequency generator cancer cure? These were some bad people and they knew exactly who I was and where I sat at this very moment. I wanted to call Hebrone, but didn't know where to reach him. Smash was dead, drowned in the Atlantic Ocean. Shack Runnels would come in an instant, but that wasn't a good idea. I was suddenly alone, and for the first time in my life, a little scared.

Nancy Wiseman could be in danger. I called her office and got through to her nurse.

"She's with a patient; she'll have to call you back."

"I don't care if she's elbow deep in a vagina, tell her I need to talk to her now."

There was a short pause, and then Nancy came on the line.

"That was not a very nice thing to say."

"They murdered both pilots of the helicopter; you need to be extremely careful, hire a bodyguard, or call John Quincy Adams, the sheriff in Newton County. Tell him everything and see if he knows an ex-cop or PI who would be available."

"You're scaring me, Jay."

"You need to be scared; these are evil people who will do anything to achieve their objective."

"What about J.D.?"

"I don't hold much hope."

"Okay, thanks for the advice."

"You'll get some protection?"

"Yes."

Sitting at the small, round table next to the window in the room, I felt as if I was flying through tenebrous skies or like Homer's heroes who must steer their fragile Barks through the symplegades on the journey home.

At four o'clock there was a knock on the connecting door to the Natenberg's room. It was two hours before we were to meet for dinner, what did they want now?"

Ashtoreth stood in the door with a glass of champagne in her hand. Her long hair hung down over her shoulders, every strand perfect and in its place. The ski pants and heavy sweater fit her tight body like a glove, reminding me of Beverly Richmond. John stood over by the table pouring the bubbly into flutes.

"We talked to the bartender, asked if he had a good champagne, to our delight there was a vintage 2000 Dom Perignon, and it was only three hundred dollars a bottle. John and I thought we'd share it with you since you've been so kind to us. Please come and have a glass before dinner."

"You are kidding, a vintage 2000? I know this wine; in fact there is a case in my cellar. I've only had it once, at a tasting a couple of years ago."

"Yes," John said, handing me a glass. "It should be mature now and last for another three or four years."

His wife spoke up. "It is fresh, crystalline, and sharp. The nose unveils an unusual dimension, an aquatic vegetal world with secret touches of white pepper and gardenias. It then reveals an airy, gentle richness before exhaling peaty scents."

John smelled the wine, and then took a sip. "Ah, toasty aromas meld into freshly cut flowers, apricots and pears with sweet notes of mint and licorice that linger on the finish."

He handed me a glass. I noted the tiny bubbles racing to the top of the flute and admired the straw-gold color. I smelled deeply. They were making a big fuss over the champagne, but if it was as they described, well they should. The nose seemed a little off to me, but I did get some of the yeasty crispness and big fruit. Tasting the wine, I got some pear and apricots, but also something bitter that I couldn't identify. Maybe it hadn't quite aired enough. Another sip and I got the same bitterness.

"You say the steaks are good here?" John asked.

"As good as any I've eaten and they have some excellent Italian reds from good years."

"Ah, Italians, we love the big Brolios, Barbarescos, Brunellos, and anything from Biondi Santi."

Another sip of the Dom Perignon proved if anything that the bitter taste was even worse. Then I felt the first dizziness and knew instantly.

"You son of a bitch, you drugged me."

"What are you talking about?"

My eyes blurred, I felt myself sliding to the floor. My world ceased to exist.

Case History of Dr. A.Z. Beacham

FEMALE—The patient developed left side breast cancer. Surgery was not an option due to risk factors from advanced scleroderma. Dr. Beacham treated the patient with Radiowave therapy whereupon her breast cancer resolved completely and her scleroderma began to resolve. The patient has not required any medication for her scleroderma for three years.

Chapter Seventeen

I am so cold and lying on the ground in the snow. The chilly stars of Orion glitter above. I gaze up at the hunter's belt and jeweled sword. Alnilam, Alnitak, and Mintaka. The stars looked the same as when seen from a frozen Mississippi hay field.

I am so cold and do not know where I am. I have no coat, no shoes. I can't stop shivering. What time is it? I curled into a fetal position. My back hit a chain link fence. I moved to the edge of the warm water. I thought I knew everything there was to know about time. Time as it related to waiting. Time in a holding pattern, burning precious fuel. Time waiting in line to take off, burning fuel. Time flying three hundred miles around a squall line, burning fuel. Low fuel lights on, engines spooling down as time depleted fuel. Time was doing strange things to me now. Trying to confuse me.

Quo Vedas—where are you going—Peter said to Jesus. "What is it to you?" He replied.

I am so cold. Indignities are odd things. There is an inverse relationship between the intensity of the indignity and the time elapsed since its occurrence. It was from this I learned the wisdom of Santayana's observation that *skepticism is the chastity of the intellect, and that it is shameful to surrender it too soon.*

My mind is foggy. I am so cold.

Solomon made himself a palanquin, an enclosed seat born on the shoulders of several men. Abishag was his wife, the fairest in the land.

"Hey!"

I turned and saw a double-wide woman with her hair in a net staring at me, smacking gum, her fists balled tightly on her ample hips.

"You gonna lay here all night? I have to clean."

"I am so cold."

"Then get up."

"I'm sorry, I was at best a difficult, recalcitrant, and recidivist teenager—alcohol—cigarettes—airplanes—girls were my only interest. My sense of responsibility developed late in life."

When I looked, the woman was gone. What is happening to me? Am I dying? Am I dead? What had I learned flying the Dharma Road? Flying does not take place in a reified sky. I am cold and I am scared. When you have faced your own demons, the demons of others will not frighten you. The last desperate words of grown men, good and bad, are often a child's cry—'Mama.' How awful to have to pretend to be brave when you are not. Maybe that's the definition of bravery. Do not lie to yourself about being brave. When telling the truth is the most difficult choice, it is almost always the right choice.

Is this my time? When I was young, I wanted my time and when I had my time I used it up, but is it my time to die? I have known people who have died long before their bodies fell to the ground. The world is full of people droning on, sitting in front of the TV, waiting to die, living only for small sensations of scandal or vicarious catastrophe that they can witness from afar. Boredom is the pathology of the depressed or the unimaginative. Ceasing to grow is a failure of nerve, because it is not what our psyche demands.

I am cold; my brain doesn't want to work.

Do I have the guts to pierce the diaphanous membrane between this tangible, frangible world, and the other, perdurable world that lies on the gossamer side of conventional reality? Is life what happens when we have other plans? I do not want to die, I have reasons to live. I want more moments of life, happiness, and sorrow. I am a bold-spirited man who wants to take off in my airplane in rain and fog and darkness to fly in dangerous skies. I do not understand what is happening.

Hold on to the fence—get up—you are strong—you can do it. What is that inside the fence? Is it a grave marker? Is this my grave? I am so cold.

Pulling myself up, I could not feel my toes. Dizzy, the world began to spin. This just cannot be real. *"Fear not,"* an unfamiliar voice said. *"What is not real, never was, and never will be. What is real always was and cannot be destroyed."*

The grave is enclosed by the chain-link fence. There is a building nearby and the security light shines on the tall headstone. I can read a name, "Cody, William F. "Buffalo Bill" Cody." Who would name someone after a buffalo? It is not my grave.

Staggering to the building proved useless, it was closed and locked. There was a road out front, maybe that will lead somewhere. The snow is ankle-deep and I have no shoes. Why am I here, where is here?

A car, headlights, someone is coming. I tried to stand, but kept reeling to one side. The car stopped. An old woman got out.

"Do you need help?"

"I don't know."

"Come, get in the car."

"Okay."

The heat felt wonderful. It was an old car, a Cadillac or Lincoln, but its heater put out warmth.

"I'm Talitha Cumi," the old woman said. "I was once dead, now I am alive. Are you injured?"

"I don't know."

"I will drive you to the convent, I am a nun there. They will help you."

• • •

I was dreaming. Buffalo Bill Cody, sure, I knew of him. I've been to the museum on Lookout Mountain, not the one in Tennessee, but Colorado. I visited the grave site. It's just up the mountain from Golden, Colorado, home of Coors Beer. So, I'm here? Is this real?

I woke with a start to bright lights. A woman bent over me, she had a hard face and a stethoscope around her neck. She turned, said something to someone I couldn't see. "We have to get his core temperature up. Keep bringing the warm blankets."

Looking down at me, she asked, "Do you know where you are?"

"Some place warm."

She laughed. "What year is it?"

"Twenty-ten, Obama is president; Osama Ben Laden is still hiding in Pakistan. Who are you?"

"Do you know your name?"

"Leicester, do you know yours?"

"I'm a doctor and you are in the infirmary of the Pueblo Del Este Order of the Catholic Nuns. We are going to help you. Can you tell me what drugs you've been taking?"

"I don't take drugs, drink very little, exercise daily, and eat healthy." Pueblo Del Este? Why does that sound familiar, I wondered? "What is that drip running into my arm?"

"Something to help you. Do you know how you got to the museum?"

"No. What's your name?"

"I'm Sister Mary. Mr. Leicester, you have taken some powerful drugs. You could have frozen to death. You wore no coat, are barefoot, and your core temperature was down to ninety-three degrees. That's hypothermic. You are lucky to have made it to our door."

I was dizzy again, the room began to spin. I closed my eyes and it stopped. Was this really happening? Was Doctor Sister Mary real? Am I dreaming? Dom Perignon—it was bad.

"Mr. Leicester, can you hear me?"

"Yes."

"You need to stay awake and talk to me."

"I want to thank Sister Cumi for helping me."

"You want to thank who?"

"The nun who drove me here, Sister Talitha Cumi."

"There is no one here by that name. You showed up alone, knocked on our door."

"She drove me here in an old car, said something strange like, she'd been dead and was now alive. You have to know her, she works here."

"Get some rest, Mr. Leicester. The drugs can produce some wild hallucinations."

I closed my eyes and saw the buffalo. It was not alive, but stuffed. Yes, it was in the museum, the 'Buffalo Bill Museum and Grave.' My flight crew and I visited the museum on a layover in Denver. We drove to Golden, toured the Coors Beer brewery, saw the mountain stream run into the building and not come out. We guessed they used a lot of water making the beer. Someone there told us about a winding road up to Lookout Mountain to the museum. The drive was supposed to be worth the trip. It was.

The old nun was back. She bent over me and I could smell her.

"Sister Cumi, the nuns say they don't know you."

She made the sign of the cross, clasped her hands together. *"Ephphatha,"* she said, and then disappeared.

"Jay, wake up. Can you hear me?"

I opened my eyes and saw an angel.

"We need you to stay awake."

"Susannah? Susannah Ward? The champagne was bad."

Sister Doctor Mary appeared in my view.

"You know this man, Sister Ward?"

"Yes, I met him just before transferring here. A neighbor of his in Union, Mississippi, is a good friend. We had dinner together, the three of us."

"What does he mean, "The champagne was bad?""

"I have no idea, but he is knowledgeable about wine."

"What's his occupation?"

"Has something to do with airplanes, a consultant of some kind. I can call my friend in Mississippi, and get any information you need on him."

"I'm right here, nuns, just ask me."

"Good, Sister Ward, do that."

"No, don't call Rose; she'll only worry, please."

Susannah leaned over the bed. "It's going to be okay, Sister Mary is an excellent physician. She'll take good care of you."

"I saw Sister Cumi again, she was back. Ask her what '*Ephphatha*' means."

"It means 'Be opened.' It's Aramaic," Someone in the background said. "Where did he hear that?"

"He's been hallucinating about an aged nun who supposedly drove him here in an old car. Called her 'Talitha Cumi,' but he was found knocking on the door, alone."

"Oh, my goodness, that's another Aramaic phrase, it means, '*Little girl, I say to you arise.*' Jesus said it to bring Jairus' daughter back alive, one of only three people that he raised from the dead."

From somewhere else in the room, I heard a voice, "There was a Sister Cumi here back in the forties. She used to drive every morning down to Golden, to deliver fresh bread from the bakery. She ran off an icy road one dark day, went over the side and was killed."

"Alright everybody," Sister Mary said, "Let's just treat the patient. We can get to the miracles later."

• • •

I woke slowly, it was dark. My mind was clear and I could sense a presence in the room. I had no idea where I was, but for some reason seemed thankful that I was warm.

"Jay, are you awake?"

A dim lamp turned on, someone approached the bed. The voice sounded familiar.

"It's Susannah Ward. I've been taking care of you for a few days."

Everything came rushing back: J.D. missing, Aspen, Nancy, Denver, the Natenbergs, the spiked champagne.

"How did I get here?"

"Someone evidently left you for dead not far from here. You almost froze to death. No one knows how, but you made it to the convent on your own."

"Big coincidence. Me, you, this place."

"Well, God works in mysterious ways."

"How long have I been here?"

"Four days. I called Rose. She wanted to come, but it was best that she didn't. We're keeping her updated on your condition."

"Somebody drugged me."

"We know. Sister Mary, our doctor who's been taking care of you, got your blood work back from the lab; she can tell you what was in your system. She seemed surprised you survived."

"I've got to get out of here; other people could be in danger."

"Sister Mary will be in to see you early this morning. You can talk to her about your condition."

"I have to go to the bathroom."

"I'll get you a bedpan."

"No, I can make it."

"Here, I'll help you up."

I was shaky and had to sit on the commode, but I made it.

. . .

Sister Mary showed up shortly after daylight.

"Well, Mr. Leicester, you look better this morning. How do you feel?"

"My mind is clear, doctor. Whatever you did for me, I appreciate it."

"You are quite welcome. I've been consulting with a Doctor Nancy Wiseman; she's explained some things and has been very helpful."

"It's a simple question, doctor, am I going to be okay?"

"Yes, you should make a full recovery. Your body temperature got a little low, but there shouldn't be any lasting effects from that. As far as the drugs in your system, they've been counter-acted and flushed out. There may be some bad dreams or flashbacks, but this should resolve itself with time."

"Have you called the police?"

"No, you had no gunshot wounds, so I'm not required to report your condition to them. Do you wish me to call the police?"

"I do not."

"Good. Then if you continue to feel good today, and gain your strength back, you should be able to leave tomorrow. In the meantime, Sister Ward will see to your needs. I'll check on you this afternoon."

"Thank you, Sister Mary."

"Would you like some breakfast?" Susannah asked.

"Yes I would, and access to a phone."

. . .

After eating food that was plain, but with a taste more wonderful than any I've ever had, and served on dishes older than dirt, I took a warm shower, feeling the strength returning to my body. Emerging from the bath, I found, laying across the bed, a fresh set of clothes, even a pair of tennis shoes the correct size. I had no idea where they came from, and thought it impolite to ask.

Susannah returned carrying a down-filled jacket.

"We have to cross over to another building for the phone. You'll need the coat."

"Thank you."

Looking at Susannah, she had an early morning, unretouched dark beauty that made my heart roll over as a dolphin does in the sea. It is a beautiful movement and only a few people in this world can feel it and accomplish it. She had chosen a life of service to her faith. It was a loss to the men of the world, a victory for God.

Following her down a snow-covered path to a small building constructed of field stones, I appreciated the jacket and the tennis shoes. The sky was clear and it was cold enough that our breath was wispy exhaust that dissipated quickly into the crisp, clean mountain air. Inside, the sun shining through the stained-glass windows, quilted the sanctuary with the faint rose light of Jesus' blood. In the back, through a low, wooden door was a small office. It was a functional space with a desk, phone, and a file cabinet. The only sign of the twenty-first century was a small electric heater, one that used ceramics rather than metal coils.

"I will leave you alone to make your calls," Susannah said. "There are some chores that need my attention. I'll return in half an hour."

A tiny window let in enough diffuse light to illuminate a small oil painting depicting the angelic face of a young woman wearing a Habit. One side of the face was partially hidden by the angle of the dim light. I remember someone writing that all masterpieces of art contain both light and shadow.

"Rose, how's my cat?"

"Jay, are you alright?"

"I'm fine. Someone took a dislike to our nosing around where J.D. was concerned, but they must have figured I was too dumb or too ugly to kill. They tossed me out in a snow-covered field in the middle of the night, and guess where, right in the front yard of Susannah Ward. If it had not been for you, I'd have been among strangers. She's been assigned to see to my every need and, as you know, I have a lot of needs."

"You'll never change, but at least I know you are okay. When are you coming home?"

"When J.D. Ballard is found."

"You should come now."

From somewhere I heard an odd, though familiar voice say, "Stay close to home."

I looked around, no one was there.

"Jay, are you still on the line?"

"I can't give up now, Rose. I owe J.D. that much, not to mention the fact that I owe someone payback for trying to overdose me and freeze me to death."

"Please be careful. I'll tell Nancy you called."

"No need, I'm going to phone her now. There are some things she needs to know. Say hello to B.W. for me."

· · ·

"Did you get some protection?" I asked when she answered the phone.

"Yes," Nancy said, with a voice that seemed far away. "I called Sheriff Adams in Newton County and, after listening to the whole story, he assigned his best investigator to me even though I live and work outside of his jurisdiction. Mentioning your name brought groans and sighs, but seemed to evoke some form of resignation. What's it between you two?"

"We go back a few years. Take his advice and be even more careful. The Natenbergs drugged me, left me to freeze to death in a snow field, or had it done, but they are operatives in this thing against J.D. They may come after you."

"But we know who they are and where they live. They will be easy to find and will lose everything; their practice and freedom."

"I know, it doesn't make sense. Sheriff Freuchen ran a check on them, they came back clean. It does not add up. I'm going to call him after we hang up."

"The doctor at the convent read me your labs, you'll be fine. She's pretty sharp. You're lucky to have her looking after you."

"Yes, I'm a lucky man. I'll be in touch."

"J.D.?" She asked, reluctantly.

"I don't know, Nancy. It looks bleak."

· · ·

"I ran the Natenbergs, they're clean."

"I know, Pete. There's something here that doesn't add up."

"Let me make some calls. Where can I get in touch with you?"

"When they release me from this Nunnery, I'm going back to Denver, to my motel room. You better let me call you."

"Okay, and Leicester, I'm glad you made it through alive."

"Yeah, thanks." I hung up the phone.

"What are you doing here?"

"Who's asking?" I said, looking up from the small desk into the dim light of the tiny room.

"I am."

The personal pronoun came out like a bullet, echoed through the stone walls and fell silent. I shivered, sensing something from the depths of my soul, invisible, coming not only from my own decades of life, but from millennia of manhood.

She was a very old woman with long scraggy hair that seemed to be blowing in a breeze although there was no wind in the tiny office. She was so emaciated that I could see the clavicle, acromion, and the coracoid process. It was like looking at one of those cheap plastic Halloween skeletons. The fatty tissue seemed to have been mostly reabsorbed, an attempt by the body to find sustenance.

She pointed a long, crooked finger at me. Behind her, the painting of the angelic face of the young nun was illuminated. Her voice crackled, "A terrible theft has been perpetrated upon you and it has left a lesion on your heart that will never heal."

For some reason, I said, "Bad things happen in this world."

"Do you believe it will be any better in the next?"

"Yes, I do."

"Their worm will never die, and the fire is not quenched."

"Who are you?"

"I gave you a ride from the grave."

"You're the nun who died in the car crash?"

The finger waggled back and forth. "Their worm will never die, and the fire is not quenched."

There was a noise at the door. The old nun vanished. Susannah Ward appeared in the doorway.

"Are you alright? You look pale."

"I was hallucinating again."

Something had been taken from me. I was still an able and confident man, but something had slipped away from me and left behind an emptiness I could feel inside myself. I wondered if it was waiting for me all this time and was inevitable.

Case History of Dr. William Hiatt

FEMALE—A lumpectomy and axillary clearance for a proven carcinoma in the right breast was performed prior to Dr. Hiatt treating this patient. The patient had an infiltrating duct carcinoma in the right breast with two secondaries in the right axilla when Dr. Hiatt treated her. The patient was treated with Radiowave therapy and had no evidence of activity in her disease some five years after her treatment.

Chapter Eighteen

The taxi sat idling in front of the Catholic Order of Pueblo Del Este while I said my goodbyes to Sister Mary and her staff. Sister Ward walked me out of the building.

"I'm sorry we didn't meet ten years ago, Susannah, maybe things would've been different for both of us."

"You wouldn't have liked me back then. I was not a very pleasant person. I drank too much, slept with every man who appealed to me and had a well-stocked wine cellar."

"Are you happy in this life?"

"God has taken me under his wing, Jay. I am comforted, and know eternity has a place for me."

"Goodbye, Susannah."

"So long, Jay. Take care of yourself, and give my love to Rose."

. . .

"Head toward Centennial Airport, driver, there's a small motel a couple of blocks from there, Rhodes Inn, that's my destination," I said to the man whose nameplate read Hussaine Mustapha. He typed in the motel on a dash-mounted GPS and the route appeared instantly—technology!

"You a priest?"

"Do I look like a priest?"

"No."

"Then I'm not."

"Why are you at the nunnery?"

"Resting."

"Okay, if you don't want to talk, this is okay. Praise Allah."

"Yeah, praise Allah."

With tip, it cost me a hundred dollars for the trip. Mr. Mustapha and his "Allah" drove away with a smile.

My first order of business was a phone call to Sheriff Pete Freuchen of the Pitkin County Sheriff's Office in Aspen, Colorado.

"Impersonators, Jay. The real Natenbergs have not been out of Burlington, Vermont, in almost a year. I've confirmed that fact."

"They are good, Pete. Even had knowledge of a local artist who lived in the area years ago."

"They could've been from there, hence choosing the Natenbergs as a cover."

"True. What about the two helicopter pilots, anything come from that?"

"Not that I've heard. Seems like a professional hit, though the caliber of the weapon they used puzzles me. The local sheriff said it was a forty-four. Most hit men use small stuff, like a twenty-two. But what I really can't figure out is why they let you live."

"Me either. I hope J.D. Ballard fares as well."

"We got nothing from the estate," Freuchen said. I could hear him light a cigarette---the flick of a Zippo lighter. "I don't think anything will come from the two pilots. You're going to have to come at this from a different angle."

"If you got any ideas, I'm listening."

"I don't, but be careful. Next time they may decide not to let you survive."

"Or maybe they didn't think I'd make it, drugged up and left lying out in a field in sub-zero temps."

"Good point, your guardian angel was looking out for you."

"She has a name, Talitha Cumi, drives an old Cadillac with a good heater."

I gave Freuchen the number at the Rhodes Inn. He promised to call if any new information developed. Placing the phone back in its cradle, I sat on the side of the bed not knowing what to do or where to go, and hoped the hallucinations would stay away.

. . .

How had I survived the drugs, the cold, or was I allowed to live for some unknown reason? Maybe my guardian angel was looking out for me as he had on many occasions, especially while at the controls of an airplane. It is a fact that while flying, a pilots condition is fragile, perilous, and at the mercy of powers and principalities over which we have no control. It would be logical, perhaps prudent, not to get out of bed in the morning. But then who would fly our passengers to their destinations? If the risk is not taken, the meaning of life is violated. Only boldness can deliver us from fear.

As a young copilot, I flew with a Captain who, on our first trip, said to me, "I am not here to fit in, be well balanced, or provide exemplar for others. I am here to be eccentric, different, perhaps strange, perhaps merely to add to our little society, to the great mosaic of being. But I will teach you things to save your life and the lives of your passengers." I knew I was in good hands.

Then there were Captains I flew with who should not have been pilots. They were drunks, losers, more trouble than they were worth. They were the future dead, I thought. The sad thing is that their passengers would be dead along with them. My guardian angel flew with us, sitting on my shoulder. I did not hate these men. I don't hate anyone because I don't particularly care about anyone enough to hate them. But for these pilots I held little regard, and for one, I felt only distain.

For some, making Captain too early or surviving a horrific crash—it makes them into bullies which is the first step toward disaster; true disaster, I mean. My guardian angel protected me from these pilots, also.

I have survived a Captain where I quickly learned to avoid engaging in a conversation contrary to his opinion unless you had a degree in rhetoric, a high threshold of pain for invective, and an unlisted phone number. He would get so vitriolic as to be unable to fly the airplane, as if his hand were palsied and not connected to a fully functioning central nervous system. Here too my guardian angel flew along with me.

Ah, the mystery of life. I have sought to respect that mystery always. Learning to live with ambiguity is learning to live with how life really is, full of complexities and strange surprises, like my recent survival that would have killed most people. Voltaire observed, *"Doubt is not a pleasant condition, but certainty is certainly absurd."*

I suddenly felt like a man heading into the second half of life. What value do we serve in this period? We all have labored for home, family, identity, retirement. I always sought to win the game of life, and only now do I realize how much I've been played by the game. I played hard, willingly, thinking I was winning something. But in the end there was nothing to win, or what I did win really didn't matter. The second half of life is a summons to the spirit, to ask and answer for ourselves, uniquely, separately, what matters most?

Please, guardian angel, don't ever leave me.

I pace the room like a bear in a cage, not sure of what to do next, my thoughts depressing, but at least there were no hallucinations. I need to find J.D. Ballard, but how? The two who were impersonating Doctor John and Ashtoreth Natenberg have probably disappeared. The people behind this were powerful and moneyed, the next move was theirs.

I tried to rest, to think of other things, but kept returning to J.D. and the two helicopter pilots and this mystery of my own mortality. I wanted to come to grips with it. My goals had changed. I prize depth over abundance, humility over arrogance, wisdom over knowledge, growth over comfort, and meaning over peace of mind.

Life is meaningful precisely because it is finite. Death is only one way of dying; living fearfully, living partially, is our common, daily collusion with death.

EROS and *LOGOS*: One the life force, the desire that wishes most to connect, to build, to combine, to generate with others. The other, archetypal power and necessary twin of *EROS*. This is the dividing, separating, differentiating energy. In our bodies and minds, both energies are continuously manifest. The one wishes merging, connecting; the other splits, divides, and diversifies.

My mind will not quit. Maybe I left Sister Mary too soon. I got under the covers.

· · ·

At six o'clock, I crawled out of bed feeling much better, my mind clear, and I was hungry. It seemed like years ago, but I remembered a great meal in this little motel restaurant, and Beverly Richmond. I hoped the bartender who served me that night was still working.

After a quick shower, I turned on the TV and watched the news while dressing. There was nothing about two helicopter pilots shot dead execution style on the airport ramp in Boulder, but much on Obama Care and out of control government spending, and a little about two wars our nation was engaged in on two fronts, Iraq and Afghanistan/Pakistan. I could solve healthcare in two minutes; vote out Nancy Pelosi, install rigorous tort reform, and allow health insurance companies to compete in all states. The two wars, a little more complicated, but done in six months. I'd seek out and destroy all terrorist with no regard to borders or politics. Stop them at all costs, and never bring to trial captured terrorist in civilian courts. Easier said than done, but at least it wouldn't drag on causing untold deaths of our young American soldiers.

· · ·

Sliding onto the barstool, I recognized a familiar face behind the bar.

"Ah, Mr. Leicester, welcome back," the tender said, spotting me.

"You remember my name?"

"How could one forget a man who walked out of this place with a woman who, for a week, had rejected all other advances?"

"Vintage 2000 Dom Perignon, you remember that bottle being ordered?"

"Certainly, last week, a couple from Vermont, seemed to know their way around a wine bottle. Why?"

"They shared it with me. What else to you remember about them?"

"Arrogance, the woman especially. Made you want to slap her."

Could this tender be trusted? I needed a confidant, so I took a shot.

"They spiked the champagne, knocked me out, and left me to freeze to death up on Lookout Mountain."

"Damn, what a waste of vintage champagne." He grinned. "I'm kidding. Why would they do that? Did you know them?"

I told him about J.D. and the cancer cure, most of it anyway.

"What do you want out of me, Leicester?"

"Someone who I can count on. Trust. I'm alone; the bad guys are going to come at me again. I need to know if strangers come through here asking about me."

"Hell, everybody that comes through here are strangers, it's a motel. You seem like a nice guy, I'll keep my ears open. Sit tight, I'll be right back."

Looking around the bar, I noticed only two other people were there, a young couple sitting in the same booth occupied by Beverly Richmond that first night we met. They were nursing beers and paying attention only to each other.

The bartender returned with a bottle of 2000 Dom Perignon and began removing the foil.

"Seems like you deserve this. It's on the house. I'll help you drink it."

He sat two flutes on the black marble bar, and poured the champagne. "What's your name?"

"Joseph Arimathea, call me Joe."

"Okay, Joe, I'm Jay."

We sipped the wine, it was good, not the best champagne I've had, but worthy of note. At least this bottle was not laced with a bitter-tasting drug that produced unconsciousness and wild hallucinations.

"Do you know the story of the monk, Dom Perignon?" Joe asked, holding his flute up to the light.

"I do. Contrary to popular myth, he did not invent sparkling wine, but did much to perfect it, including a thicker glass bottle that would not explode during the second fermentation."

"'It's like drinking stars,' was his most famous quotation." Joe took a sip and set his glass on the bar. "Do you have an opinion about whether vintage champagne ages in the bottle?"

"I can tell you with certainty, my bartender friend, that despite much nonsense written to the contrary, champagne improves in the bottle, after disgorging (a process where the cork is removed and the sediment is ejected and a '*dosage,*' a little sugar syrup, is added which determines the dryness or sweetness of the finished wine) hardly at all. Most very old champagne found to be in good condition—and they can be superb—have been aged in the original cellars before disgorging, with the sediment still in the bottle."

"I do believe you know your wines. It is a pleasure to share this with you."

It was fun to drink the champagne with Joe the bartender. I was more relaxed than at any time during the last two weeks.

We finished the Dom Perignon and I was suddenly hungry. Joe and I shook hands. He promised to keep his eyes and ears open, and to let me know if anything or anyone looked suspicious. I promised to stop by for a cognac after dinner.

The strip-sirloin was outstanding accompanied by an Italian Barolo that married perfectly with the meat. I was relaxed, mellow, and a little drunk as I headed for the room having decided to pass on the nightcap. The champagne plus the red wine was enough alcohol.

Approaching my room, I met two women walking down the hall, one of them looked vaguely familiar, however in my alcohol induced euphoria, I paid little attention, merely nodding to them. I only wanted eight hours of uninterrupted sleep. Sticking the card key into the slot, I opened the door.

The gun barrel felt cool against my neck.

"Inside, Mr. Leicester, and don't be stupid."

My hands were cuffed behind my back with plastic ties and a cloth sack placed over my head. The eight hours of sleep were not going to come.

Case History of Dr. William Hiatt

FEMALE—The patient had a squamous cell carcinoma of the floor of the mouth which was removed prior to the patient seeing Dr. Hiatt. The patient refused further surgery. Dr. Hiatt treated the patient for a recurrence of the squamous cell carcinoma in the floor of the mouth. A biopsy indicated the growth was malignant. Dr. Hiatt gave two courses of treatment with Radiowave therapy with a thirty- eight day period between treatments. Three years after the last treatment there was no evidence of the disease.

Chapter Nineteen

I was driven from the motel in what was probably a limo. How they succeeded in getting me from the room to the car without being noticed is anyone's guess. Several other people were present, I could hear them speak. After what seemed to be about an hour, the car stopped and we got out. I instantly knew that we were at an airport. I could smell it, had smelled it thousands of times—jet fuel. An onboard auxiliary power unit was running and it made a lot of noise. I was led up a flight of stairs and placed in a seat. Someone fastened my seatbelt. It was a big jet, (my head didn't reach the headliner) but I had no idea what kind of airplane. It could've been a Gulfstream, Boeing Business Jet, or Falcon. I listened to the engine start; there were only two, which narrowed the type down a little. In just a short period of time, we were airborne, heading I knew not where, nor why.

No one said anything, no one approached me. It was as if I was suspended in a black void. I tried to count the minutes after takeoff to judge how high we climbed, and after what I estimated to be about twenty-five minutes we leveled off and the aircraft accelerated to its cruising speed. Counting again, I wanted to estimate how far we would travel. I knew we were up around thirty-nine or forty-one thousand feet and the airspeed would be around five hundred miles an hour, so at least I would have some idea how far we'd flown from the Denver area.

After about an hour we started our descent, and soon I heard the landing gear come down and we turned onto final approach. After landing, we taxied for what seemed an extraordinarily long time, then we stopped and the engines spooled down. Nobody moved, nothing was said, it was eerily quiet. Then I felt the airplane jerk. We were being dragged by a tug, probably inside a hangar. My head hurt and I needed to go to the bathroom. Someone unbuckled my seatbelt, and led me by the arm off the plane into a car.

"Well, Leicester, old boy," I said to myself. "You've got yourself into a mess now. Where are you Talitha Cumi, my guardian angel?"

We drove for what I estimated to be about forty-five minutes, and then I was led into a building with the antiseptic smell of a hospital. Someone pulled the cloth cover off my head, the bright lights blinding me. I seemed to be standing in some kind of lab, all stainless steel and sterile.

My eyes soon adjusted to the light and I knew I was in a room used for autopsies. I'd been in many like this on other unfortunate occasions. Three people were with me. One being the woman described as the pilot who flew J.D.'s Citation and the one who had placed the warnings on my motel room door, along with two men who I'd never seen before. I was hoping the two who impersonated the Natenbergs would be present; there were some things I wished to say to them.

There was a body lying covered by a sheet on a table. No one said a word. The woman who had blond hair, but not the cheap wig she'd worn as a disguise, walked over and pulled the sheet from over the head of the body. There lay my friend, J.D. Ballard. When one has seen enough dead bodies, you learn to tell if someone is asleep, unconscious, or dead. At the moment of death there is a primary flaccidity, then two to six hours later, rigor mortis sets in. After twenty-four to forty-eight hours rigor turns into secondary laxity usually in the same order it began, then the body cools: algor mortis. The second or third day after death putrefaction starts to show as a green discoloration and moves over the body. Then one smells the sulfur gas as bacteria starts to eat the body away. The smell of putrefying bodies is distinctive.

My friend was deceased. Sixty years old, here was a whole life. A whole life of learning to creep and crawl and walk and talk and love and hate and make money and woo and wed and have children and sicken and now die. We only have one death to endure. Then we enter eternity for all time. Just one death and we are free forever. I wondered if it was possible to capture some kind of truth at the instant of death. To learn the secret of everything that matters? My knowing J.D gave his death depth, for it was anyone's death. My death or yours—for here was an unnecessary death; assassination.

Easy, old boy, don't lose it here in front of these—people.

They should be glad my hands are constrained behind my back.

My shock and grief at J.D.'s death turn to nothingness. I try to describe to myself what nothingness feels like, but I turn mute and wordless, and prove unworthy of the task. My conscious is a lost continent where all the jungles have impenetrable canopies, all mountains are alpine, and all rivers contain strange currents of desire and intrigue.

Anger starts to boil, becomes uncontrollable, a black rage. It's gut-check time. What am I going to do, what can I do? I start to shake.

"Control, gain control," I hear a wise old Captain tell me. I fly in the left seat, my first trip in command, the Check Captain along for the ride. The night is stormy; the aged airliner shakes violently as if it will rip itself to pieces. The right engine starts to fail and the firelight comes on. We are starting to get in trouble and I am getting behind the airplane. There are fifty-six passengers aboard; they cross my mind, their safety depends on me.

"We're ten miles from touchdown, the weather is five-hundred overcast with two miles visibility; piece of cake." "What's the wind?" "Down the runway." "Shut that engine down and run the emergency checklist," I say. He does it.

I'm catching up with the airplane and starting to think, acting like an airman, when suddenly lightning strikes the tip of the left wing, runs across and out the right wing, a huge ball of light explodes off the tip. The instruments cease to function, we are both blinded for a moment. "Now concentrate," I hear him calmly say. The radios and instruments return to normal. We are still flying. I move the controls gently and settle down on a steady course. We pass over the final approach beacon, let down the gear and start our final descent, which is always the most complicated and demanding in accuracy. The Check Captain takes a box of matches from his pocket and lights them one after another under my nose. I am heavily engaged in trying to hold course and altitude exactly. This is the real thing, not some simulator exercise. It counts. "What the hell are you doing?" I am bewildered. If I were not so extremely busy I would brush the flame away. It is difficult to see the instruments beyond the flame, and he holds it just close enough to make breathing difficult. I blow out the match, he lights another. I am fifty feet too low, we are swinging off course, and our speed is falling off. "Steady…" His voice is calm without malice or mischief. I fight to keep things in order. As one match after another flares before my eyes, I become infuriated with him. He is a sadist, sick with weird complexities. He is afraid I will do a good job. To hell with him. I will keep everything as it should be regardless of his interference.

We break out of the clouds exactly at required altitude, the speed is right, and we are on glide slope and centered down the middle of the runway. The Check Captain shakes out his match and sits back in his seat. I glance at him, my anger doubling when I discover him smiling. We will have this out on the ground.

As we park at our arrival gate and shut down the one good engine, he snaps the logbook closed, puts a heavy hand on my shoulder. "Anyone can do this job when things are going right. Think, control your anger. In this business we play for keeps."

Looking around the room at these people, at J.D.'s body, I again see the Check Captain's matches flaming before my eyes. Even though distracted by the pounding of my heart, I remember that airman and his matches and their incalculable worth. I quit shaking.

The woman spoke, "We are sorry about your friend, his death was unexpected."

I said nothing, will myself to remain silent, the rage was still subsiding.

"There are circumstances of which you are unaware, Mr. Leicester. Things are not always as they seem."

As calmly as I could, I said, "You kidnapped me from my motel room, handcuffed with a hood over my head, flew me to an unknown location and show me the body of my friend and have the audacity to say things are not as they appear."

"An autopsy has been done to determine why Doctor Ballard died. He was administered some drugs that, in themselves would not have caused his death. We are, even though you may not believe it at the moment, saddened by his death and I assure you it was unintentional."

The absurdity of the woman's statements brought the rage back, I fought to control it.

I blurted out, "He died during the commission of a felony, it's murder, pure and simple." I sounded like a District Attorney.

The two men and the woman looked at each other as if they expected my comment and had discussed it.

"Who are you people, where am I, and what do you want from me?"

"All in good time, Mr. Leicester. Come, I want you to meet someone."

"I'm not going anywhere until I know who you are."

"My name is Doctor Saidoreh Doreh. The rest will have to wait, I'm afraid."

"Would you at least take these cuffs off?"

"We know you to be a powerful and sometimes violent man, Mr. Leicester, for now the cuffs remain. Follow me, please."

I shrugged and followed her, the two men trailing behind. What else could I do?

We walked down a hallway that resembled a hospital corridor. Seeing a door marked "restroom," I stopped. "Please, I'm in pain."

Doctor Doreh nodded. The men took me in and assisted with my clothes. Relief was immense.

We entered a large room resembling a small suite. Lying on a hospital bed was an old woman who appeared to be asleep. To my astonishment, on a table beside the bed sat J.D. Ballard's frequency generator, the one missing from his airplane.

Doctor Doreh said, "Mr. Leicester, this is my mother. She developed a skin cancer, melanoma, on her right groin. The cancer metastasized, spread to the liver, lungs, and spine. After conventional treatment with chemotherapy and radiation, the tumors continued to grow. She was given less than six months to live."

I looked at the old woman; there was a familial resemblance to her daughter. She appeared resting, her breathing easy and regular. My mind was racing, trying to put things in some semblance of order. Why bring me here? What connection could this possibly have to J.D.'s death, the two dead helicopter pilots, the suppression of the cancer cure, the frequency generator sitting on the table next to the old woman?

As if reading my thoughts, the doctor motioned for me to follow her from the room. We went down a corridor to a rather plush office.

"I will explain all of this, Mr. Leicester, and I am sorry, but for the moment you must remain restrained."

"What time is it?"

She glanced at her wrist. "Almost four a.m. I realize you are tired, and so am I, but the time of day is unimportant. What is necessary is that we conclude this whole thing now, this minute. What we decide here in the next hour may affect this whole nation, maybe the world."

I almost laughed. She must have me mixed up with someone else. I'm a lowly aviation consultant from the back woods of Mississippi. Whatever I say or do wouldn't bother the coyotes running on my back eighty much less the nation or the world.

Doctor Doreh leaned back in her chair and wiped both hands over her face as if removing water after a shower, and then she smoothed the blond hair back over her head.

"Mr. Leicester, I am one of the six people who control the pharmaceuticals, the American Medical Association, and all cancer treatments and organizations in the United States and most of the free world."

I knew it was a small group, but only six?

"So you are responsible for having my friend J.D. Ballard killed, for the deaths of the two helicopter pilots?" I started to become angry, sat on the edge of the chair, and tested the cuffs holding my hands behind my back.

"I've caused no one to die, Mr. Leicester. I've spent my whole life dedicated to healing people. Calm down, sit back and listen to what I've got to say. We don't have much time."

I felt tired, my mind was confused, out of its normal element, fragile. J.D.'s death struck me somewhere between normal grief and pathological grief; mourning and melancholia. Listening to this woman, this Doctor Saidoreh Doreh, was not something I wanted to do right now. I needed rest, sleep, some time to let my brain reboot.

"No!" I said, standing, straining at the cuffs. "Not now. Give me a room where I can sleep. Put a guard at the door, put ten guards there, I don't care, but take these damn cuffs off. Give me time to think, to get my thoughts in order and rest. I promise, after that I will listen to what you have to say about my kidnapping, the three dead, your mother, the frequency generator cancer cure machine beside her bed, and your involvement in all this, but not now."

She rose from the chair; a sudden light seemed to shine in her eyes like wood reaching its kindling temperature and bursting into flame. "Very well, you have eight hours, but no more." She nodded at the two men.

I was led away, through a side door into a small room with a bed. It looked like an on-call room, some intern quarters where a few minutes of sleep could be grabbed between patients.

"Turn around, Mr. Leicester; I'll cut the cuffs off. You would be well advised not to create a fuss," one of the men said. "I assure you we can handle the situation."

"I gave my word."

"We'll come for you at the appropriate time. Sleep well."

Rubbing my wrists, I sat on the bed. It felt wonderful to have the freedom to move my arms, even though confined to this small space. Spotting the light switch, I darkened the room and lay down. *Nune, verno inter saxum et locum durum sum,* I muttered aloud. Now, I really am between the rock and a hard place.

For some reason known only to my guardian angel, my brain switched off like the lights. The next thing I knew, someone was shaking me. It took a moment to remember, and then it all came rushing back. It was time to meet with Saidoreh Doreh.

"There's a shower, Mr. Leicester," the man who'd cut my cuffs off said, pointing to the bathroom. "You can put on the hospital scrubs laid out on the chair while we have your clothes cleaned."

"Where are we?"

"Doctor Doreh will tell you what she wishes for you to know."

"What time is it?"

"One in the afternoon."

Looking at my watch confirmed what I suspected; we were still in Mountain Standard Time. This had to be Salt Lake City. The side trip that was made when J.D. was abducted went to Salt Lake, but for what reason?

The shower was what I needed. I felt refreshed and rested, ready to deal with the good doctor, the one who professed to only wanting to heal while bodies lay all around her.

Putting on the scrubs, I wondered if the old woman with the melanoma, Doctor Doreh's mother, was treated with J.D.'s frequency generator. Did they bring him here for that purpose, to administer treatment? That was over three weeks ago. Had he refused to help? What did he die from? How was the old woman's health today? Lots of questions for the doctor, and one of the first and most important that I intended to ask was what am I doing here.

"Come, Mr. Leicester, we have prepared something for you to eat."

We went to a room with a conference table laid out with food. To my delight there were coffee, bagels, scrambled eggs and some kind of sausage patties that were wonderful, I thought maybe venison that was highly seasoned to perfection.

"We will leave you alone, and when you are finished Doctor Doreh will meet with you."

"Yes, I'm sure."

Eating slowly, even though famished, I formulated the questions I wanted answered. I needed to unravel the complex trigonometry of the radical thought that silence could make up the greatest lie ever told. I did not want Doctor Doreh to remain silent about anything, all must be revealed.

Out the window of the conference room, the sun blistered the snow on the far mountains with a seething gold, then a flare of red, followed by a pink-fingered rosy hue. Sitting the coffee cup in its saucer, I wiped my mouth with a crisp-laundered cloth napkin, and pushed my chair back from the table. A feeling of dread swept over me at the thought of the upcoming meeting, but it is a poor thing for anyone to fear what is inevitable.

Case History of Dr. William Hiatt

FEMALE—The patient had breast cancer and was taking hormones to control the disease. The hormones proved to be ineffective. Dr. Hiatt treated the patient with Radiowave therapy. Eight years and three months after the last treatment no evidence of malignancy was present.

Chapter Twenty

This time we went to a room less opulent, but much more intimate, with large, comfortable chairs and a small fireplace burning brightly. There was no desk or file cabinets, only a small end table that held a telephone. Tiny windows, high up near the ceiling, allowed afternoon light to enter, drawing geometric designs on an opposite wall. Saidoreh Doreh sat in one of the chairs facing the fire. She did not rise when I entered.

I think my arrival had shaken something loose in her, had touched her in a long-buried place. So she decided to open up under all the protection that fire and cold and darkness could provide when a soul has a hummingbird-like moment and decides to fly toward the high, urgent places. This afternoon her soul was a living thing born by firelight. She told me her history, one I think she'd never told anyone. But why? Was it because of what had occurred with her mother? The death of J.D. and the helicopter pilots? Or the high stakes involved with the radio wave cancer cure?

She rose from the chair and added two sticks of wood on the hot embers. The fire blazed higher, crackling into sudden light as the wood reached its kindling temperature and burst into flame.

Deciding not to push things, I crossed my legs, lay my hands in my lap and watched the fire. I would let events flow as I felt they would. The gates had been opened, and now patience was my best weapon. Hebrone

Opshinsky strangely came to mind. I once watched him play solitaire with a deck of cards sixty-eight straight games until he won. Getting up, he looked at me, and said, "Patience," then walked away.

Doctor Doreh was a small fine-boned woman with a long face and narrow head. Her smile exposed teeth which were long and white with healthy gums. She sat down, crossed her legs and knitted her fingers on top of a knee. Her nails were clean, closely clipped and protected with a layer of clear polish. There was a shine to her blond hair just like the nail polish. Behind her, out the row of small windows, the sun moved in its arc, changing the shadow patterns on the opposite wall, and there was nothing one could do to prevent or stop that movement.

"Mr. Leicester, the people I am associated with are some of the most powerful in the world outside of politics, and believe me, we are involved in that to the extent we get what we desire. These people have two gods, money and power; they are an anomic group and could care less about the health and welfare of patients. I know, for until a short time ago I counted myself as one of them. We control the pharmaceuticals, the AMA, FDA, and all companies and organizations involved in medicine—all of it, including controlling the boards of major insurance companies."

She paused to see if I could grasp the scope of her statement. I did, but remained silent.

"When something comes along that threatens our power, we act quickly and decisively. In this instance, two concerns cropped up almost simultaneously, an engineer from Houston, Texas, with leukemia and your friend, Doctor J.D. Ballard. The situation in Texas resolved itself; Doctor Ballard would not go away."

I recrossed my legs, smoothed out the green scrubs, and said nothing.

"You are familiar with the Royal Rife Frequency Generator?"

"Somewhat," I answered.

"Rife did some marvelous things, but was far ahead of his time. His major problem was the unwillingness to share with the medical community the inner workings of his inventions, the microscope and wave generator. Unable to duplicate the experiments with any degree of success resulted in great skepticism and thereby cries of fraud and quackery. However, there was enough patient improvement after treatment by local doctors that he kept the company viable, though barely. His failure in the art of diplomacy and politics was his undoing. Money and power rules the world, not the science."

"So none of Rife's machines worked?" I asked, wanting to learn exactly what her thoughts were on Rife and his frequency generator.

"Some trials on patients had one hundred percent cure rates, but Rife wouldn't play the game and was shut down. The treatment of cancer evolved into what it is today and he was forgotten. Then John Kanzius developed leukemia, revised the frequency generator and somehow got the M.D. Anderson Cancer Research Center interested. Then Doctor Ballard appeared on the scene and things began to escalate. Media attention started to generate interest. Kanzius went at it the wrong way, he injected the tumor cells with tiny bits of gold, used the frequency wave generator to heat the metal, killing the malignant cells leaving healthy ones undamaged. Then the leukemia killed him before he could perfect his treatment or realize that the use of the metal was unnecessary to the procedure. However a two million dollar grant was awarded one of Kanzius' doctors to continue work on the theory. The news show, *Sixty Minutes*, did two segments on Kanzius, one before he died and one after."

"So you and your little group were afraid my friend would team up with the M.D. Anderson people and you would lose your money machine? To hell with the lives that would be saved if the frequency wave generator could be funded and brought into the twenty-first century."

She sat up straight in the chair, wrung her hands. A bead of sweat appeared on her temple. She seemed to shiver and the skin on her arms goose pimpled and assumed the consistency of a freshly plucked chicken.

"Mr. Leicester, it's so much more complicated than you realize. Forget the patient for a moment and think about the people world-wide who work in this industry whose livelihood depends on the thousands of companies involved. If all these failed, what would they do?"

"You have the audacity to weight that against the hundreds of thousands dying from cancer each day? You can't be serious?"

"No, you're right, of course." She got up and paced the room. "It was all so simple. Rife was forgotten, mainly due to all the quacks that started selling the frequency generators in the seventies and eighties and nineties, claiming to cure everything from ingrown toenails to tonsillitis. However a few people like Doctor Ballard knew the truth, and they would not go away."

"You and your group decided to do away with Ballard, get him out of the picture?"

"If we were to do that, someone else would be just as persistent about the Rife machine. We wanted to reason with him, show him scientifically why the machine didn't work, and why he must quit promoting the treatment."

"But you couldn't do that."

"No, and for two reasons. Ballard couldn't be bought, and the machine worked."

"Your mother?"

She ignored my question.

"We planned to meet with him in Aspen, hired some people to see that he showed. No harm was to come to him. Then weather caused our airplane and Doctor Ballard's to divert to Denver."

"You were following him in your airplane?"

"Yes."

"What happened in Denver?"

"I introduced myself at the Centennial Airport. My mother was gravely ill and I begged him to fly to Salt Lake and treat her, teach me how to use the frequency wave generator. Then he could continue on to Aspen. He was very accommodating."

"You didn't tell him you were a member of a group planning to shut him up?"

"No. We flew in his plane to Salt Lake and started treatment on my mother."

"Why were you and another man flying J.D.'s Citation when you left Denver?"

"He offered to let me fly; it was him that flew copilot. The other man was my assistant."

"What happened when you arrived in Salt Lake?"

"He started treatment with his own machine, showed me how to continue, and due to my mother's condition, suggested we run the generator six hours a day, seven days a week. There was a misconception, going all the way back to Rife's first machine, that the body couldn't absorb the dead tissue from large tumors all at once without becoming toxic, so treatments were stretched out over months. That hypothesis proved incorrect."

"It's been three weeks, how is your mother?"

"A full body scan was done yesterday. She has no trace of malignant cells."

"How wonderful for you and her. Why isn't my friend sitting here with us toasting the successful cure with a glass of champagne instead of lying dead in your morgue?"

Doctor Doreh hung her head, leaned forward in the chair.

"I'm waiting, doctor. Why is J.D. Ballard dead?"

She sat up, looked me directly in the eyes, and said, "I lost control of the situation. The meeting in Aspen was going to take place, I couldn't stop it."

"So you went along with it, even though the man was saving your own mother's life. You are a piece of work. How can you live with yourself?"

"Doctor Ballard refused to go back to Colorado, he wanted to stay and follow the progress of my mom's treatment. However, things were already arranged. People had flown in and were waiting. He was given oral and then IV drugs and prepared for travel. I left my mom in the care of my best people and went along, thinking to at least ameliorate the situation."

"You flew his airplane to Aspen, and then carried him to the estate. I know for a fact that he couldn't walk when he got off the plane. He had to be helped into the limo."

"Yes."

"What occurred at the house on Traveler's Ridge?"

"You know about that place?" She seemed surprised.

"I've been there, saw where the helicopter landed in the corral to take you to Denver. The ones your little group hired to run things are not quite as smart as they should be, more like careless. Hard to believe the ineptness."

"Something went terrible wrong. Doctor Ballard would not shake off the sedation. Either the drugs, dosage, his system, or some underlying condition he had that we didn't know about—he just never recovered."

"It was decided to fly him to Denver in a helicopter?"

"They have an outstanding trauma center there, but he died enroute."

"Six medical doctors and you let a man die from some stupid drug? You administered them, or somebody did, that makes you all guilty of murder. But why was it necessary to kill the pilots?"

"The people my group hired made that decision. It was out of my hands."

"You flew J.D.'s body from Denver here, to Salt Lake?"

"Yes, in my private plane. I wanted to find out what killed him."

"You realize I have to be silenced, along with Nancy Wiseman, Sheriff Pete Freuchen, and maybe others to keep the monopoly safe."

"According to our operatives, none of that would be a problem. There are many ways to silence the opposition. But I have a proposal."

"This ought to be interesting." I said with as much sarcasm as I could muster.

She handed me a file folder.

"I would like for you to look over what's inside. I will give you a half an hour alone to scan the contents of the folder, to see what's proposed. We can discuss any questions you may have."

It took me five minutes to go through the pages in the folder. It was an insult, a slap in the face. A black rage began to build. A thought crossed my mind that if I was going to die anyway, I would take her with me, now. Then something else slipped through the rage, another plan, one where everybody may benefit. I decided to listen to what Doctor Saidoreh Doreh had to say.

When she returned, I handed her back the folder. She looked hard at me, searching for some sort of reaction, some acknowledgment of her proposal. It took a Sisyphean effort to keep from telling her how ridiculous the idea seemed. I looked at her knowing that the only source of the truly ridiculous is affectation.

She sat down, crossed her legs. "Your thoughts, Mr. Leicester?"

"A memorial to J.D. Ballard? Building a memorial to him does not change the fact that he is dead, murdered."

"You missed the point; it's not a memorial, but a research center. I have a theory, Mr. Leicester; the only thing that never changes is that everything has to change. I've changed my mind about the radio wave treatment of cancer."

"On account of your mother, just one case?"

"Partly, but I've done a lot of research, the treatment works. Here's what I'm prepared to do." She stood, walked to the center of the room, turned, and faced me. "I am a very wealthy woman, several billion dollars. If you were to total the wealth of my five colleagues and me, it would be more than Bill Gates and Warren Buffet combined. I point this out so you'll know that what I propose is entirely possible."

I stood, clinching my fists. "You think you can shut me up by flouting money in my face and building a memorial to my dead friend?"

Not fazed, she stood her ground, never batted an eye.

"I own forty acres of land adjacent to the airport. On that land will be built the finest cancer research facility this nation has ever known, surpassing M.D. Anderson. The sole purpose will be destruction by radio wave of malignant cells. I will pay construction cost, fund operations with an endowment of one hundred million dollars, plus another forty million will go for equipment and salaries. The center will be named: *J.D. BALLARD/ROYAL R. RIFE CANCER RESEARCH CENTER."*

"All I have to do is keep my mouth shut about three murders?"

"Hundreds of thousands of lives can be saved."

"Your colleagues agreeable to this?"

"They know nothing about it. You and I and one other person are the only ones who are aware of this proposal."

"Who's the other one?"

"Doctor Nancy Wiseman."

I was stunned. "Nancy, but why…?"

"I offered her the director's job. It was an offer she couldn't refuse."

"She accepted?"

"She wanted to talk to you first but, yes. My plane has been dispatched to bring her here today."

I sat back down; there was a lot to think about.

"You know nothing about Nancy Wiseman. What expertise do you think she has for running a one hundred and forty million dollar cancer research center?"

"I know everything about her, from the day she was born, to what she had for breakfast this morning."

"You're simply eliminating someone who can tie your little group to three murders, not to mention the atrocities perpetrated on millions of people who died of cancer because of suppression of a noninvasive, cheap treatment that could have saved them because of your greed."

"No, Mr. Leicester, you are overlooking the big picture, the research center will expose all that."

She had me there.

Stepping up close to me where I sat, she said, "Three deaths, two by overzealous operatives and one accidental, is a small price for the benefit coming to mankind, don't you think?"

"You won't get away with it."

"That's our worry. The question is whether you are on board or not."

"The other five members of your group are going to lose a fortune. What's their reaction going to be?"

"My problem, not yours."

The door opened.

"Mr. Leicester, we have your clothes, would you like to change?"

"Yes, thanks."

The man left the clothes and departed.

"What time is Nancy due to arrive?"

"Three o'clock."

"We'll need some time alone, in strict privacy."

"Absolutely."

"This whole thing stinks," I said, retrieving my clothes. "I don't like any of it."

"Even the radio wave research?"

"It's a fine idea. I just don't like how we got here."

"I'm going to be with my mother, Mr. Leicester, make yourself at home. If you need anything, knock on the door."

"I'm still a captive?"

"Yes, I'm afraid so."

Doctor Saidoreh Doreh left. I changed out of the hospital scrubs, sat down and looked through the folder containing the proposed cancer research center data, and awaited the arrival of Nancy Wiseman. My friend J.D. Ballard cast a shadow over the pages in my lap.

Case History of Dr. Ernest Grissom

FEMALE—Slowly enlarging mass in the left calf. The tumor was partly removed. Histology was a myxoid lipsarcoma and myxoid sarcoma 14cm long which was incompletely removed. After treatment with Radiowave therapy by Dr. Grissom no recurrence of the disease was found after eight years and four months.

Chapter Twenty-one

The walls seemed to close in around me. I felt that I was among a brood of vipers and was sticking my arm inside the den, feeling around for the longest one. *Take note of what you are seeking, for it is seeking you,* the flickering flames from the fireplace seemed to scream out at me. There was no way I could let three murders go unpunished. My conscious would not allow that, it is not who I am. However, Doctor Doreh's point that the number of lives to be saved must be considered. It is not always easy to reconcile two sides of any truth.

Getting up, I went to the fireplace and added two more sticks of wood, merely for something to do. The late sun caused the light and shadow on the walls in the room to resemble a clerestory, but this was not a church. I became like an anesthesiologist, giving anesthesia, knowing that the drugs have a thoroughly baffling mode of action. No common chemical structure or effect to explain their alterations of pain and consciousness. They seem to act by dissolving mysteriously in the membrane of the nerve cells—more a physical than a chemical phenomenon, and they themselves cause twelve thousand deaths annually due to related problems.

Nancy's arrival would be welcome, her input invaluable. My idea for everyone to gain from these circumstances needed her approval. She was an intelligent person, and I knew her thinking would be like a patient's write up in a chart; the order ritualistic, the phrasing formulaic, and the emphasis and reasoning constrained.

I stared at the lambent flame in the fireplace. It was good to be alone; though I was sure someone was listening or watching. I prefer to be by myself, away from the rest of the world. I am never lonely, and sometimes wonder if this is a good thing. When I am alone, I do a tremendous amount of thinking, but there is a tendency to form my own opinion about everything. Books have been my only escape from this—my salvation. I turn to them for a direction other than my own—something I get from very few other people.

I walked to one of the windows and looked out. Clouds were beginning to amass and planes of sunlight, like sheets of amber glass, angled through the thickening layers. To the west a flight of wild ducks etched themselves against the mountains, blurring, then etching again and I knew no man was ever alone in this world.

J.D. came to mind, his body lying in the autopsy lab. I felt curious—not ill but suddenly empty—it was the way a blow to the stomach could make you feel. It was an odd thing, but true, that the death of a friend could affect you almost as much as a member of the family. I had experienced it before, when news reached me of the death of a pilot I'd flown with, or an almost stranger like Doctor Victor Frank. I felt empty for a spell after learning of his unfortunate accident. I liked the man; I just didn't expect him to die.

Maybe now is not the time to think about J.D. Now is the time to think of only one thing, that which may keep me alive and a cancer research center funded.

This is a temporizing world, fading into uncertain shades of grey. The great conundrum is what is worth living for and what is worth dying for. I chose not to live for a nationalization of this great country into some western European socialist/democracy, uncontrolled spending that will bankrupt this nation, or healthcare run by our government.

But what is the alternative? I know enough about myself to know I cannot settle for one of those simplifications which indignant people seize upon to make understandable a world too complex for their comprehension. These people adopt grotesque simplifications—black

Muslim organizations, Klucker Klan's, terrorist groups, nudism, nihilism—in hope of finding the *answer*, because the very concept that maybe there is no answer, never has been, never will be, terrifies them.

Pacing in front of the fire, I said aloud, "Yes, Leicester, maybe you should be made a 'Prophet' by God." I believe in the Holy Trinity. Just look at the universe and you'll know. I think the closest we can get to awareness of God is when we see one man, under stress, react in…in a noble way, a selfless way. The billion dollar church buildings, with multi-thousand congregations and the television sermons of "organized" religion with the formalities and routines are not for me. Maybe for other people who need routines, rules, examples, taboos, object lessons, sermonizing. I don't. Give me Rose's "Little old church in the wildwood," real religion—and no title of "Prophet."

The door opened. A man entered wearing a starched lab coat, and there was an "M.D." after his name. He was a big man who looked as if he worked with his hands. He reminded me of a young Sheriff Pete Freuchen without the years of tobacco ruin. Nothing wrong with someone who works with their hands. Ernest Gann ran a fishing boat. Cezanne had been a butcher. Renoir a carpenter, and so was Jesus the Nazarene. Emerson had been a Hod carrier.

"You need anything, Mr. Leicester?"

He knew my name.

"Do you know if Doctor Nancy Wiseman has arrived?"

"I understand the plane just landed."

"What killed Doctor J.D. Ballard?"

"I'm sorry, that's not under my purview."

He left, closing the door behind him.

Watching the flame in the fire, I began to feel like the person attempting suicide, who jumped from the Golden Gate Bridge, only to survive. He said that the last thing he saw as he leapt over the railing were his two hands on the rail. At that moment—frozen in time—he realized he'd made a terrible decision. But it was too late. Was my decision to play both ends against the middle wrong, or too late? Did

I have the courage to proceed? What was courage? Ian Fleming said, *"Courage is a capital sum reduced by expenditure."*

Nancy Wiseman came through the door. She was dressed in a well-cut black suit brightened only by a gold pin, a Caduceus. Her ash-blond hair hung shoulder length. Her hazel eyes had a cool, impersonal expression I found unsettling. There was nothing bucolic in her appearance.

She shook my hand as if we were strangers.

"We need to talk," she said with an indifference that was annoying.

"Yes, but not here." I glanced up at the ceiling.

She nodded.

We were led to an inner courtyard with trees that seemed stark and bloodless against the winter sky. The sun was almost down, a narrowing red lozenge on the cloud-streaked horizon. It slipped out of sight behind the mountains. The whole western sky became smoky red, as if the sun had touched off fires on the far side of the world.

We wore no coats, but the temperature did not seem cold. We walked a few hundred feet in silence, stopped and faced each other. There was much to say, but neither of us wanted to start. It was as if we must form a comitatus, however unnecessary palaver would be awkward and inane.

"Did you ever love J.D. Ballard?"

Her eyes betrayed her, there was hurt at the question, then anger, after that understanding.

"Because I took the job offer to run the Research Center?"

"Yes."

"Doctor Doreh was informed that I needed to talk with you first."

"You didn't need my permission to hide three murders, one your boyfriend, for money and prestige."

"Come on, Leicester, you are more intelligent than that. There are other things to consider. I knew you would have ideas and thoughts, I wanted to hear them. You may not believe it at the moment, but I have an angle or two of my own."

"It would be interesting to hear them." I was almost shouting.

She turned her back to me, bowed her head. She turned back around; a tear ran down her cheek. The tough Nancy Wiseman was actually crying. Something about this whole scene suddenly seemed real, and made me change my confrontational demeanor.

"The lawyers are the key." I said, softly.

"What?"

"We have to get her lawyers to draw up the contract for the funding of the Research Center so that no matter what we do in the future the money will be forthcoming."

"But how…?" She gestured with both hands.

"It's complicated, and we don't have much time. My bet is that they want your directorship contract signed tomorrow, and my signature on a nondisclosure form concerning the murders."

"If we do that, all is lost."

"There's never been a contract this side of heaven that couldn't be broken, Nancy. The key is to somehow keep the funding no matter what happens."

"I've had the same thoughts, and knew you'd be thinking along these lines. That's why I wanted to talk to you first."

"Let's go inside." I took her by the elbow. She was shaking.

We were escorted back to the room with the fireplace. Doctor Saidoreh Doreh was waiting. She looked us over, not with distain, but with an impatience which said that time was important, maybe more than important. Time was running out. If the other members of her elite group got wind of her defection, the consequences could be severe.

"Have you two reached agreement?"

"What's the rush? You have a dinner date?"

"Don't be crass, Mr. Leicester. You know very well the reasons to finalize this arrangement. The lawyers are in the conference room waiting. Can we meet with them?"

Nancy stepped forward. "Yes, though there are a couple of stipulations we insist be added to the contracts, if they are not already there."

"Name them."

"As I see it, there are two concerns. One, if something happened to you, the Research Center would continue to be funded. Two, if for some event unrelated to either myself or Jay, the deaths are tied to you and your group, nothing changes with the Center."

"The funding is set. The money will be in escrow, to be controlled by you as director at your discretion. As far as Leicester is concerned, his agreement will be a little more ironclad. But I'm sure we can work out the details. Shall we go meet with the attorneys?"

The meeting went much more quickly than expected. Nancy signed her contract, contingent upon my agreeing to a nondisclosure of any involvement of Doreh or her group in the deaths. These lawyers were either ignorant or a bunch of idiots, maybe both. How could they prove I wouldn't use a third party to blow their little scheme apart? It was impossible. They did insist that the funding cease if any of the members were indicted. Neither of us would sign if that clause was included. Doctor Doreh had them remove it.

When the session was over, we went back to the private room. I wanted J.D.'s body flown back to Union for burial. Nancy needed a month to hire another doctor to take over her practice in Philadelphia before assuming her duties overseeing building of the Research Center.

Doctor Saidoreh Doreh stood before us looking as if a huge weight had been lifted from her shoulders. But deep in her eyes something floated that appeared evil. I don't think she knew that it was there. "The results of the autopsy will take another week. Dr. Ballard's body will be ready for transport in the morning. My plane will take you both back to Mississippi, along with the remains. A suite has been reserved for you tonight at a local resort. I will pick you up at ten a.m. and take you to the airport. So, if all is in order, I'll say goodnight."

· · ·

The resort was Five-Star, resembling a French Chateau. The décor was for the dedicated skier, wealthy skiers. Our suite forded a breathtaking view of the surrounding mountains. Sadly, darkness had settled over the area and we only got a fleeting glance. The morning sunrise should be spectacular.

The living area provided a huge fireplace and all the amenities one would expect. Bedrooms were even more lavish. I would not mind staying for awhile; it would be easy to get used to.

A bottle of champagne cooled in a bucket of ice and a tray of hors d'oeuvres sat on the bar. A note said we were welcome in the dining room; a table awaited us until ten p.m.

While Nancy went to freshen up, I lit a fire and opened the champagne, a Cristal from a good year. We had not talked about J.D.'s death and I wanted to draw her out, see how deeply hurt she truly was. I might have seemed a little cruel to her at the hospital, but the effect garnered what I wanted it to. She cared about the man, but she dealt with death daily, so her reaction would be expected to differ from the layman. I once asked my personal physician what the hardest thing was about practicing medicine. He said having a patient die you'd become friends with, or grown to like. Doctors have to distance themselves from the emotion, inure themselves from the loss, otherwise they would go insane. Sipping the champagne, I decided not to breech the subject tonight. We both needed to relax for a few hours. Maybe I'd bring it up on the flight back to Mississippi, or after we landed and began making plans for J.D.'s burial.

Nancy emerged from the bedroom and I handed her a glass of the wine.

"No more of the business at hand, my dear Doctor. Let's relax, have a nice dinner, and get some rest. We can begin anew tomorrow."

. . .

The dining room was elegant. The Maitre d' insisted I wear a coat, which he provided from a closet reserved for rednecks like me. High-back, comfortable chairs and a table adorned with the finest linen, silverware, and dishes awaited our comfort. The chef was doing duck breast in a sauce I was unacquainted with, and we both decided to try it. From the wine list, brought by a Sommelier with a Tastevin draped from his neck on a gold chain (which if real was worth more than I earned in months), I selected a French burgundy from a year known to be a good one.

"Ah, a Domaine Romanee-Conti, excellent! The gentleman knows his wines. However may I suggest the '05. The '02 is going through a stage where it is not quite right."

Looking hard at him, I tried to guess if he was being an arrogant showoff hiding behind his Tastevin, or truly being helpful. A slim man, he appeared around fifty. His eyes were clear, but deep wrinkles etched his face, and with graying hair, gave the impression he was older.

"You are thinking bottle age or something else?"

"We're not sure, but I assure you, sir, the '05 is drinking much better."

"Than let's try it."

The Sommelier was right about the Romanee-Conti, or at least that the '05 was drinking well. I was enormously impressed by it; an incredibly rich, fantastically concentrated wine. It had a deep, lively color; a huge, dry tannic and alcoholic wine that married perfectly with the duck. Nancy thought it the finest wine she'd ever tasted. And so went the meal. At the end, a small serving of Stilton cheese and a glass of '77 Ware's port finished a wonderful dining experience.

The waiter offered a cigar, which I accepted, and cognac, which I declined, having noted a bottle in the suite. There was a balcony and I thought that if it wasn't too cold, I could enjoy the cigar there.

As we passed the natatorium, several couples were enjoying the pool. Two of them eyed us intently as we paused for a moment to watch the steam rising. There was a faint aroma of chlorine seeping under the glass doors.

Back in the suite, Nancy joined me for a glass of the cognac, a rare Hennessy that I'd not tasted. Out on the balcony we found the temperature cool, but not unpleasant. Lights on the mountains provided a spectacular view. Had the circumstances been different, this would have been a perfect night. However, the circumstances were not different, and so goes life.

When the cognac and cigar was finished, we were relaxed, pleasantly tired, and decided to get some rest.

As Nancy started to her bedroom, she stopped, turned and faced me. "Thanks for tonight, it was something I needed."

"Sleep well, Doctor Wiseman," I said with true affection.

Case History of Dr. Ernest Grissom

FEMALE—This patient had abdominal mesothelioma and was suffering from systematic lupus erythematosis (SLE). The patient was treated conventionally however her health slowly deteriorated. When the patient was treated by Dr. Grissom the patient had a left sided pelvic mesothelioma of the peritoneum. The patient was treated repeatedly using Radiowave therapy. Two months after her final treatment the mesothelioma had shrunk considerably and the ascites had almost disappeared. Three and a half years after her first treatment there is no evidence of the SLE and x-rays of her chest and abdomen indicated that the peritoneal mesothelioma had disappeared.

Chapter Twenty-two

The view from the balcony at sunrise was even more spectacular than imagined. Nancy and I both rose early and, though neither was hungry, ordered a pot of coffee and bagels. We watched the way the shadows etched their way across the high ridges and in places, the sunlight glinted off the snow making them blaze as if the mountains had been inlaid with billions of tiny rhinestones. We both uttered alliterations meant to be silent, but forced aloud by the beauty.

There are many arguments one could marshal to give evidence of the existence of God. There is scientific evidence pointing to that fact. For example, whatever is in motion must be moved by another, for motion is the response of matter to power. In the world of matter there can be no power without life, and life presupposes a being from which emanates the power to move things, such as tides and planets. Or there is the argument that says nothing can be the cause of itself. It would be prior to itself if it caused itself to be, and that is an absurdity. Then there is the law of life. We see objects that have no intellect, such as stars and planets, moving in a consistent pattern, cooperating ingeniously with one another. Hence, it is evident that they achieve their movements not by accident but by design. Whatever lacks intelligence cannot move intelligently. A bullet would be useless without a gun and a shooter. What gives direction and purpose and design to inanimate objects? It is God. He is the underlying, motivating force of life. I saw all this in the morning sun lighting the mountains.

"You alright, Jay?"

"Yeah, just doing some introspective thinking."

All too soon it was time to meet Doctor Saidoreh Doreh for the ride to the airport. In the lobby, the two from the natatorium sat sipping coffee and reading the newspaper. They eyed us as we walked through to the limo. I gave them cursory thought.

As we pulled out onto the ramp to the airplane, I saw for the first time the type of aircraft that transported me from Denver to Salt Lake with my head covered by a cloth sack. It was the Airbus Corporate Jet. This version carried the designation, A318 ELITE. It is the same type of aircraft USAir's Captain "Sully" landed in the Hudson River in New York, making him an instant national hero for simply doing what he'd been trained to do. I remember my neighbor, Shack Runnels saying, after my rather negative comment about the "Heroism," that maybe every so often we need a national hero. I couldn't argue with that.

I had never flown or, while I could see, flown in one of Airbus's corporate jets, so I thought this could prove to be interesting. The same size as Boeing's 737/BBJ, the interior of this airplane had to be seen to be believed. Set up for fourteen passengers, it was like entering someone's living room. Except for the small windows along each side of the fuselage, one would not know they were aboard an aircraft.

Things have changed in airplanes over the last eighty years. While the dash and peculiar character of the men and women involved changed very little, the considerable differences between aircraft greatly diminished. Today they all look the same on the outside. The jets are safe, easy to fly, and most of them economically efficient. The combination of these virtues has, at least to me, washed much of the color from the flying scene. The overall dominance of glass cockpits run by computers, wedded to iron-willed bureaucracy, has completed air transports personality. Commercial aviation has grown up and, in one sense, died.

The interior of Doctor Doreh's personal chariot was elegant and reminded me of a long ago era where aircraft flew low and slow and the

Matson Steamship Company, a diverse corporation long engaged in Pacific Ocean commerce, decided to offer a new form of transportation to their customers. Aircraft were outfitted with comfortable seats and elegant décor. Above the windows were full-length panels of mahogany veneer expertly carved with the familiar Matson insignia. Flight attendants were selected for eye appeal and wore uniforms created by Parisian designers. Long tables were installed in the rear of the cabins for dining, with seating for eighteen at a time, presided over by the Captain, and alternated by the First Officer.

The cuisine was superb, created by an onboard chef, served by a steward with a napkin properly folded over forearm. The menu offered an assortment of appetizers, bluepoints and Dungeness crab, with a pleasant Riesling to stimulate the taste buds. Next would come a roast with a big Cabernet followed by a baked Alaska cleverly molded into the shape of the very aircraft in which they flew.

This flying in such grand style was deliberate, and the calculated results were most satisfying to Matson officials. Offering air travel one way and the option to sail back on one of the company's steamships was ever popular to customers.

I had the unique and great privilege to fly as First Officer for the company for six months until Juan Trippe, whose Pan American airplanes flying the same routes half empty, pointed out to the Civil Aeronautics Board that Matson was violating the law, specifically the Civil Aeronautic Act which specified that no surface carrier could be engaged in scheduled air transportation. Within weeks Matson was forced to withdraw from the scene, and I sought a flying job elsewhere.

Saidoreh Doreh led us up the steps to the cabin of her corporate jet. A uniformed steward pointed out safety features and amenities available to us.

This aircraft took interior custom design to new heights, with rare wood veneers, bird's-eye maple, nubuck leather, mood lighting and semi-precious stone inlay work. The bedroom suite offered a shower and an electrically operated bed surrounded by mirrors.

The aft cabin zone offered "mini-suite" executive seats, all of which converted into beds and were equipped with 20-inch LCD monitors, pull-out tables and retractable ottoman seating for guests.

The so-called "Smart Cabin Automated Dimming System" allowed the passengers or crew to "dim" a window from clear to opaque with the push of a button.

After the tour, Doctor Doreh said, "Nancy, I'll see you in thirty days. Construction on the Research Center can begin immediately under your complete supervision." Turning to me. "Mr. Leicester, had it been under different circumstances, I think we could have become friends." She reached out to shake my hand.

"Yes," I said. "You're not riding with us to Mississippi? Maybe we could get to know each other better, have a little fun?" I wanted her to smile. Her smiles would level out the harshness.

"No, there is much to do here, and there's my mother to see about."

"I want that frequency generator returned. Give it to Nancy."

"Certainly."

She turned, nodded to the steward, and deplaned.

The door was closed and the engines started. Nancy and I sat in comfortable chairs. We could have been in anyone's living room, a well-appointed living room. This aircraft, the Airbus A318 ELITE, was like art that has been formed as an integral part of function.

The cockpit door stayed locked for the entire flight to Meridian, Mississippi. A much different atmosphere from the Falcon 7X flight I took from Houston a lifetime ago. It truly did show professionalism, though; keep the cockpit sterile and safe. Oh well, I for once behaved myself and instead thought about the contents of the cargo hole.

All too soon we touched down in Meridian. An ambulance waited to take us to Union. We'd arranged for Stephen's Funeral Home to handle the services.

My old friend, Earl Sanders greeted us with a handshake and a smile.

"They must have ordered fuel?" I said.

"Two thousand gallons. I owe you for this one."

"I had nothing to do with it. They wouldn't even let me visit the cockpit."

"Wise men, this flight crew. I'm sorry about J.D."

"Thanks."

"Let me know. Annie and I will attend the service."

"You are a good man, Earl Sanders."

We got in the ambulance and headed for Union.

At the funeral home, I phoned the Newton County Appeal.

"Hello, Jack. If you'll give me a ride out to the cottage, I'll tell you a story…"

Little did I know that this "story" was about to take a dramatic turn that would change many things.

. . .

Nancy's car was at the Philadelphia airport, and after Jack dropped us off at my cottage with a promise for a more detailed interview later, I'd given him a brief synopsis; I drove her to retrieve the vehicle.

Pulling up beside the would-be Hummer, I asked her again if she knew of any family J.D. might have that needed to be notified.

"Not that I'm aware. He never spoke of family, saying only that he had no siblings and his parents were deceased."

"I'll handle the arrangements, if it's okay with you," I offered. "One of us needs to go through his things, see if there's a will. It needs to be done before the State steps in and takes over."

"I have a key to his place," Nancy said. "Maybe we can meet tomorrow and do it together."

"Sure."

. . .

Stopping by Rose's place on the way back to the cottage, I found her in the back yard holding a dead cat, tears streaming down her face, her eyes, grey and watery, like olives left too long in a jar.

She looked at me. "The older I get, the more I believe every living thing is one of a kind."

I thought that she may be right.

"We brought J.D.'s body home."

Her attention focused now, not on the dead cat, but me. "Does he have a burial plot? I have several; we can let him rest in one."

"I don't know, Rose. Nancy and I will go through his papers tomorrow. Maybe we can find out."

"Will you help me with this?" She held out the cat.

"Yes."

I dug the small hole in the "Pet" cemetery where there were at least a dozen markers. It was a special place for Rose; she loved her animals as people. When we were done, she insisted that we make coffee and talk.

Stirring a big dollop of Tupelo honey into the thick, black, aromatic liquid, I told her the story, much as I'd related it to the publisher of the Newton Appeal. At the mention of the Rife/Ballard Cancer Research Center, tears again streamed down her face, for Rose had been cured of cancer by J.D. Ballard and his frequency generator.

She was brave with her illness, and I only found out when it was in the latter stages. She contended that nothing happens until it actually happens and you live your life up until then. She believed a thing is only bad when it is bad. It is neither bad before or after. One must simply have the ability to suspend the functioning of the imagination. Learning to suspend your imagination and live completely in the moment with no before and no after is the greatest gift one can acquire. It is the opposite of all the gifts one usually had. That is what makes it such a rare thing, and why it is so prized by one when they have it.

I have often mused that she was right, and remembered what Hemingway wrote in his book, "*Dangerous Summer*" on the three requisites for a bullfighter: *Courage, skill in his profession, and grace in the presence of the danger of death.* So it was with Rose English. Then from somewhere I know not came:

By my troth, I care not: A man can die but once; we owe God a death. Let it go which way it will, he that dies this year is quit for the next.

Leaving Rose to weep for her dead cat, I drove to the cottage and reacquainted with my big Siamese, B.W. He curled up in my lap, nuzzled my chest and purred. In his case, it was more like a loud vibration shaking the whole house.

Building a fire, I opened a good bottle of Petit Syrah, and sat watching the flames, smelling the wood smoke. Suddenly I had a moment of *La Recherché du Temps Perdu,* and decided that I did not like killers, not the soldiers or those who killed to save themselves or others, but the professional who killed for money. They should be made to stay with the body, all mucus, and steaming blood stench and gouted excrement, the eyes going dull with the final muscle spasms. Then, if he is, in all parts and purposes, a man, he will file that away as a part of his process of growth and life and eventual death. But, if he is perpetually, and hopelessly lost, he will lust to do it again, with no hope to save his soul.

I went to bed early, hoping there would be no dreams. I was not so lucky, there were many and they were frightening.

· · ·

Driving out of the cottage early in the morning, the trees in the hollows seemed stark and bloodless against the grey sky.

We went through J.D.'s things, finding a will. It was filed less than a year ago, leaving everything to Nancy with stipulations that a percentage of the estate be used for research on the frequency generator. Surprisingly, he left the Cessna Citation to me. There was a burial insurance policy that included a plot in the Union City Cemetery.

Nancy showed little emotion. In his work shed, a stand alone building near the house, we found two completed frequency generators with wide metal plates upon which one could rest their feet while receiving the waves through them. Instructions showed the feet must be protected by a saline-drenched cloth to protect from burns. Nancy said we should each take one before authorities showed up. I agreed.

We stopped back by the funeral home and provided them with the information. We were told the service could be held day after tomorrow at two p.m., if that was acceptable. We said that it was fine.

Dropping Nancy off at her house, we agreed to meet for lunch at my cottage on the day of the funeral.

. . .

The funeral home was full. It seemed everyone in town came to pay respects to J.D. Ballard. But then that's the way people are in this part of the country—God's country. It's one of the reasons I like living here. A long line of cars followed the hearse to the cemetery. Rose's preacher from the little old church in the wildwood said a few words and we dispersed—Dust to Dust.

Nancy, Rose, Shack and his wife, Annie, and Earl Sanders, who had driven up from Meridian, and I, all met at the cottage. We opened some old bottles of champagne I'd been saving for just such an occasion and toasted the life and accomplishments and contributions and friendship of our friend. This time Nancy couldn't hold back the tears, and neither could I.

After everyone left, I fed B.W., added more wood to the fire, and sat commiserating on my own life, what people would say about my accomplishments in this world. Would anyone open a bottle of champagne and toast my life spent aloft. Or maybe no one would show up for my funeral. Then it dawned on me how much of a loner I've truly been, and that frankly I didn't really care if anyone came to mourn me. Today was about J.D., not me.

I made a sandwich from some roast beef nearing its expiration date, drank some two day old Merlot, and watched the fire. After that, I was tired and went to bed.

. . .

The phone rang early. B.W. sat on the table next to the bed, listening to the ring and looking at me as if to say, "Are you going to answer that thing, or do you want me to?"

"Leicester."

"Hello, Jay. Pete Freuchen."

"High Sheriff, what's going on in the mountains?"

"They killed your girl."

"Beverly Richmond? Deputy Plaxco? Who Pete?"

"Doctor Saidoreh Doreh. Sniper, long range, head shot."

"When? How did you…?"

"It's big news out this way. She was getting out of a limo at the airport to board her private jet. Feds are looking into it; they'll probably contact you and Doctor Wiseman."

"Thanks, Pete, I appreciate the information."

"Take care of yourself, and don't forget my cancer cure machine."

Hanging up the phone, I lay back in the bed, my thoughts racing. Nancy, I needed to call her.

. . .

"Oh, Jay, no." One could hear the anguish in her voice.

"I'll pick you up at your office at noon, we can have lunch and talk."

"Yes, that will be fine."

I showered and tried to think of all the possibilities this opened up. Would they come after me? Nancy? Would they attempt to stop the Cancer Research Center, attack the contract she signed with high-powered attorneys? What about Doreh's family? Did she have anyone other than her mother? The "powers that be" can't overtly protest too much. It would expose them.

Brewing coffee, I dressed and went out on the porch. It was cold, but tolerable. The sky was clear, though advection fog lay over the land like a silky film. It made things damp and moisture dripped from the trees, making the woods look beautiful in the rising sun. There were four dead now; J.D., the two pilots, and Doctor Doreh. How many more? It was time to stop this, if it could be stopped.

. . .

Picking up Nancy, we drove to a small restaurant and sat in a booth.

"I got a call from one of the lawyers soon after you hung up," she said, rubbing at a spot on the table. "He informed me of the death."

"Did he say anything else?"

"No, only that he'd let me know when the memorial service would take place. She will be cremated as soon as the body is released."

"We must attend. It's important that we do. We can take the Citation. You need to have someone look carefully at the papers you signed."

"As soon as I returned, I sent a copy via FedEx to a professor of contract law at Harvard. He's an old friend. He promised to let me know next week."

"Good."

"Jay, do you think they'll come after me, or both of us?"

"I don't know, Nancy. If they'll kill one of their own, they are capable of anything. I do know this; they can't kill all of us. Sooner or later it has to stop."

Returning her to her medical practice, she said she'd let me know as soon as there was information on when the memorial would take place. We would fly out the day before.

. . .

We took off at sunrise from the grass strip. Frost made the runway glisten like a long pane of glass. The sun appeared like a foreign diseased thing, glowing down a red contagion on the farmland and to me it seemed defective, a tired speck at the edge of a vast unseen interstellar black and wore that harsh steely look of defeat. Soon we were above the winter haze layer and the grey overcast did not appear so ominous. Cleared up to thirty-five thousand feet, we pointed the nose of J.D.'s Citation toward Salt Lake City, Utah. If the weather and winds held, we could make it non-stop. Denver was on the route, if we needed to refuel. The memorial for Doctor Saidoreh Doreh was at ten o'clock tomorrow morning.

Climbing through flight level 290, we topped the cloud layer and flew along under blue sky. We are a people who expect the day to be sunny, the body young, full of vitality, and, who, when the clouds form, the marriage fails, the erection wilts, the mind slips, seek for the psychiatrist who passes out the tranquilizers.

I am flying as Captain today because I felt like being in command. It was a strange day for me. There was no understanding the feeling. It was simply there. I felt cold, unsheltered, perplexed. Looking over at Nancy, the sunlight slanted indirectly through the cockpit window behind her head and seemed to silhouette her as the tints in the glass caused enigmatic patterns in its rays. I watched her hands. She had a habit of touching each fingertip to the pad of her thumb repetitively as if she were counting or keeping a beat, or playing a musical instrument. It seemed an absent-minded habit, like some people do when they hum.

She remained quiet, somehow sensing my unrest. Her silence reflected her level of intelligence. I began to relax. The day was starting to feel smooth, pebbled with the nostalgia of other long ago flights. I watch the clouds pass underneath, their shapes and color enticing as butterflies. For the first time in days, I am at peace.

Nancy looked at me. She seemed to be one of those people who always have reflections inside their eyes, like ghosts or memories no one else can see.

"Salt Lake is reporting clear skies, calm winds," she said. "My calculations show we'll have thirty minutes of fuel on arrival. Want to try it?"

"Let's proceed," I said.

We made Salt Lake with no problems, caught a cab to the same resort we stayed in before and, to the amusement of us both, the same suite. Reservations in the five star dining room were a little harder to come by. We could be seated only at six or nine-thirty. Nancy wanted the six o'clock seating. It suited me.

Case History of Dr. Hiram Gibson

FEMALE—*The patient was diagnosed with right breast cancer with blindness in right eye and a cough. Vitamins and homeopathy were tried with little results. When patient was treated by Dr. Gibson for one month the mass in the breast disappeared, sight returned to the blind eye, the cough went away and all pain ceased. Blood tests (CA 125) came back negative. Two years post treatment patient remains cancer free.*

Chapter Twenty-three

The church was full to overflowing. We sat with one of the lawyers who'd handled the contracts, in fact, the one who phoned Nancy, informing her of Doctor Doreh's death. It was a long service. A lot of people spoke, some were friends, and many politicians who wanted nothing other than to be seen and heard. Saidoreh's mother sat up front in a wheelchair, but had to be taken away after an hour. Finally, it was over, and the lawyer said he needed to meet with Nancy, at the hospital, later that afternoon. It was important. She agreed.

Back at the resort we had a late lunch, then went up to the suite.

"Well, here it comes," I said. "They are going to find a way out of the funding for the Research Center."

"Then they better be good. I got an e-mail from my friend at Harvard, the contract is solid."

"You want me to come with you to the meeting?" I offered.

"I think I can hold my own."

"Okay, then I'll go out to the airport and nose around. Maybe we should stay another night, get an early start in the morning."

"Yes."

The lawyer sent a car for Nancy. After she left, I walked out on the balcony. The temperature had dropped suddenly, but the sunlight was gold on the bare trees, and there was a tannic smell in the air that I associated with the end of winter.

The Concierge said there was no problem with us staying another night, and a cab would be waiting to take me to the airport when I came down.

The ride to the FBO was one I'll remember. The driver played loud middle-eastern music over bad speakers that sounded like dying chickens. Paying the fare, I walked away thinking the man had Van Gogh's ear for music.

Ordering a load of fuel for the Citation, I told the girl behind the counter we'd be leaving in the morning around ten o'clock. She made a note for the line crew. Two men dressed in suits sat in the waiting area and looked vaguely familiar. They paid no attention to me. Maybe they were a corporate flight crew I'd crossed paths with at another airport.

Nothing at the FBO proved interesting, so after an hour I caught a taxi back to the resort, thankfully this time with a driver from Pocatello, Idaho, who loved country music.

Passing through the lobby, there were six people sitting about who eyed me intently. Paranoia was raising its ugly head.

Looking out the big windows toward the mountains, it occurred to me that the only thing in this world worth anything is the strange, touchingly pathetic, awesome nobility of the individual human spirit.

Around five o'clock, I heard the door lock open. Nancy entered walking stiff-legged. I prepared for the bad news. With awkward steps, she moved closer and a raging smile spread until it looked as if it would split her tight face open and spill out whatever hid under those black eyebrows, right out onto the floor. She threw a small purse at a chair, looked at me.

"Saidoreh Doreh left a sizable trust fund to care for her mother," she said with less sarcasm than I expected.

"That's nice, and…?"

"The rest she left to the Cancer Research Center, including the Airbus jet. All told, almost three billion dollars. The lawyers read her will, or at least the parts that concerned me. Jay, she named me the Executor of it all. I didn't even know the woman."

"It's a done deal, no protests?"

"Not a dissenting voice in the room."

"Are you going to accept this?" I asked. "It's a huge undertaking, a radical lifestyle change, not to mention the danger?"

Nancy sat down.

"That's a good question."

There was a knock on the door.

"You expecting someone?" I looked toward the bedroom where my magnum lay in a ditty bag.

"No."

Retrieving the trusty old revolver, I peered through the peephole and saw two well-dressed men. One held up a gold badge.

"State your business."

"FBI, we need to talk with Mr. Leicester and Ms Wiseman."

Keeping the chain fastened, I cracked the door.

"Put the credentials up closer."

They looked legit. I opened the door, holding the magnum behind my back.

The next two hours were some of the most intense conversations I've ever been a party too. The agents were thorough, professional, highly intelligent, and knew more about Saidoreh Doreh and her secret organization than I thought possible.

They were years away from indictments, either for murder or white collar crime, but the investigation would move forward, daily, weekly, monthly, yearly, until it reached its conclusion.

What surprised me most was their knowledge of the radio wave frequency generator, its suppression, and how it related to their case. When the interview was over, I felt much better about Nancy's safety, should she choose to stay in Salt Lake. Those who would want to harm her or halt the Research Center were made aware they were known and being watched.

. . .

The Five-Star restaurant lived up to its reputation again. We sat quietly in an atmosphere conducive to fine dining. Ordering a bottle of the resorts best champagne, a vintage Dom Perignon recommended by the Sommelier, we celebrated Nancy's rise to head an empire with a single goal, to perfect a treatment for cancer; an alternative to mainstream medicine. A single mission to better mankind. We also knew that, at least for the near future, the threat from those who control power to halt the research, had been put on notice. We were also smart enough to know that this battle was not over, not by a long shot.

I toasted to her success, to which she replied, "Remember this Jay, Destiny controls the passes to the top. It is not important, really, how far you go, but how you make the trip, and always pay your own way."

"Well said."

"I'm going to stay here," she said, resolutely. "There is much to be done. I can handle any business back in Mississippi, by phone. I have another D.O. who will take over the practice, so there's no real reason to go back."

"What about your house?"

"I'll get a real-estate agency to sell it; movers can pack everything and ship them to me. If I have to return, the Airbus is available for a quick trip."

"I understand. You promise not to forget us; me, Rose, Shack."

"No, I'll never forget any of you, and you'll come and visit, see how the J.D. Ballard/Royal Rife Cancer Research Center is progressing."

"It's a promise."

. . .

I left Salt Lake City, Utah, the next morning at ten a.m., heading to Aspen, Colorado, to deliver a cancer curing frequency generator to Sheriff Pete Freuchen. The same one used on Saidoreh Doreh's mother. I planned to stay for a few days, see some old friends, ski down Bunny Slope, and dine in favorite restaurants, clear my mind.

The tower cleared me to land, and on short final it occurred to me that there is a moment when an idea either puts on flesh or is forgotten, squirms into possibility with the red stretch of any birth or vanishes without a trace. This trip to the old mining town needed to materialize.

George Barrows guided me to a parking space. It was good to see him. The noon sky was cloudless; stamped copper roofs on airport buildings gleamed like rubbed coins and threw angled shadows that were so precise they seemed painted on the runway and ramp. The air was dry, though sharp with the blue smells of ice and invisible winter.

"Come in," Barrows said. "Catch me up on everything."

We went into his office. It was as Spartan as I remembered with few Objects'd Art of aviation, a working man's space. We talked for an hour, and when I finally finished gushing out all that I needed to say, a kind of cathartic release, he simply nodded. He was probably processing the information, but to me it showed intelligence by not overtly analyzing my soliloquy.

"Call Pete for me," I said. "Tell him I'm on the ground and to come pick me up."

Sheriff Freuchen arrived a short time later. Telling Barrows that my stay in Aspen would be four or five days, and to please take care of J.D.'s Citation until then, we drove away from the airport heading for Freuchen's office.

I, as with Barrows, told Pete all that had transpired since we'd last talked.

"They're going to get away with murder," he said, with anger, the muscles in his jaw tightening into knots. "That stinks."

"To high heaven, Pete, but what can be done?"

In his office, I gave him the frequency generator, explained how to operate it, the three frequencies, and their times of usage. He peered at the machine as if it were some fearful animal that could attack at any moment. I hoped he never had occasion to use it, but if he did, then it was up to him to conquer the little black box.

I left Sheriff Pete Freuchen to keep law and order in Pitkin County,

Colorado. For the next five days, I ate at all the fine restaurants; the Copper Kettle, the Red Onion, and some new establishments that didn't impress me, drank the best of fine champagne, and wines, skied Aspen and Snowmass Mountain for exercise, rode on a horse-drawn sleigh up into the mountains to a dinner cabin with ten other people, ate grilled steaks before a fireplace large enough to walk around in, while listening to live music from a local band, and made love to a woman I thought about asking to be my wife.

On the fifth day, I woke before daylight, watched her plod barefoot to the fire and add wood. She had that perfect proportioned body and the skill trained into it to satisfy any man. In any block a stone mason can see many things, but a master sculptor can see but one. In his eye no two blocks of marble are alike, and the thing he sees is the thing for which the block was created. In her, I could see that the master sculptor had been at work.

She got back under the covers, her naked body cool up against me.

"You're going to leave today, aren't you?"

"How did you know?"

She didn't answer, rolled over to her side of the bed. Most women have a level of trust in men whom they love that men seldom earn or deserve. As a rule, we do not appreciate that level of trust until it's destroyed.

I watched the silver liquid moonlight flow over the bed, squeezed through the place where the curtains overlapped. It was spectacular that splash of light. She had called it the Wolf Moon, sometimes called the Old Moon, when the wolf packs would howl outside the villages in the dead of night.

"You knew I'd have to go."

"Yes."

I was flooded with feeling. With this new found sense came a falling, a desperate clawing fall down an acrid chasm toward despair. Over the past weeks something in me had died, sadness welled up in my gut and burned out through my eyes with tears.

. . .

Barrows had a friend who worked in the tower. He phoned him and asked that I be the last departure for the evening before the curfew. He gave him the "N" number of the Citation. We were instructed to monitor the ground control frequency, and the controller would get my clearance from Denver Center and give me an engine start time.

Barrows and I sat in the cockpit with an auxiliary power cart running the electrical system and talked while awaiting clearance.

"You coming back this way anytime soon?"

"Ah, George, who knows. Life in Mississippi is so good I don't think I'll ever want to leave."

"Yes, that's the way it is with me and these mountains."

"November One Juliet Delta, Aspen Tower, we have your IFR clearance, and you are good for engine start."

"Roger, we're ready to copy."

"Goodbye, George, take care of yourself."

After engine start, Barrows disconnected the power cart and I taxied to the end of the runway. It was dark now, and my eyes were adjusting to the cockpit lights. Carefully following the checklist, since I was alone, I stopped short of the active runway. When all was ready, I called the tower for takeoff clearance.

I have lifted my aircraft from runways perhaps five thousand times and I have never felt the wheels depart from mother earth without knowing the uncertainty and the exhilaration of first born adventure. Cleared up to flight level 240, I had little time to do other than pay close attention to my trusty Citation, run the checklists, and fly the gauges. Finally cleared up to thirty-five thousand feet, I began to relax. Leveling off and accelerating to cruse speed, I heard the ding, ding, ding of the over speed warning horn. The airplane, being light, with only me aboard was like a young galloping colt, she wanted her head. Pulling back the power, I said, aloud, "Easy girl, slow down, it's a long flight."

To fly in unbroken darkness is at times unreal to the point where the existence of other people seems not even a reasonable probability. The mountains, the plains, the forests are one with the darkness, and darkness is infinite. The earth is no more your home than is a distant star. The Citation is now my planet and I am its sole inhabitant. The night takes me into its realm, envelops me entirely, leaving me out of touch with earth, leaving me within this small moving world of my own, living in space with the stars.

Being alone in an airplane at night with nothing to observe but your instruments and your own hands in semi-darkness, nothing to contemplate but the size of your small courage, nothing to wonder about but the beliefs, the faces, and the hopes rooted in your mind, is an experience that can be as startling as the first awareness of a stranger walking by your side at night and realizing that you are the stranger.

Denver passes off the left wingtip. Looking down, I think of the big cities, the dirty windows, the huffing smokestacks, rusting skeletons of groaning bridges, the ever present flow of yellow-painted cabs, constant blowing of horns, squealing of tires and brakes. I hate cities, and thank God for the little cottage in the wildwoods.

Now I look out the windscreen at the stars and think of the probabilities of life beyond earth. There are two hundred and fifty billion stars in our galaxy. If we assume half of these will have planets with an average of five per sun, then we have sixty-two and a half billion capable of sustaining life. If we take one percent of that, we have six hundred and twenty-five million on which life can be. Now, if we take only one tenth of one percent of that figure we see there are six hundred and twenty-five thousand planets with intelligent life in our galaxy alone. And there are billions and billions of galaxies!

It is now near midnight, I am hungry, and the fuel is running low. To land in Union, it must be daylight. I will stop, refuel, get something to eat, and kill a few hours so as to arrive at my destination at first light.

. . .

"Good morning Meridian Approach, November One Juliet Delta with you thirty west with information Alpha, descending out of ten thousand for three, in bound to Union International."

"Morning One Juliet Delta, altimeter is 30.06, cleared direct to Union. Are you going to be able to see the strip?"

"I think so. It's starting to get daylight, although there's some ground fog forming. I'll let you know turning final."

"Roger."

Using the usual visual cues, I turned onto final approach and in the dim light was able to make out the grass strip. "Meridian, One Juliet Delta, field in sight, you can cancel the IFR."

"Roger, One Juliet Delta. Have a good day."

Slowing the Citation as much as I dared, I crossed the boundary and touched down, extended the thrust-reversers and came to a stop. Taxiing back to the hangar, I shut down the engines, hung my head, and slumped in the cockpit. I was tired. It had been quite an adventure. It seemed like the end of something.

From the files of Dr. Wan Hunsing: Colorado: 2010

A sixty-three year old law enforcement officer presented with bilateral, end stage lung cancer. No hope was given and usual treatment followed. Patient treated himself with home-made radio frequency generator for a period of six months. Last CT scan of lungs showed no sign of disease. Details of treatment and pathological examination are documented for your purview. To our astonishment, cure seems complete.

EPILOGUE

Ten years later

I sat in the chair on the front porch of the little cottage in the wildwood, propped my feet up on a cedar post, set a snifter of cognac on a side table, and carefully cut the end off a Charlemagne cigar. It was a clear, spring day. The grass was greening and the trees were budding. In the hollow to the north, briars were blooming and if not cut soon would overrun the woods, making walking impossible.

Sipping the warm cognac and tasting the aged tobacco from the cigar was bittersweet. I was alone in these woods. All my friends were gone. Rose English was buried in one of her plots out on the highway next to her daughter, Alella. In the end, she refused pain meds and went about dying the way she went about living, one thing at a time, and when everything was done but dying, she did that, as we all do, for some divine purpose that seemed increasingly arcane, increasingly arbitrary, and increasingly baroque in its cruelty. At least it seemed so to me the older I get. Shack Runnels lay not far away, having died from an infection after a young bull gored him in the leg. Hebrone Opshinsky was killed when the plane he was flying crashed into a mountain in Central America. They say it was pilot error. I never believed the final accident report. I buried my cat, B.W., on the hill behind the pond next to Savage, my German Sheppard.

Life is winding down here in these woods in central Mississippi, a place I've always considered God's country. I closed my Aviation Consulting business last year. It just wasn't any fun anymore after my friends died.

Nancy Wiseman continues to run the *J.D. Ballard/Royal R. Rife Cancer Research Center* in Salt Lake City, Utah. Much has been accomplished in the search for a cancer cure. The wave frequency generator has been successful in all but rare forms of malignancy who's MOR (mortal oscillatory rate) has yet to be discovered. The treatment is still forbidden in the U.S.; however several countries have had one hundred percent success rates in ninety-five percent of patients. The battle continues.

Off to the south, a flock of turkeys are feeding their way across a hayfield. A lone coyote sulks along a fence row, eyeing the birds, but without the pack, he's not sure what to do, so he trots on toward the creek bottoms to the west.

The sun sets behind the cottage and color fades from the fields and trees. Silence envelops the countryside. Even the animals sense that it is time to rest. A lone hawk soars high in the clear sky, availing itself of the last thermal of the day. The ghosts emerge and quiet voices speak unintelligible sentences, shadows cross my vision and disappear. I am not insane. It has been this way since moving to this hill in the deep woods twenty years ago—these ghosts and voices and shadows. At first they frightened me, but I soon learned they meant no harm.

A cow lowed far away, then a second time. Tears came to my eyes at the sound, bringing forth memories of Rose English and Shack Runnels, two cattle farmers who were much more to me than mere friends. They were part of my life.

Now the wind is calm, not a breath stirred. The cigar smoke rose in a vertical shaft to the ceiling of the porch and spread out like a micro-burst from a summer thunderstorm; a phenomenon that had killed so many of my fellow pilots before we learned how to detect and avoid them. I hoped this smoke formation would not have such effects on my lungs.

I went inside and poured another glass of cognac. It was one of those days that called for a second glass.

"What now, Leicester?" I thought as I sat down on the porch, automatically looking for my cat, forgetting where he lay up on the hill. I took a long drink of the Martel. "What does life hold in store for you? What fate lies in wait on the morn?"

"Are you feeling sorry for yourself?" I heard Rose say. "Get your sorry ass up and do something worthwhile."

I missed Rose. Even in death she could cheer me up.

"Here's to you, old woman." I raised my glass. "You did good."

It was dark now, the glass empty, and the cigar out. A lone lightening bug winked its glow for a mate in the scope of trees to the east of the cottage. The stars were shinning, blinking strobe lights from aircraft high up in the sky interrupted the silent vista. It was a nice night. I hated for it to end. But as with the sweet hours of youth, all must pass. A song by Iris DeMent came to mind:

And ya know the sun's settin' fast
And just like they say, nothing good ever lasts
Go on now and kiss it goodbye
But hold on to your lover 'cause your heart's bound to die
Go on now and say goodbye to our town, to our town
Can't you see the sun's settin' down on our town, our town
Goodnight

Up the street beside that red neon light
That's where I met my baby on one hot summer night
He was the tender and I ordered the beer
It's been forty years and I'm still sittin' here

I've buried my Mama and I've buried my Pa
They sleep up the street beside that pretty brick wall
I bring 'em flowers about everyday
But I just gotta cry when I think what they'd say

Now I sit on the porch and watch the lightenin' bugs fly
But I can't see to good, I got tears in my eyes
I'm leavin' tomorrow but I don't wanna go
I love you, my town, you'll always live in my soul

But I can see the sun's setting fast
And just like they say, nothing good ever lasts
Go on, I gotta kiss you goodbye
But I'll hold on to my lover 'cause my heart's 'bout to die
Go on now and say goodbye to my town, to my town
I can see the sun has gone down on my town, on my town
Goodnight, goodnight.

I got up and went inside.

FINAL THOUGHTS

Like Coleridge's Ancient Mariner I had a compulsion to tell these tales, but unlike the Wedding Guest, who "cannot choose but hear," you reader could have closed the books at any point and I would never have known the difference. Nevertheless, it has been a delight to have you along for the adventure.

Let's pour one more glass of cognac and light another cigar before you leave. Let's raise a toast to Jay Leicester, Rose English, Jack "Shack" Runnels, Hebrone Opshinsky, Andrew "Smash" Bullard and, last but by no means least, to that brilliant medical doctor, friend, and bibliographer, Edgar Grissom, who started it all.

THE END